With best regards
and good wishes

11/21/81

Rachamim
(Forgiveness)

From Darkness into Light

a novel by
Ray Naar, Ph. D.

iUniverse, Inc.
New York Bloomington

Rachamim
From Darkness into Light

iUniverse books may be ordered through booksellers or by contacting:

iUniverse
1663 Liberty Drive
Bloomington, IN 47403
www.iuniverse.com
1-800-Authors (1-800-288-4677)

Because of the dynamic nature of the Internet, any Web addresses or links contained in this book may have changed since publication and may no longer be valid.

ISBN: 978-1-4401-5134-7 (sc)
ISBN: 978-1-4401-5136-1 (dj)
ISBN: 978-1-4401-5135-4 (ebk)

Printed in the United States of America

iUniverse rev. date: 6/30/2009

To: Youssef, my "kavass," whose marvelous stories enchanted a little boy's life.

To: Commandatore Giuseppe Castruccio, a noble human being who risked his career and his life to save many Jews from Salonica from certain death.

Author's Note

In a preface to his book *The Far Side of the World* Patrick O'Brian states: "Perhaps few authors are wholly original as far as their plots are concerned. It is a truism to add that whatever one creates is a regurgitation, in a different form of all the experiences one has been through and all the knowledge one has acquired."

O'Brian further states that, "general appropriation is not quite the same as downright plagiary and in passing it must be confessed that the description of a storm's first aspect on page 310 is taken straight from William Hickey, whose words did not seem capable of improvement."

It is in that spirit I "confess" that the comic encounter between the Greek mountaineer and the Italian soldier (see Chapter 7) bears some resemblance to an incident described by Louis De Bernieres in his magnificent novel *Corelli's Mandoline*. To my discharge, I shall say that I became aware of the resemblance after I proofread *Rachamim* for the umpteenth time and getting a sense of *deja vu* reading these few paragraphs. It took me a much longer time to track this unconscious plagiarism to its source.

Forward and Acknowledgement

Rachamim is a work of fiction, but some of David's early years and memories in Salonica are my own and I did not want to let them die. The descriptions of the persecutions of Salonica's Jews are accurate and were documented in M. Molho's (ed.) *In Memoriam: Communaute Isrealite de Salonique, Thessalonique, 1973*. Commandatore Giuseppe Castruccio, consul of Italy, in Salonica saved, indeed, many Jewish lives and it is to him that I dedicate this book.

Everything else in *Rachamim* is pure fiction, although readers may be interested in part of a clipping from the *Jerusalem Report* as follows:

> Divers are set to start searching off the Greek coast for a sunken boat believed to hold up to $24 billion worth of treasure stolen from the Jews of Salonica by a Nazi administrator.
>
> The operation was initiated by a Greek Christian in his 70's who asked to remain anonymous. Earlier this year, he walked into the office of the Salonica Jewish community and announced that he knew the spot off the Peloponnesian peninsula where the boat had been scuttled, explaining that in 1958 he spent time in jail with Max Menten, the German civilian boss in Salonica during the war.

I was not aware of the above report when I wrote the first draft of *Rachamim*.

How can one thank those who helped write a book? The influences acting upon a writer start at birth and continue through his/her life. I shall give it a modest try. I want to thank my father and mother for giving me, among so many precious gifts, their love for the written word. I remember very fondly my teachers at the Lycé Français de Salonique who taught me, even as a small child, to think and encouraged me to write. I wish to thank all the writers whose works I read and inspired me.

I express my gratitude to my patients. They taught me tolerance and understanding, and I am proud that, at least for some of them, I was what Dr. Rosen was for David. It is because of them that I was able to write the dialogue between David and Dr. Rosen in a realistic fashion.

I wish to thank Sr. Corinne of the Benedictine Sisters of Pittsburgh who typed the initial draft of the manuscript and put up with my vagaries and demands. I thank my friend and assistant, Sarah Slevinski, without whose knowledge of computers, good humor and patience with my abysmal ignorance of this new cybernetic world, this work would never have been submitted.

I want to express my appreciation to my son, Walter, for reading the manuscript and making appropriate suggestions.

But when all is said and done, it is my wife's love, faith in me and encouragement when I was ready to give up that made this book possible. With her I share my joy and pride.

Chapter 1

Mavropotamos

The sassy wind successfully challenged the sun and the bright blue sky. April in the mountains of Northern Greece saddled both winter and spring, and breathing the cold air was like drinking from a cool mountain spring. From the lookout rock, one could see forever, tall mountain peaks covered with snow, meadows in the valley, emerald green ornamented with garlands of white.

Mavropotamos, population 528, was perched like an eagle's nest along the side of the mountain.

It was Monday morning, a beautiful sunny day when one throws away the winter's cobwebs, lets the fresh air in, and feels cleansed and rejuvenated. An April day when children sing and hopes soar and plans are made for the future. Yet this Monday was different. There were no sounds of children going to school, no mules or donkeys tied to the rail in the village square, no bicycles against the walls. The stores were closed except for the taverna, and even the taverna was empty. Yet, one could sense people behind the closed doors. Every once in a while, a storeowner would peek outside, then precipitously go back in and retreat behind the safety of his door or window.

A little girl set off running through the square, and Kyra Elene, her mother, took after her like a flash, scooped the child under her arm, and hurried back to the safety of her home. Pater Demetrios, the village priest, stood in front of the church clothed in a black robe with a tall black hat. He was a very old man, gnarled as an olive tree, solid as an oak. Occasionally, he would gaze into the distance then would pace back and forth like a faithful sheepdog protecting his flock.

1

The silence was deafening and seized one by the throat as if depriving one of oxygen. Bodies were tense, and hearts beat faster. Husbands looked at their wives with apprehension, and parents looked at their children. There were few young men in the village, but there were sparks in the eyes of the old men, and fists clenched and opened, some in fear, but mostly in anger.

The Germans were coming.

There were some men huddled in the square. Their uniforms and short carbines were those of the Italian military. Yet there was nothing martial about them. They were all in their late forties and early fifties, bulging in the middle, looking around with embarrassed, sometimes apprehensive glances. Sergeant Raffaele, the group's non-commissioned officer, towered above his soldiers.

"These poor bastards," he said, "God knows what the Germans will do to them," and he spat with anger against the wall.

"Precious little we can do," said another man. "Just wait."

Their leader was different, somewhat younger, tall, elegant with a military cape negligently draped over his shoulders. His name was Francesco Venchiarutti, and he commanded the Italian garrison at Mavropotomos: twenty men with carbines, one Howitzer that could not fire, and a Fiat staff car that had seen better days. He didn't try to hide his nervousness, and cigarette followed cigarette, which he kept crushing under his feet. There certainly was a sense of foreboding in the air.

The Germans were coming.

There stood, at the entrance of the village, a statue of Kolokotronis, a hero of the Greek independence, and these words were inscribed on the socle of the statue: "Better one hour of free life than forty years of slavery and jail." The Greeks took their freedom very seriously, and most of Mavropotomos' young men had joined the partisans, the Andartes. Their unit, however, operated far from Mavropotomos, and there was a tacit agreement between the Andartes and the Italian garrison: the Italians would not bother looking for the partisans, and the partisans would leave the village's occupying forces strictly alone. The unspoken understanding pleased everyone. The Italians felt an affinity and secret sympathy for the Greeks. Besides, being that almost all of them were into middle age they did not relish the prospect of pursuing will-of-the-wisp partisans through icy mountains, and the partisans felt reassured that their families in the village would have some semblance of protection and would not be retaliated against.

And then, two days earlier, a couple of German soldiers had been shot by guerillas a few miles from the village.

Venchiarutti stomped on his half-smoked cigarette and thought grimly, *How could this happen so close to the village? Who are the idiots who did it? How the hell am I going to deal with the Germans when they come?*

And, indeed, they came.

Kosta, a bedraggled sixteen-year-old, almost killed himself climbing down from the lookout rock. Venchiarutti saw him running, flailing his arms like a wild semaphore, but he could not hear his words at first. The youth was breathless when he finally neared the square.

"They are coming, they are coming," he managed, then kept running to spread the word through the rest of the village.

A dusty grey Kubblewagon, with an officer and two non-commissioned officers, was followed by two truckloads of soldiers. The three vehicles stopped in the center of the square, and the trucks disgorged a large number of SS troopers, who immediately formed a strategic perimeter around the Italian soldiers.

They were young, tall, grim faced, and looked formidably efficient. Their leader approached Lt. Venchiarutti and gave him a Nazi salute.

"Heil, Hitler, Sturmbandfuhrer Otto Kleindienst."

The Italian offered a lazy, almost insolent, military salute, barely touching the rim of his cap. "Lt. Venchiarutti, and may I ask what you are doing here, Hauptman Kleindienst?"

"Sturmbandfuhrer," corrected the German.

"Yes, of course, whatever. I still want to know what you are doing here."

The German turned beet red under the thinly veiled sarcasm, the Italian's dismissal of the SS officer's military title, but Venchiarutti's flawless German intrigued him; yet, it took him a moment to regain his composure while he looked fixedly at his Italian ally.

The two men were a study in contrast. Both were tall, lean, well-built. The German, however, was much younger, maybe in his mid-twenties, blond and blue-eyed, and stood ramrod straight and unsmiling. His hair was cut short and his uniform--immaculate, except for a thin film of dust--fit him to perfection. He wore his hat at a jaunty angle, and there was an iron cross around his neck. His expression was not only serious, but had a touch of arrogance. Lt. Venchiarutti slouched a little, his dark hair was a shade too long, and he wore a slight grin, which seemed to indicate that he took neither himself nor the vicissitudes of life very seriously.

Venchiarutti had noted the German eyeing him with curiosity and tried to soften his earlier insolent remarks. "I spent some time in Berlin," he explained, "a few years just before the beginning of the war. A stage with a German law firm. I still would like to know, Herr Kleindienst, how can I be of service?"

"Two SS soldiers were ambushed and killed not far from here, Lieutenant, and I was told to investigate and take all proper measures so that such atrocities will not occur again. Of course, I count on your cooperation."

You bet, thought the Italian. *I believe I know what these proper measures are.* He sighed audibly and put his most charming smile forward.

"I think, perhaps, we shall be more comfortable discussing the matter in the taverna. Why don't you follow me?"

Without waiting for the German's answer, without a backward glance, Venchiarutti led the way. Kleindienst hesitated a few seconds, shrugged, and followed. At the door of the taverna, Venchiarutti courteously stepped aside.

"After you, please."

The taverna was small and stone-paved. It took a while for the two men to adjust to the semi-darkness after the glaring sun outside. A scent of *ouzo* and stale tobacco lingered. There were a few tables and some wooden benches. A print of the Acropolis and another of the Isle of Santorini adorned the walls. The owner, Mastrandoni, a burly man in his fifties, leaned against the wall and made no effort to welcome the two officers. He was bareheaded and wore a white shirt buttoned up to his neck with white sleeves and a long apron which could not hide Greek Army boots.

Venchiarutti sighed again. *Sighing is getting to be a habit*, he thought.

He pulled a bench and motioned to the German to sit down.

"The man's enthusiasm at our presence leaves somewhat to be desired, but his wine is quite good," Venchiarutti said.

Turning to the host, Venchiarutti ordered a bottle of red wine and appetizers.

Mastrandoni disappeared in the back room, while the two men studied each other in silence, neither liking what he saw. The German had the beginning of a sneer, and his thoughts were betrayed by his contemptuous attitude. *A decadent aristocrat*, said his sneer, *a shadow of a soldier for whom victory, glory, and discipline have probably no meaning*. In contrast, Lt. Venchiarutti no longer smiled. There was something sinister and evil emanating from the young German, something that he sensed but could neither touch nor define. The German gazed at him without blinking; his smile was not a smile but a leer, and his body was straight and rigid. There was strength in him but also ferocity. Venchiarutti felt a shiver down his spine. He remembered that same feeling when, as a child, he had seen a cobra in the zoo. This man was dangerous and could not be taken lightly.

Mastrandoni came with the wine and the food. The wine was good, indeed, with a full body and a slightly, not unpleasantly tart aftertaste. The appetizers were sizzling, and the bread was freshly baked.

Venchiarutti forced himself to be cordial.

"It has been a long time since I have had the opportunity to speak German, and I hope it is not too rusty. I kept some wonderful memories from Berlin." He did not add, *Before you bastard Nazis took over.*

"Your German is perfect, Lieutenant," said Kleindienst, somewhat mollified, "but unlike you, I haven't had the pleasure of living in Berlin. Just passed through it a couple of times. I am from Stuttgart myself." Kleindienst was pleased. "Indeed, a pleasant coincidence. I am sure that I can count on your cooperation in fulfilling my duties as efficiently and as rapidly as possible."

Venchiarutti's eyes narrowed a little. "And what exactly are these duties, Herr Kleindienst?"

The German frowned at Venchiarutti's omission of his SS military title.

"My duties are fairly simple. At dawn, the population of this den of murderers will be executed and the village destroyed. By eleven o'clock tomorrow morning, we shall be on our way."

"Everyone? Women and children as well?"

"Everyone."

"From a practical point of view, is this advisable? You know that it will stiffen their resistance and, perhaps, result in even more German casualties."

"I know no such things. On the contrary, I believe that it will serve as a salutary example to others who might think of defying the might of the Third Reich. Besides, even if I did agree with your estimation of these people's character, these are my orders."

"Herr *Sturmbandführer* Kleindienst," this time, Venchiarutti emphasized the military title, "you are a German officer. Would the massacre of women and children be consistent with your military honor?"

"I believe we have totally different conceptions of military honor, Lieutenant. To obey my orders, no matter what they are, and to die for my Führer and my country define my honor and the honor of all German soldiers. The death of these poor specimens of humanity causes me no concern. I would destroy all of Greece if it brings Germany closer to victory."

A silence followed, heavy, deadly, punctuated only by the buzzing of a fly, who could not quite determine whether to stay in the taverna or allow itself to be seduced by the pencil of golden brightness showing between the wall and the half-closed door of the taverna.

"Herr Kleindienst, you are a military man and, undoubtedly, a very bright one. You hear the front line news. You know as well as I that we are losing this war. Massacres, as the ones you plan, will bring terrible retributions upon our people. For the sake of your countrymen, if not for the sake of humanity, I implore you not to carry out your plan," said Venchiarutti.

The German smiled. "Lieutenant, if you were under my command, I would have had you arrested for your defeatist attitude. As it is, I must inform you that I shall report your comments to your superiors upon my return. And you are wrong. Germany cannot lose the war. As soon as we render operational the new weapons that the Führer has promised, the military situation will be reversed."

Lt. Venchiarutti felt an insurmountable physical lassitude, a sense of helplessness he had never experienced before in his life. He could do nothing; he could say nothing to sway the arrogant, sneering incarnation of evil in front of him, nothing to thwart the monstrous deed that would be accomplished in less than twenty-four hours. He felt a spasm of rage. He could kill him, kill him now, and perhaps his own soldiers could prevent the massacre.

As if he had read his mind, the German added, "Don't even think about it, my Italian friend. Even if you could kill me, which I doubt, my second in command is aware of my orders and will carry them out to the letter."

"Herr Kleindienst, I am legally in charge of the occupying force in this village. You are interfering with my authority, and I will not allow you to do so."

Kleindienst stood up, but there was nothing threatening in his attitude.

"Look," he said simply. Venchiarutti followed him to the door. The twenty-man Italian garrison had been disarmed. The men were sitting on the ground, surrounded by Germans pointing sub-machine guns at them.

Venchiarutti did not look back, he opened the door and walked outside; the fly preceded him, unable to resist the larger rectangle of sunlight. Bitter burning tears of rage and despair gathered in the corners of his eyes, which, nevertheless, remained dry. He turned suddenly, and the German almost bumped into him.

"Let my men go," Venchiarutti said.

"Of course," replied Kleindienst. "They are free, but we must keep their weapons. You may keep your sidearm, Lt. Venchiarutti."

Venchiarutti nodded and walked away. The Germans had come.

Chapter 2

Mavropotamos

After his brief encounter with the SS officer, Venchiarutti returned to his quarters. It was a spartan room with an army cot in one corner, a foot-locker, a small desk, and a chair. There were pictures on the desk, but he could not look at them. These pictures of happiness belonged to a different world and had no place in a village which was about to die. He sat in the straight-backed chair, impervious to the cold wind blowing through the open window. The luminous dial of his watch indicated 10:00 p.m. It would be a long night, perhaps the last for many people. Then, the clamors and screams started.

Unable to stay in his room, he returned to the center of the village, and from a side street in the shadows, he witnessed the apocalyptic scene. Machine guns at the ready, the SS men kicked in the doors of the old houses and emerged, dragging behind them men, women, and children desperately holding on to their door jambs. They soon realized the futility of their efforts and docilely followed their tormentors, women in tears holding their children by the hand, men with flashing eyes, carrying some meager possessions, trying to look straight ahead. One of the SS troopers shoved a woman who was not walking fast enough. She stumbled, fell, and her man, an elderly but husky fellow, grabbed the German by the shoulder and swung him so violently that the man was turned around and lost his balance. A second German pointed his Schmeizer at the Greek, while a third smashed him in the kidneys with the butt of his weapon. The man fell to his knees, and the German swung his weapon again. They were approximately a step away from Venchiarutti. The Italian officer came out of his hiding place swiftly, stepped up, and interposed himself between the two. The two Germans hesitated for a minute, then shrugged and marched on. Venchiarutti helped the Greek to his feet; there were no words exchanged, no thanks given. He was the enemy.

"*Raus, schnell, Schweinerhund!* Outside, quick, swines!" the Germans screamed, three words that had become familiar to millions of slaves throughout the continent. Then, gradually, the screams diminished, and the ensuing silence almost hurt. The village was deserted; even the animals were gone. A sudden noise startled the Italian. It was a door that a gust of wind had slammed. Then there were more noises. The doors of most houses had been left ajar and were further opening and closing with the whims of the wind. The wind came down from the peaks. Venchiarutti remembered a documentary he had seen as a child of old abandoned cities in the American West; only the tumbleweeds were missing.

But those cities far away had been abandoned. This village was being murdered. There were no tumbleweeds, but there was a child's Evzone beret, a doll, and a few battered suitcases, pitiful remains of those who were about to die. At least Caesar's gladiators could defend themselves. These poor people would be slaughtered like lambs.

He entered the empty taverna. Two tables had been thrown against the walls, and two chairs were broken. *Mastrandoni must have put up quite a fight,* he thought. He went behind the bar and poured himself a glass of *ouzo* that he swallowed straight. The fiery liquid failed to steady him. He wandered around the deserted square for a while longer, and at last he returned to his quarters. He cursed silently and angrily. He was angry at himself, angry at the stubborn villagers, at the Germans, and above all, at the crazy, senseless fate which put him, an up-and-coming successful lawyer in Rome, in charge of a small garrison in a God-forsaken corner of the Greek mountains.

He closed his eyes and pictured the peaceful garden of the large villa in the outskirts of Rome where he was born and where his parents still lived, the well-kept flower beds, the alley with a bench on which he had spent countless hours with a succession of beautiful young women, each unique and each having elicited in him a sincere and undying love. Then Stella came, and as soon as he met her, he knew that the bench had finally served its ultimate purpose.

They had met at a charitable gala affair. He did not relish such parties, but he had accompanied his mother, who had been one of the organizers. His father had been away in Paris on business, and he had never been able to say no to his mother. He had noticed Stella right away, almost hiding in the shadows of a marble pillar. After all these years, he still remembered very vividly what she wore: a very simple, long linen sheath contrasting beautifully with her tanned face and honey-blond hair. Her hair was drawn back, revealing exquisitely sculpted features and deep dark eyes. She wore a gold medallion, and the young man he was then had been stunned. She was like an apparition out of a storybook--tall, regal and beautiful.

He approached her, but suddenly, all his sophistication left him, and he could only stammer, "My name is Francesco." She smiled, and to him her smile was like the dawn of a beautiful summer day. They sat side by side and exchanged a few words. When the evening was over, he asked her permission to call on her parents. They were married a year later.

Stella came from an impoverished but old, distinguished Roman family, and both sets of parents approved of their union. There was a depth to Stella which matched her appearance. A graduate of the University of Rome, she was endowed with a brilliant mind and an unending curiosity. The old bench must have been surprised at the kind of discussions that he and Stella often had during their courtship. Stella was more than a wife in the traditional sense of the thirties and forties. She was a partner and a companion. Unlike so many couples of the Roman aristocracy, he and Stella were truly devoted to each other, and occasionally, when they visited his parents, he would look at the old bench with a glint of mischief in his eyes, but without nostalgia and without regrets.

He and Stella had bought a smaller villa adjacent to that of his parents, and much to his father's disapproval, he had entered law school. The older Venchiarutti frowned at such activities. As far as he was concerned, a wealthy, well-born, and well-bred Roman should devote his life to appropriate leisure activities such as racing, traveling, playing endless games of tennis, and, as a concession to modern times, occasionally controlling his investments. Yet, he was sure that the old man was secretly proud of him. He had quickly risen to the top of his firm, and for a while, he thought of dabbling at politics until the ascent of Mussolini and his black-shirted fascists. Something in his aristocratic nature rebelled against the vulgarity and brutality of the New Order. His sense of justice and fair play quickly became offended at the high-handed tactics of this new breed of Italians, and since neither he nor his father kept their views to themselves, their family soon became *personae non grata*.

He was worried about his father, and the two of them had long and not always optimistic conversations in the old man's study, an airy, sunlit room with books and trophies lining the walls.

He remembered a balmy Sunday afternoon, one of those luminous fall days in Rome when everything was quiet and peaceful. His father had retreated into his study for an inordinately long time. Somewhat concerned, Venchiarutti had knocked at the door and went in without waiting for an answer. His father was slumped in his heavy desk chair and seemed so tired.

"Papa, are you all right?"

The old man smiled and nodded. His son went behind him and put his hands on his father's shoulders. The old man reached over and held his son's hand.

"It's good that you are here. Pour me a cognac, and pour yourself one."

They sat side-by-side for a while, savoring each other's presence, the declining afternoon sun, and the ruby liquid in the crystal glasses.

"I am worried about you, son, but I am worried even more about our country. In so many ways, we were a model for the rest of Europe, and look at us now. Our beautiful Italy, run by a bunch of goons with no principles, no sense of history."

The old man sighed and swirled his cognac in his balloon glass. Francesco remained silent for a few minutes. He could well understand his father's anguish in as much as he shared it.

"How long will this go on, Papa? Our people love their freedom. We are not Germans who worship authority. How long can we put up with this rabble without rebelling?"

The older Venchiarutti cast a sidelong glance at his son. He wondered how long it would take his son to reach the inevitable conclusion. Italy had to liberate herself from the yoke of shame. Unknown to Francesco, his father had been in contact with some circles in Rome, whose disgust and anger at Mussolini were still in the talking stages but would soon translate themselves into action. He was loath to involve his son in such activities. He did not care what happened to himself, but Francesco had to remain in the clear for the sake of his grandson.

"The day will come, my son, perhaps sooner than we think. Still, the war may end even earlier."

"Do you really think so? Hitler seems more formidable than ever. He is piling up victory upon victory in Russia and..."

His father interrupted him with a gesture, got off his chair, selected a book from a shelf, and in his beautiful baritone voice, read to his son:

> *The snow was falling. They were defeated by his conquest. For the first time, the eagle bowed its head. Somber days! The emperor slowly retreated and behind him burned Moscow in flames.*

"This, my son, was written by Victor Hugo about Napoleon. You see, Francesco, Hitler will beat the Russians, but Russia will beat Hitler."

Francesco always marveled at his father's erudition and wisdom. "So many millions will die until then."

"Yes," replied his father, "and worse than the lives lost, worse than the blood shed, it is the spirit, the soul of Europe that this man is destroying, and I am ashamed that we are part of it."

Francesco heard the anger and the sadness in the older man's voice. He went behind his father's leather chair and put his hand on his father's shoulder. The older Venchiarutti reached for his son's hand, and although now almost forty, Francesco experienced the same reassuring sensation as when he was a little boy and held his father's hand.

"I love you, Papa."

"Go now, Francesco. I need to be alone."

The Venchiaruttis were shunned by many of their neighbors, and over time, the volume of Francesco's legal business quickly declined. This state of affairs did not bother him much, but he was deeply saddened by what was happening to his beloved country. He was wealthy enough to live without the income of his legal practice, and he was quite content to spend his days with Stella and Bruno, their beautiful ten-year-old. Then thunder struck. In spite of his age--he was nearing forty-one--Francesco had been called into the army. He still recalled his anger and the cold feeling in the pit of his stomach as he discussed his draft notice with his wife and parents, especially his father.

"You cannot refuse to go, Francesco. We shall lose the war, but it's still our country." There was sadness in the old man's voice, a resigned sadness as when one speaks a painful but inescapable truth.

Stella was silent, but tears slowly flowed from her beautiful dark eyes. She held Bruno tightly, and he knew her pain and her fear. Francesco's fleeting thought was escape. Perhaps he could hide, perhaps escape into Switzerland. He just could not run away, although running away was not only the wiser but, perhaps, also the nobler thing to do. Somehow, for reasons he did not wish to analyze or understand, he just could not run. He glanced at Stella, and she smiled through her tears.

"We'll be all right, don't worry about us," Stella assured him. "We'll move into the big house with mother and father. Just come back to us." And that was all.

But that was not all. He could not run away, but his whole being rebelled at the idea of being a cog, even if only an insignificant one, in Mussolini's war machine.

As Francesco sat silently with his family, his mind played an inner dialogue as he tried to piece together his circumstance:

Who would I be fighting for, Mussolini and his goons?

What else can you do?

I could go to Switzerland and take my family away.

Then what? You would have to come back one day.

No one would hold it against me.

That is not the point. They would probably be happy for you. But they will suffer and starve and die while you and your family will be safe.

That is as far as he could go with his internal dialogue. Sometimes words like "honor" and "duty" would come to his mind, but he would still them, not knowing where "duty" and "honor" lay. The bottom line was that, like Danton, the French revolutionary, he could not leave his country behind.

Leaving his family behind was not easy. On the day of his departure, Francesco's family lined up in front of the big house: his parents, Stella, Bruno, Giovanni the gardener, and Maria the cook, who had been with the family since long before his birth. Francesco shook Giovanni's hand and gave Maria a hug. He kissed his mother and hugged his father tight. Then he scooped Stella and Bruno into his arms.

"My loves, my loves, my loves."

"We'll be all right, my husband. You make sure you come back to us."

He smiled in return, a little ashamed at his overwhelming emotion. Truly, he was not worried about them. Indeed, they would be all right. He was horribly frightened, however, at the thought that he would not see them again. He got into the waiting taxi, leaned out of the window, and waved until he could see them no longer.

After a perfunctory basic training, Francesco was awarded as first lieutenant commission. He thought ruefully, *I must be the oldest first lieutenant in the Italian army.* His first assignment had been to command a small garrison in a village in Greece with the gloriously pompous title of Military Governor of Mavropotamos, population 528, not including dozens of small irascible donkeys and innumerable goats. Mavropotamos was an eagle's nest, perched in the middle of inaccessible mountains, and its inhabitants were as proud and intractable as eagles.

When he had first arrived with his small group of aged reservists--apparently someone in Rome, in his infinite wisdom, had lumped all these elderly warriors together--he had felt a deep sense of foreboding not at all helped by the villagers' attitudes. They would walk by him and his men, tall, straight, rigid and unsmiling. All of them--men, women, children (even the goats, he could swear)--would look straight through him as if he did not exist. He had requisitioned a room on the second floor of a small house in the center of the village. From his window, he could see the *plateia* (town square), the hub of all commercial and social activity. Across the street was Mastrandoni, the tall burly fellow with a stained apron but an immaculate white shirt and army boots, who looked more like a mountain brigand than a tavern owner. Francesco spent long hours at his window, and once, out of sheer boredom, he had tried to count the donkeys, but he soon gave up; there were too many of them.

One day, he entered the taverna on an impulse and sat at a table. Studiously, the taverna patrons avoided his glance, and nobody came to serve him. He snorted loud enough to be heard and left in disgust, promising himself never to return.

Eventually, he ventured into the hills and became seduced by the savage beauty of the mountains. He learned to take long walks, sit on a rock, and look at what seemed like an infinity of blue and gray mountains reaching to the end of the world. Sometimes he had the curious sensation that he was part of it all, that he was an eagle soaring high up in the sky. Those were the very rare times when he would think of Stella and Bruno without a deep sense of hurt. These moments were like an intense, physical sensation and would not last long. When they passed, they would leave him with a feeling of awe but also with a vague sense of guilt and embarrassment, as if he had partaken of some god-like but forbidden delight.

He worried about his men. He knew they felt alone and vulnerable. When they first reached the village, he had not allowed his men to be billeted in private homes for two reasons: first, he did not want his unit to behave like a conquering army, and requisitioning one room for himself was, as he thought, bad enough, but in that he had no choice. Traditionally, the commanding officer could not share his men's sleeping accommodations. Secondly, he wanted his men together so that they could find support in one another. They had spent the first two weeks under tents while building a wooden barrack large and comfortable enough for twenty-five men. He would, sometimes, join them in the evening and partake in melancholic *canzonnette Napolitane* or listen to the fine tenor voice of Sergeant Raffaele. Occasionally, one of the men would turn around to dab a tear from his eye, and the others pretended not to notice.

Gradually, however, the villagers' attitudes changed, perhaps because, like his men, the citizens of Mavropotamos were all middle-aged. There were few young men to be seen, and Francesco guessed that, while some had died during the Albanian Campaign, most had joined the partisans. Such questions were not asked, and if asked, were never answered. Perhaps also because Italians and Greeks were alike in so many ways and felt a sense of kinship which neither group shared with the Germans. Perhaps because his men were the least militaristic military unit he had ever seen, although as an inveterate civilian he was not an expert on the subject.

Francesco chuckled as he remembered the event that first led to the change. Sgt. Raffaele, he of the fine voice, was leading a squad of five soldiers through the village square when he turned around and marched backward while counting cadence, watching his men. He bumped into the rear end of a jackass led by a burly Greek villager. Not to be outdone, the jackass turned around and hit Sgt. Raffaele with his head, and the tall sergeant fell to the pavement. Witnesses to the incident ran to the scene, and the five

Italian soldiers automatically formed a semi-circle, rifles at the ready. The moment was pregnant with expectation and tension. Lt. Venchiarutti moved to intervene, but in the end no intervention was needed. Raffaele's soldiers turned around and, seeing their leader on his rear end staring at the jackass, burst into uncontrollable laughter, and in no time, an Homeric wave of laughter swept the square. Sgt. Raffaele, somewhat sheepishly, picked himself up, patted the jackass, and gave a cigarette to the appreciative owner of the animal.

Whatever the reason, the thaw was welcomed and had made Lt. Venchiarutti and his small detachment feel less vulnerable and less isolated.

The real turning point had been when Francesco was invited by some of the village elders to share a drink of *ouzo* under the big oak tree in the village square--apparently the taverna was still out of bounds. He spoke no Greek, and they spoke little Italian, yet, they managed to communicate. Photos were passed around, and he felt sheepish as he became aware of his huge, satisfied grin over the villagers' approval of Stella and Bruno. At times like these, the constant ache of not being with Stella and Bruno dulled somewhat, and he would think of them with a curious feeling of joy--joy that they were part of him, such a wonderful part of him and that these hard, primitive men knew and understood his feelings.

They discussed many subjects except two that always remained taboo. These were the lieutenant's opinion of Italy's fascist government, and the presence of partisans in the mountains. Francesco would often remain silent and stare at the milky liquor in his glass when these topics were discussed.

Many months went by, and he was lulled into the comfortable belief that he and his men would, perhaps, weather the end of the war in Mavropotamos and eventually return home. The village was tranquil; he knew that there were partisans operating in the mountains, but they left Mavropotamos strictly alone. His orders were to keep the village peaceful but not to venture into the mountains in pursuit of will-of-the-wisp partisans. This gentleman's agreement suited him and his men quite well until the day when the peace of his little world was suddenly shattered.

ဢ

That peaceful world had existed until two days ago, and already the village seemed like another life and another world. Venchiarutti was sitting at the same window, looking at the never-ending blue mountains, which he had learned at first not to be afraid of, then to admire, and then to love.

Hard as he tried, Lt. Francesco Venchiarutti had never been able to understand and relate to his German allies. He had met some of them before; they could be charming, sociable, well-mannered, then suddenly they would turn into wild beasts, robots of incredible efficiency, with no thoughts of their own and certainly devoid of human feelings. He had tried to talk to the German commander. The man was not a bad sort; he was friendly, likable enough, but there was something bizarre about him. He seemed totally unaffected at the prospect of a deed as monstrous as killing 528 civilians. He had listened with near bewilderment to Lt. Venchiarutti's arguments and, very politely, had replied, "I wish I could help you, Lieutenant, but these are my orders--good night." The bastard was probably sleeping quite soundly.

Venchiarutti sighed, snuffed out his cigarette, and stepped outside. It was pitch dark; the cold was, indeed, penetrating, and he raised the collar of his great coat. The huge barn where the villagers were held sat at the outskirts of the hamlet. The pattern of the rounds of the two sentries was quite simple; they circled the building in opposite directions. It would be easy to get close and behind them, but it would be difficult to neutralize them; he did not want to kill them, and besides, he could not afford noise. He stumbled, almost fell, looked down, and picked up a stubby chunk of wood about a foot long. He faded into the shadows, blending into the wall of the barn. The first sentry passed him, and Venchiarutti hit him in the back of the neck. The second sentry walked toward him, and Francesco hit him in the stomach. As the man bent over, he clobbered him on the top of the head. Venchiarutti paused briefly, bent over, and made certain they were both still alive. He rubbed his hands rather smugly. By George! He did not think he had it in him. With a chuckle, he realized that in his four years of army life, during this most violent of all wars, hitting two German allies in the pit of the stomach and the back of the neck with a chunk of wood had been his two most violent actions. Time was running out. He opened the barn door and was almost suffocated by the stench. Fortunately, his Greek by now was passable.

"I took care of the sentries. Hurry up into the mountains. May God be with you."

The villagers knew better than to waste time, and in a few moments the rear of a bedraggled column had disappeared among the rocks. It was then that reaction set in and his legs started to shake, his head spun, and he sat down for what seemed an eternity.

When he felt able to walk again, it was too late. A German patrol was almost upon him. As he ran, he could hear them yelling, heard shots, felt a blow on the back of his head, and he lost consciousness.

Chapter 3

The Mission

It was May in Washington, D.C., a beautiful, sunny day with only a hint of the oppressive heat which would arrive in the summer. The pavement and the leaves on the trees were bright as if recently washed. May 5, 1976, to be exact. America was getting ready to celebrate its bicentennial and the events of World War II belonged to a different era and a faraway place.

A tall, well-built young man, wearing a conservative, well-fitting blue suit entered the Shoreham Hotel. His name was David Castro. He sat down on a comfortable leather chair in an inconspicuous corner of the lobby and watched the entrance. *Old habits die hard*, he thought with an amused grin. As usual, the hotel hosted some convention or other, and the ornate lobby was full of business suits with white nametags on their lapels and briefcases under their arms. Here and there was a sprinkling of women, but even they, in their serious dark, charcoal gray attire, could not manage to enliven the deadly dull crowd.

At five to eleven, the three men walked in, and David shook his head in wonderment. The nature of the stereotype changes but stereotypes remain, and junior State and FBI people certainly lived up to theirs. Bill had not changed much, a little on the heavier side maybe, but he still had the same friendly smile and slightly disheveled appearance. David felt a wave of affection for his old friend; he let Bill and the other two men walk by and settled back in his chair. He would give them ten more minutes before going upstairs. Seeing Bill, even from a distance, stirred so many memories, some pleasant, some painful. He closed his eyes and allowed himself to remember.

They had met almost twenty years ago while serving in the same outfit in Korea. David had been transferred there shortly after his basic training at Fort Knox. Basic training had been one of those unforgettable experiences which one remembers with mixed feelings, not knowing whether to laugh or cry at the memories. At that time, he had only been in the States for six months. His English was very poor, and his knowledge of American society and customs was nonexistent. Sick of counting and carrying merchandise in a department store, he had joined the army on an impulse. He had a hard time understanding commands, and on the drill field, it was not at all unusual for him to turn left while his squad turned right. The firing range was another of these tragi-comical situations where he would never hear the command to fire on time, and his rifle would start after all other rifles had ceased firing. In the deadly silence which follows the simultaneous discharge of eighty rifles, the discharge of his weapon was, to say the least, conspicuous, and did not endear him to his platoon lieutenant. This came to pass, however; his English improved rapidly, and the fact that, in spite of his poor timing, he always had the best score on the rifle range brought the members of his platoon around, including his platoon leader. While none of the other recruits were close to him, they respected him. His shyness, as well as his obvious desire to be left alone, discouraged advances and friendliness. He avoided closeness, yet often felt lonely. The other men in the outfit kept a respectful distance. He did his work well, often more than his share, but his serious, almost austere mien discouraged friendliness, and his physical appearance discouraged hazing; he was six foot two, and his well-proportioned, muscled body conveyed an impression of power and agility.

There was one soldier, however, who did not take no for an answer. In spite of David's coolness and distant demeanor, this soldier kept sitting next to him, never missed an opportunity to engage him in conversation, and, more than once, helped David out of an embarrassing situation. Bill's perseverance eventually paid off, and David gradually warmed up to the young soldier. Yet, while David listened to Bill with pleasure during their conversations, he never talked about himself.

How clearly he remembered one day in Korea, a lazy Saturday afternoon, a blue sky, a warm but not oppressive heat, the almost empty barrack. He was reading on his bunk when Bill stopped by, stood there for a minute, and with his infectious smile said, "Well, what do you say, David? Let's go paint the town red." He chuckled, remembering how odd the concept of "painting the town red" had sounded to him. He had been touched by the invitation.

His initial reaction had been to decline as he always had, but, somehow, the empty barrack and the sun slanting through the window stirred in him an unexpected wave of nostalgia and loneliness. He shrugged, smiled, and said, "Hell, why not?" It took him ten minutes to shower and get into his Class A uniform.

Their "painting the town red" had been quite tame, indeed--at least in the beginning. They sat at a table in an out-of-the-way bar in the outskirts of Seoul and talked for a long time as beer followed beer.

Bill was a pure, unadulterated WASP, at least in terms of his background. Born in Pennsylvania into a well-to-do family, he had been destined since an early age to a career in politics or the military. At the age of eighteen, he had almost been disowned by his grandfather for choosing a large northeastern university instead of West Point or an Ivy League college. The old gentleman almost had a fit when, after graduation, Bill joined the army as a lowly enlisted man rather than apply for commission. It was characteristic of Bill that he preferred to remain an enlisted man when he could have had a commission for the asking. Bill's father, however, did not seem to mind.

Staring through his mug of beer, Bill chuckled, "I always had a feeling that Dad had wanted but never dared tell Granddad where to get off, and I was doing it for him. For whatever reason, he and Mother always backed me up and let me do my thing, whatever it was."

It was a warm and comfortable feeling that David had rarely experienced; quiet talk, the trust developing, the peaceful cool restaurant. For the first time, he talked to Bill about himself. He described the big house where he was born in the city of Salonica, the spacious rooms with the large windows, the warm furniture with its character and history.

He remembered his mother saying, "Dad designed our bedroom suite and ordered it from a manufacturer in Paris. There's only one like it in the whole world, and then he traveled to Belgrade to buy our living room from the French ambassador who was returning home. It is a genuine Louis XV." His mother, indeed, had been very proud of her home. She was somewhat of a paradox; she valued education and, above everything else, honesty and hard work. Money and material possessions were secondary, except when the contents of her home were concerned.

David also loved his home, the room he shared with his younger sister, the huge backyard with the many trees and a mini-jungle where cowboys and Indians would encounter Tarzan of the Apes. He talked about school, about his beloved teachers who had taught him to think and question, about his friends who were now all dead. But he did not talk about their deaths. When Bill wondered about what happened to his family and what had made him come to America, David shrugged and said, "Enough about me, let's talk about you."

"David, I am so glad you are here, but what made you change your mind?"

"I can't rightly say. The barracks were too quiet, maybe. Maybe I was lonely. Besides, you are a pain when you want something, and you never take 'no' for an answer."

Bill smiled. "You're right, but it's not a good enough answer. Anyway, it doesn't matter. I'm just glad you came."

"Why did you ask me?" asked David. "Why did you go out of your way so often to help me and become my friend in spite of my sullenness? Because I know I've been sullen, sometimes rude, not only with you but with the other guys."

"No, that's not true. You've never been rude, but yes, the unmistakable message was that you wanted to be alone."

"Then, why?" insisted David.

"To tell you the truth, I don't know," Bill said, shrugging. "I often wondered about that myself. For many years, until Annie was born, I was an only child, and I always wanted a brother. Sometimes, it was a younger brother to whom I would teach things, sometimes an older brother who would protect me. No, I don't mean that I look at you as a substitute brother. Not at all. Yet, sometimes... I guess, I just like you... It's good to be friends."

They drank in silence, in the peaceful warm atmosphere of the Korean bistro.

It was dark when they left and happened upon a dimly lit alley, an alleged short-cut to the USO where the buses were waiting to drive them back to camp. In the alley, there were three young Koreans, probably in their twenties, and their intentions left little doubt as they spread out in front of David and Bill.

Bill swallowed audibly and his voice was a little shaky. "David, let's give them what they want and get the hell out of here."

David gently put a restraining hand on his friend's arm. He was neither angry nor afraid but felt as if his chest wanted to burst with excitement. It was a sense of exhilaration that he did not ever remember experiencing, yet it was, somehow, a proper culmination of that strange evening. He jumped high and his flying side kick hit one Korean in the center of the chest; the man dropped without a sound. David pivoted, and his rigid left hand shot out with military precision and hit the second assailant on the side of the neck. He continued pivoting, and the palm of his right hand made a sickening dull sound as it encountered the man's chin. The third Korean was much more circumspect, and a streetlight reflected from the knife he was now holding. To the man's surprise, David did not pause; his left leg whipped the air from right to left, and the knife flew out of the man's hand. That seemed to be enough, and the only Korean left standing turned and ran.

In the dark, Bill's features were indistinguishable. He said one word, "Wow," and the two started running toward their destination. It was getting late, and the base was a long way off.

⟳

Some noisy young people walking by disturbed David's reverie. He looked at his watch. Fifteen minutes had gone by, and it was high time to join Bill and his associates. He dropped the newspaper into the trash and moved toward the elevator. There were no familiar faces in the lobby, and the elevator was empty. When he exited on his floor, he carefully looked in both directions before proceeding toward the room where the meeting was being held.

Habit, he thought ruefully. *Someday I'll be like normal people.* He stopped briefly, then knocked.

There were three men lounging in the room, a table with a glass top covered with papers, a bar in the corner with bottles and glasses, and several telephones on a desk against the wall.

Not the run of the mill hotel room, thought David. *It probably houses more such meetings than hotel guests.*

David glanced at Bill, and their eyes met, and it was as if they had just seen each other the day before.

"Hello, Bill," he said, and Bill's eyes twinkled with the same mischievousness of old. He had not changed a bit. He was almost as slim as ever, tall and elegantly rumpled, a touch of gray, perhaps, in his thick wavy hair. Characteristically disdainful of decorum, he moved over to David and hugged him. One of the other two men cleared his throat, and Bill winked.

"David, this is Tom Scorcese, FBI, and Steve Harper from State. Gentlemen, this is the man I told you about, formerly with the agency and now in business for himself, my old and very dear friend David Castro." The three men shook hands and Bill handed a glass to his friend. "*Ouzo,* David, on the rocks."

David laughed, but was touched. "All right, William, why do I feel you are fattening me up for the kill? What's up?"

The four men sat around the round table. The State Department man, Steve Harper, was a tall but frail man with sad brown eyes and was neatly, almost fastidiously dressed. He had a precise and clipped diction, as would be expected from a junior State Department official, but with none of the arrogance that characterized so many of his colleagues. Rather, he seemed reserved, almost shy or tired.

Bill's FBI colleague, Tom Scorcese, was a large, beefy man with deceptively sleepy eyes which, seemingly half closed, missed nothing of what was going on. He looked rumpled in his blue suit, but not in Bill's elegant manner. He was a working class cop, thought David, and not one to be taken lightly. He sensed that one should keep one's guard up with Scorcese, yet he could be trusted.

It was Harper who started the briefing.

"Mr. Castro, it all began over thirty years ago, more precisely in 1942, in Northern Greece, in a fairly large city named Salonica."

David stiffened and shot a glance at Bill, who shook his head imperceptibly. He decided to say nothing, took a seat, and let the man from State continue.

"Salonica, at that time, had a large and very sophisticated Jewish population. In 1942, racial laws were applied to that Jewish community, and a systematic deportation of Jews from Salonica to Auschwitz resulted in a complete annihilation of a very vibrant community. Out of 75,000 Jews, only about 1,500 survived. The assistant Gestapo chief in Salonica was an SS colonel named Johann Richter. As the war drew to an end, SS Colonel Richter disappeared, dropped off the edge of the world, and was never heard from again. All efforts to locate him were in vain.

"In 1951, a German refugee by the name of Dieter Von Eckardt settled in Detroit, Michigan. As far as we and immigration authorities know, Von Eckardt came from an old Prussian family whose members had been opposed to the Nazi regime and were occasionally persecuted by Hitler's henchmen. Von Eckardt did well for himself, eventually started his own engineering firm, and presently counts himself among Detroit's millionaires. He kept pretty much out of the limelight and raised a model family, two sons and one daughter. No scandals, no problems. In spite of their money, they are not ostentatious and live a relatively simple life. Neither State nor the FBI would have bothered with them if it weren't for the fact that several months ago we were informed by the Israeli government that, according to information gathered by the Mossad, model citizen Von Eckardt is none other than ex-SS Colonel Johann Richter. The Mossad's evidence, however, is circumstantial and would not stand up in court. We did some digging of our own and found that low profile Von Eckardt had some discreet but sustained contact with the P.L.O. and members of neo-Nazi organizations. Nothing illegal, mind you, but rather incompatible with the image of a respectable, solid businessman which he has always projected.

"Recently we have received some additional information from the Mossad, and this is where you, Mr. Castro, come in. It seems that there lived in Salonica, at that time, a talented Jewish historian by the name of Assael. Dr.

Assael survived the massacre by hiding out in the Italian consulate in Salonica, under the protection of Commandatore Castruccio, the Italian representative, known for his anti-fascist leanings and humanitarian attitude toward Greek Jews. Rumor has it that, while in hiding, Dr. Assael chronicled and managed to document much of what was going on in his home town. Unfortunately, shortly after the liberation of Salonica, Dr. Assael died of a heart attack on his way to Israel; of course, back then, it was called Palestine. His chronicles were never found. While in hiding, Dr. Assael had become quite friendly with an Italian officer--Captain Venchiarutti, now a successful and respected attorney in Rome. If anyone knows the whereabouts of Assael's documents, it can only be Venchiarutti. Perhaps Commandatore Castruccio also knew, but he has been dead now for several years. At any rate, next week, Venchiarutti will be in Athens to address an international conference of distinguished jurists. We would like you to contact him and, if the chronicles exist, persuade him to turn them over to you. Our relations with the government of Greece, although friendly, are not on the best possible footing, and the government of the United States would rather not become officially involved. We could, of course, approach the Greek foreign ministry directly to ask for their assistance. We cannot be sure, however, that, should they find the documents, they will turn them over to us in their entirety. A CIA operation is out of the question. The risks involved are too great. If anything were to go wrong, it would not help our prestige and our relationship with the Greek government. As you may know, the Greeks are rather touchy about foreign secret services operating on their soil. It would not do at all for our CIA to receive such publicity. We would like you to do this as a private citizen. At first, hearing it sounds like a rather routine mission, but there may be ramifications of which we are not aware. There always are in the case of former Nazi bigwigs."

David had stopped listening long before the man from State had finished his presentation. It seemed centuries ago; he had been only nine or ten, and he remembered standing at the corner of the street where he and his family lived and watching long, interminable files of Greek soldiers returning from the battle front. He remembered how tired they were, looking neither right nor left, just plodding along. The Germans came the next day. Tall, blond young men, not unfriendly, riding dirty, dusty tanks and trucks. For a little boy, these were exciting days. No school, no homework, parents too concerned to maintain discipline.

"Don't come late, son."

"No, Dad, I won't. Don't worry." But he always returned home long past curfew, much to the chagrin of his parents, who constantly worried that something could happen to the little boy. They were right, of course, although nothing had ever happened. Yet, these were dangerous times, and their fears were not exaggerated.

The city looked eerie after curfew. In the dark and the utter silence, the boots of German patrols sounded like rumbling thunder. He was afraid, of course; his heart would beat faster, and sometimes his knees trembled. Yet, it was a delicious sensation that he had never experienced before. He and his two best friends, Jack and Freddy, would hide in the dark. It was almost like a game to see how close they could come to the Germans without being detected. They were terribly afraid, but the danger seemed unreal. Deep down, they knew that nothing could happen to them. It was just a marvelous game. A whole year passed before they realized that it was not a game at all. Then the bad things started to happen.

"Well, Mr. Castro... What do you say?" The voice brought him out of his memories.

"I'm sorry," said David, "I guess I was daydreaming there for a moment. Of course, I'll accept the mission. After all, that is how I make a living."

The man from State smiled a tired, somewhat relieved smile.

"O.K. Bill will brief you on the logistics."

∾

The airy café in Georgetown, with its crisp and yuppie chic, was a far cry from the seedy little place in Seoul so many, many years ago. Yet, the same feeling flooded him, the camaraderie, the warm sense of being accepted; it was real, tangible and he knew that the experience was shared. It was good to be together again.

"All right." Bill smiled. "Let us get the essentials out of the way. Delores is fine, healthy, and as beautiful as ever and sends her love. Your godson is a tough little five-year-old, and I have registered him at a karate school. Tang-Soo-Do, no less... And David, this caper is on the level. Salonica is just a coincidence. They don't even know that you come from there. The agency clearance was sufficient, and no background check was run on you."

David had flown to Washington five years ago, at the birth of Bill's first born, Frank. Bill and his Peruvian wife, Delores, had decided that he would be Frank's godfather, and holding the baby had been a strange experience, indeed. Uncontrolled tears had flooded his eyes, and he knew it was neither sadness nor hurt. It was as if he had reconnected again, as if the chain broken by the death of his parents, friends, and relatives, the destruction of everything he had known and loved was being repaired and a new link forged. Bill,

Delores, and Frank had become terribly important to him. They had become his tie to future generations.

"Bill, I'll take your word for it and even if they knew, I wouldn't care. I don't belong to the agency anymore. I can afford to make this a personal matter, and you know I will."

He ordered a bottle of very cool Riesling, and for a while, both men sipped their wine in silence, each lost in their own memories.

He had, long ago, shared with Bill the untouchable parts of his life, the horrors tucked away in the recesses of his mind and which the past few hours had reawakened.

The "bad things" had started a year after the beginning of the German occupation, and they had started with a famine. His parents had protected him and his younger sister, but he remembered that every day his home seemed different. He had finally realized that pieces of furniture were disappearing one by one--fine, gold-layered antique chairs, tables, sofas traded for flour and vegetables from the countryside. One day, his father did not come home from work. It was two days before he returned, his face swollen, his clothes torn and stained with blood. The Gestapo had arrested and beaten him for some pro-Allied articles he had written at the beginning of the war in the newspaper where he worked. Shortly thereafter, they had to leave their home and move into a small apartment in the section of town designated as the Jewish ghetto.

It was at that time he began to withdraw and to be afraid. The fabric of his life, the wonderful tapestry of love and security was slowly being torn apart and disintegrating. Nothing was the same; things changed every day and changed for the worse. His father and mother could not stop the changes; therefore, he could not rely on them anymore. He had made friends in the ghetto, other children his age, but like the old beautiful furniture, they would disappear one at a time as the deportations to Auschwitz began.

Johann Richter had been a name spoken in whispers, a name synonymous with dread and evil. It was a name which had receded into the depths of his mind and which now, once more, intruded in his life. Things were different now. He was no longer afraid. In fact, he was never afraid. They had even managed to kill fear in him by taking away all meaning to his life.

This rather simple mission was a personal matter, indeed.

Outside, it was getting dark, and it was late, but he didn't care. The time spent with Bill was precious and rare, and he wanted to enjoy it.

"What are you thinking about, David?"

He glanced at his friend and smiled. "Oh, you know, the old army days. Remember? You were such a pain in the butt. It seems like yesterday, and it was so long ago."

Bill laughed and said, "If I hadn't been such a pain, as you say, you would still be sprawled on your bed staring at the ceiling and watching the flies."

David was no longer smiling. "You are right, you know, and I'll never cease to be grateful."

Bill snorted. "Cut that out and let us get down to business. In Athens, you'll stay at the Hotel Grande Bretagne, old but very plush. That is where Venchiarutti is staying. Supposedly, you represent an important law firm in the States dealing with Italian manufacturers. He has no idea what it is you want from him. When you get back to your hotel, you will find your plane tickets--non-smoking, of course--and five thousand dollars in travelers' checks. You need more, just holler. As usual, I'll be your liaison. Anything else?"

"No," said David. "I think you covered everything pretty well."

"David, one more thing, like the man said, it is a routine mission, but you can't tell with those bastards. So be careful."

"You know I will."

"On the way back, Delores and I would like you to spend a few days with us. Whatever time you can spare. So long, my old friend. Take care of yourself. We'll look forward to seeing you soon."

As Bill's taxi sped along the quaint avenue, David had a sense of emptiness, a realization of how alone he really was. He shook his head. After all, this was the life he had chosen.

Chapter 4

Reminiscences

It was five a.m., and in an empty conference room of the Shoreham, cross-legged on the floor, David was slowly emptying his mind and meditating. Unless it was physically impossible, he never missed his daily ritual. There was no flag to bow to, but he bowed to the memory of Master Kwang, the old Korean with the wrinkled face and the slanted eyes, at times cruel, at times gentle, compassionate and full of understanding. He had been in Korea only a month when, one evening, walking listlessly through the streets of Seoul, he had entered a do-jung on a whim. The class was ending, and a Korean with the face of an old man and the body of a youth approached him. He had slightly bowed from the waist and said, "Please come in, I am Master Kwang."

The old master asked no questions but was obviously interested in the tall, serious-faced American soldier.

"There is much sadness in your eyes and much anger. Sadness and anger must be harnessed, otherwise they can destroy you. You will come and learn Tang-Soo-Do."

It was so many, many years ago, and David grinned at the memory and the fact that it had never occurred to him to question the old man's decision.

He had gone the following day for his first class and made a curious discovery: for the first time in years, he became truly absorbed in what he was doing; for the first time, the bad memories receded, and for a while he felt free. Tang-Soo-Do, a military version of Tae-Kwan-Do, the Korean style karate, became more than just an obsession, it became an addiction in that it helped him forget. He would practice four, five, or six hours a day, every day

26

of the week, except when his duties kept him at the base. It was as if he stepped into a different world where nothing mattered except the complicated karate moves. His body would take over from his mind, and he would experience a sense of exhilaration as he improved to perfection a complicated form, flew through the air in executing flying techniques, or sparred with one or two opponents. He was tall, beautifully muscled, and very fast on his feet, a combination rarely encountered among Korean athletes, who were strong and agile but seldom over six feet tall. He listened respectfully and learned never to be impatient at the rituals and to follow strict discipline.

For a year and a half, he practiced with a class, and it was only then that Master Kwang talked to him again. He asked him into his office, and after David had bowed and stood at attention, he gently gestured for him to sit.

"I am pleased. You have discipline and respect. You can harness anger, and you are very good. From now, on I shall teach you myself."

David was overwhelmed but had bowed without saying a word. Every day that followed, David spent an extra hour practicing with the old master. When his tour of duty was over, he extended it by two more years. With Master Kwang, he quickly graduated to the use of weapons and excelled at it. Free fighting with Master Kwang was a heightening, almost spiritual experience.

It was as if each person entered the psychological and physical world of the other. There were no boundaries between them, and they moved in unison, feinting, kicking, blocking and punching, predicting and countering the other's moves, at times frozen in a hieratic stance like two jungle animals watching each other and waiting for the first move, at other times attacking and countering at a speed which seemed hardly believable. It was during these fast exchanges that boundaries were blurred and they seemed to become one. Yet, in an incomprehensible way, it always occurred with infinite mutual respect, and David never felt his individuality diminished; as soon as the flurry of moves and countermoves was over, each man immediately became a separate being.

He had learned to love the do-jung where they sparred, a stark but fastidiously clean place, furnished only with straw mats on the floor, a small desk and chair in a corner, several trophies on shelves, and a Korean flag on one wall. It had become a place where he found release, where he felt accepted and wanted.

Master Kwang always insisted on alternating full contact with no contact sessions. The full contact sessions were often painful, and Master Kwang did not spare him. Many a night he had crawled into his bunk with ribs so sore that he could hardly breathe, legs and arms which turned blue in the morning. Yet, David was grateful for these sessions. He learned that Tang-

Soo-Do was more than elegant, complicated, and beautiful combinations of moves; it could also be a source of unpleasant, sometimes severe pain to be taken seriously for one's own protection. This attitude served him well much later during his years as a company field agent.

The most difficult aspect of the full contact free fighting was his inability to let go. In his sparring with Master Kwang or, for that matter, with any of his fellow students, he always found it hard to let go and would always hold back his kicks or punches. Paradoxically, he never experienced that problem when he was engaged in real, life-threatening confrontations. Eventually, however, as his relationship with Master Kwang and his trust in the old master grew and strengthened, he learned to lose his fear and let go. He still remembered when it happened for the first time and the exhilarating sense of freedom he felt.

As he learned to trust himself and Master Kwang, and as full contact sessions became easier, the non-contact sessions became increasingly harder. He talked with Master Kwang one evening when all other students had left and he lingered behind as he was often wont to do.

"Why is it, Master, that in our full contact sessions I am afraid to let go and as I improve I am so afraid during our non-contact sessions?"

The old master shrugged but said nothing.

"It is," David continued, "as if I don't trust myself, but how does this work? I don't understand."

"You are right," answered Master Kwang. "You are right. You don't trust yourself. I can help you trust me, but only study and practice can help you trust yourself."

It took a long time, but eventually he mastered the exquisite sense of self-control which enabled him to unleash a lethal kick and stop it half an inch or closer from his opponent's head.

He learned to love the old man. Since the death of his parents and for a long time after his first encounter with Bill, Master Kwang was the only person he felt close to and he knew that the feeling was reciprocated in spite of the master's austere and distant mien.

His tour of duty ended, and he had received orders reassigning him to the States for discharge. On his final day at the school, Master Kwang called him again into his office, went into a file cabinet, and pulled out a tattered black belt. His eyes twinkled as he handed it to David.

"This was my first black belt more than fifty years ago. It is for you." He paused for a moment, then added, "David, always remember, Tang-Soo-Do makes life cleaner and better, but Tang-Soo-Do should not be all your life." Then, Master Kwang did something very uncharacteristic; he opened his arms and hugged the younger man. David closed his eyes and, for a split second, he felt as he had when, as a little boy, his father held him, and it was so warm and so safe.

"Thank you, Master. I will not forget."

Having said goodbye to the old master, there was not much left to do but pack and wait. Bill had left two months earlier, and David had no close friends left among the other soldiers except maybe for the first sergeant, who had seen David practice karate. Unlike many first sergeants, Sergeant O'Hagen did not believe that his purpose in life was to make other soldiers' lives miserable. He shook David's hand and wished him well. Soon a jeep, compliments of the first sergeant, came to take him to the port of embarkation. He boarded the *Admiral Greely* and looked at the Korean coastline fading in the horizon.

He probably would never see it again, but he would remember fondly its kind yet hard people. It seemed as if through his knowledge of Tang-Soo-Do he was carrying inside of him part of the soul of the Korean people, a pride mixed with self-discipline and compassion.

The days aboard the ship had been long and monotonous. He reached San Francisco and chose to be discharged there. His discharge papers in his pocket, he had rented a room in a cheap boarding house and hunted for a job. Jobs were scarce then, especially for someone like him, with no skills and the equivalent of an undergraduate degree in liberal arts. Eventually, he was hired as a delivery truck driver. He liked the work because driving forced him to direct his attention outside of himself and limited his interactions with other people to a bare minimum. His colleagues, as was the case in the army, respected him but left him strictly alone.

He increasingly turned inward, and except when driving or practicing his beloved Tang-Soo-Do, he was in a kind of haze, reliving over and over the horrible experiences of his tender early years. It was as if the dead were not dead and haunted his nights as well as his daydreams. Memories of childhood, memories of the concentration camp, sometimes vivid, sometimes hazy, sometimes distorted, filled his mind with agony. At times, he was possessed by a murderous rage, and he had an irresistible impulse to go out and smash and destroy whatever and whoever was responsible for his great pain.

More than ever, he became immersed in the practice of karate but, this time, without the guidance of Master Kwang. He had to be careful. Once or twice, he had almost hurt his sparring partners. His great strength and extraordinary skills were such that they could become lethal unless severely controlled, and he knew that his controls were getting weaker and weaker as the days went on. Sometimes, at night, he had the crazy fantasy that he could open his skull and take his brains out so that he would no longer think.

All his life, he had been fastidiously clean, and for the first time ever, he had to make a real effort at appearing neat. Sometimes he would go for long walks. It was not easy to leave his room. He would force himself to shave and shower and walk to exhaustion. He rarely would sit at the terrace of a café and watch people walk by. He loved children, yet he felt a deep pain at seeing families together. He had a crazy impulse to go up to them and say, "Please, let me be a part of you. I have no one."

Indeed, he had no one. The word sometimes resonated in his head: *Alone, alone, alone.* Once, he bought a bottle of whiskey and enjoyed the drunken stupor during which his head was empty and the bad thoughts were gone. It was only during the practice of karate that he felt free, that his body did not feel so terribly heavy and his mind could concentrate on something else.

Occasionally, he thought of drinking again or using drugs, but the teachings of Master Kwang were too strong. He would live or die on his own; he had to be in control of his life. Yet, he knew that he was losing the battle every day a little more. And then, what he dreaded most happened, and he was the only one that knew it.

He was strolling along Fisherman's Wharf on a lazy Sunday afternoon when his attention was drawn by a loud altercation between a man and a woman. There was a little girl with them. The man lashed out, hitting the woman, and the little girl screamed in fear, ran toward David, and hid behind him. The man left the woman doubled in pain from a blow to the stomach, came toward David, pushed him out of the way, and brutally cuffed the little girl on the side of the head. The child, however, turned her head at the last moment, the blow hit her on the nose, and a geyser of bright red blood instantaneously stained the front of her little dress.

David uttered, "You bastard."

The man, a burly, heavyset fellow looked at him with insane fury, picked up a two-by-four laying in the gutter by the sidewalk, and without a word, swung toward David's head. Instinctively, David raised his crossed arms, parried the blow by catching the piece of wood in the V formed by his crossed arms, then twisted it out of the man's hands and hit him on the side of the head. The man fell as if poleaxed. A crowd had gathered, congratulating David, much to his distress.

When the police and the paramedics arrived, the policeman who took David's name said, "A skull fracture I guess, but he'll survive. I wouldn't worry if I were you. Enough people were here to testify that it was self-defense." But David knew that it was not; David had really wanted to kill him.

CO

The damage to his mind had started on that first night, the night of their arrival at Auschwitz. He was barely twelve, and even almost fifteen years later, the events of that night were as vivid as if they had just happened, and they kept happening over and over again whenever he closed his eyes. The searchlights, the trucks, the Germans in black uniforms, the dogs, the long lines of new arrivals.

He was terrified, had never been more afraid in his life, holding on to his father's hand with all his strength. The Germans had come and tried to separate him from his parents and sister. He did not want to let go of his father's hand, and the German hit him, and he fell to the ground, blinded with blood and only half-conscious. He never saw his parents or sister again. More than twenty years later, he would occasionally touch the side of his head in an unconscious gesture. Something very strange had happened that night. After he regained consciousness, the fear was gone, but nothing had replaced it. He was empty, completely empty. It was as if one part of him was watching the other part in a dispassionate, detached way. He worked, he ate, he slept, but felt nothing, no anger, no sadness, no fear. He was big for his age and very strong and managed to survive.

The weeks after the liberation were very hazy in his memory, and to this day he did not remember all the details of his return to Greece. He was taken care of, learned to function again, to smile appropriately, but he made no friends and he never, never spoke of what happened in the camps. He went to school, got a degree, and worked in an office, always alone, neither happy nor unhappy. Then one day, on a whim, taking advantage of new immigration laws, he emigrated to the United States, bummed around from city to city, and eventually joined the army as the Korean War was drawing to a close.

It was in Korea that he met Master Kwang first, then Bill. The process of recovery was very slow, and it was only years later that he realized the subtle bonds established between him and Master Kwang, the very gradual reawakening of feelings, trust first, then humor, the ability to smile again, then anger and also pride.

In retrospect, it amazed him that he had trusted the old Korean so quickly and so completely. There had always been few words exchanged between them, but somehow words were not necessary. David, fiercely independent, savagely alone, listened to the old master and enjoyed being with him. Their sparring sessions were a physical and emotional experience. Master Kwang asked no questions, and David volunteered little information, and yet he felt that the old Korean knew all about him.

When Bill had come along, he had been ready for a friend his own age. In that café in Seoul, he had talked about his past for the first time in almost twenty years, and it had been okay. In different ways, without knowing each other, Bill and the old master had almost nursed his mind back to health. He would see changes in himself, subtle but pleasant changes when he least expected them.

One Saturday evening, against his better judgment, he had gone to the enlisted men's club. It was a warm summer night in August two months after he had met Bill. A dance was going on, and his normal reaction would have been to leave, but before he could turn around, he heard his name. Two soldiers were sitting at a table with two young women and were calling him over.

"David, come and join us. This is Leila, PFC Leila, and this is Sylvia, a civilian at headquarters."

"Where are you from, David?" Sylvia asked.

There were garlands hanging from the ceiling, a subtle scent of perspiration and perfume, and good jazz music, which he enjoyed.

"Oh," he joked, "I was born in the army! Thirty-year man, you know."

"Would you care to dance?" Leila was dark-haired, petite, and wore a white chiffon blouse and a blue, rather short skirt. Her gaze was frank and direct.

"Why not?"

She was solidly built, and he enjoyed holding her in his arms. The evening passed quickly, and later, in his bunk, he marveled at how much fun he had experienced that night at the enlisted men's club--a situation he once would have avoided like the plague.

Now, Bill and Master Kwang were both gone, and it was worse than before he had even met them. The Pandora's box had been opened. The feelings were no longer dead; the pain, the fear, the sadness, the loneliness, and the anger, the horrible killing rage, were there now on the surface, and he didn't know how to cope with them.

⁓

The judge had dropped the charges regarding the incident on the wharf, ruling that David had acted in self-defense. David knew better; he knew that he could have disarmed the man easily, but he had wanted to kill him, to destroy him. That knowledge sobered him. It was not so much the killing potential within him that frightened him, but rather the realization that his anger was taking over and that he was losing control of his life. It was as if he was standing on the edge of an abyss, tottering on that edge, and he could fall one way or the other.

More than ever, he kept to himself and avoided people, going to work in the morning and quickly returning to his small apartment. It did not help and, in fact, made matters worse. It seemed as if there was no buffer between him and his memories. He realized that something had to be done quickly before it was too late, and his first break came when his company sent him to a doctor for a required physical examination. He was early and found a pamphlet in the waiting room describing the services offered by a mental health clinic. He took the pamphlet with him and a week later called for an appointment. His second break occurred when he was assigned to a Dr. Rosen.

Dr. Rosen greeted him, standing ramrod straight, and his military bearing was so much at odds with his potbelly, balding head, and rumpled clothes that David almost laughed. David looked around. The office was airy and full of light; there were shelves full of books but no loose papers, no clutter. He hesitated for a moment, then looking into Dr. Rosen's eyes, he saw compassion, friendliness, and bright intelligence. He felt instantly at ease and sunk into an old, comfortable plastic yellow chair.

He met with Dr. Rosen regularly, twice a week for twelve months. It was three months into their therapeutic relationship that David could articulate what the sessions meant to him.

"When I first came to see you, Dr. Rosen, I expected answers. I expected you to tell me what to do and how to do it. I am glad you never did."

Dr. Rosen smiled gently. "If I had, you wouldn't have followed my advice and probably wouldn't have come back."

"True, true, but you listened, and I always felt that what I was saying was truly important to you. So, it was easy to talk, and once I start, I never shut up. You know how much I loved Master Kwang. You know how much he meant to me. Yet I couldn't talk to him as I talk to you. It's hard to explain..."

Dr. Rosen, sitting at his desk at a right angle from David, leaned over and patted his arm.

"Try, try to explain and, of course, I know how much you love and respect Master Kwang."

"Well, it's as if he intimidated me a little... a little... a lot. You see, Master Kwang made me aware of my strength, a strength that I did not know I had. I was embarrassed of my weakness. With you, I can share my weakness and... in ways that I don't understand, these weaknesses no longer embarrass me."

"It is as if by accepting these weaknesses as part of you, you can nurture them, strengthen them... Is it something like that?"

"Yes," said David. "The word 'acceptance' rings a bell. You know," continued David, "I think of Bill. He loves me dearly. He could listen to me forever, but somehow it doesn't fit. He knows all about me, but he knows the fact. He doesn't know the feelings. It is as if Bill is the future and what you and I talk about is the past, but, damn it, it is a past that won't go away."

Several months later into his therapy, David said, "The past, somehow, is losing its grip on me."

Dr. Rosen uncrossed his legs, stroked his chin, and asked, "Do you know why?"

"I think I do. All these horrible things had happened to a frightened, lonely boy of twelve, who was so vulnerable that he was afraid to be afraid and could feel nothing. I am no longer a little boy, Dr. Rosen. I am big and strong and not afraid to be afraid. Fear will not destroy me."

And one day, for the first time, at long last, David cried. He cried unashamedly with big, racking sobs, not like an adult but like a child in pain. He cried during many sessions, and Dr. Rosen always let him cry, simply looking at him with his gentle, compassionate eyes.

Then one day, he cried no longer. He stood up from the big, yellow chair and walked to the bay window. He stared at the San Francisco skyline for a few minutes, then turned and said, "There was a well of sadness, and it had to be emptied." It was not long after that session that Dr. Rosen and David decided to terminate therapy. On their last meeting, they shook hands and when David said, "Thank you," Dr. Rosen sighed and said, "I envy the life that is ahead of you," and David knew that he meant it.

✑

After his therapy was terminated, nothing held David in San Francisco. He liked the city, but too many unpleasant experiences had been attached to it, and it was time to pick up the threads of his life. He decided to do what he felt he should have done immediately upon his return from Korea. He called his friend Bill. Two weeks later, he arrived in Pittsburgh, Pennsylvania, where Bill and his family lived at that time. His reunion with Bill was an experience such as one goes through no more than once or twice in a lifetime. They were all waiting for him in the airport lounge. Bill's father, a distinguished looking gray-haired gentlemen, Bill's mother, slim and elegant with kind eyes and a mischievous smile, and Annie, their twelve-year old, Bill's sister. Before David could put his carry-on down, Bill had grabbed him by the shoulders and hugged him. The past two years had not weakened their friendship.

During their drive to town, Bill's family abstained from asking personal questions. It was much later, after dinner, that Mr. and Mrs. Sanders sat with him and Bill in their spacious living room and Bill's father simply said, "Bill told us how much you mean to him, David, and this home is yours. We shall be honored if you share with us some of your affection for Bill." Mrs. Sanders said nothing but reached for David's hand.

He felt no embarrassment but a deliciously warm feeling and nodded. "Thank you."

Five days later, he had rented his own apartment and applied for graduate work in psychology at the University of Pittsburgh.

と

The next three years were among the happiest and most peaceful in his life since the war. He enjoyed his studies and devoted himself to them with enthusiasm, but not with the passion reserved for Tang-Soo-Do.

This discrepancy became obvious when, toward the end of his studies, his advisor asked to talk with him. He did not like his advisor's office, a small cubicle cluttered with books and papers, but he liked the man. He was somewhat aloof and cold, yet supportive of his students and always honest.

"David," said Professor Myers, "I read the first draft of your dissertation. It is a very good piece of work, and you will have no trouble graduating. You have worked very hard, but somehow I sense that your heart is not in what you are doing. What made you go into psychology?"

David was grateful for the professor's interest and knew that he was right. He realized that he had gravitated toward psychology because of his work with Dr. Rosen and his admiration for the old man. A career in academia did not interest him, and he did not feel capable of doing what Dr. Rosen did.

"Yes, sir, I believe that you are right, but I don't know what drew me to psychology."

The professor sighed and handed the manuscript to David.

"Here, David. Nice piece of work. Let me know if I can be of help."

"Yes, sir. Thank you."

He obtained his doctorate in three years, but kept delaying his search for a job. Teaching a class or two at local community colleges provided him with enough money, and he felt content. He built a special relationship with Annie, Bill's sister, spending as much time with her as possible. She was not only Bill's sister, but she filled the empty place left when his own ten-year-old sister was killed in the war, and he became fiercely protective of the child. He did not believe in God, yet at times, he would catch himself praying silently, *Please, God, let her grow up, let her live. Don't make her suffer like Liza.*

"Uncle David, let's go for a walk through Schenley Park."

"Okay, Annie, let's go."

"I like to be with you, Uncle David. You are not like the other grown-ups. You never say 'no.'"

"Perhaps I should, Annie."

"No, no. No, don't."

He laughed and would never say no.

Yet, he was getting restless and knew that he had to do something with his life.

When he shared his indecision with Bill, his friend suggested a luncheon with his father. They met in a Greek restaurant called Athena, and David appreciated the white napkins and blue tablecloths so reminiscent of Greece. He and Bill arrived and waited for a few minutes for Mr. Sanders.

Ouzos and a bottle of *retsina* (raisin wine) were de rigueur, and it was only over coffee that they began to talk seriously.

"I am trained as a psychologist," started David. "I enjoyed my studies, but what can I do with the knowledge that I acquired? I am not cut out for academic life. I would like to be a psychotherapist, but I know in my heart that I cannot do what Dr. Rosen does. Short of opening an academy of Korean karate, which wouldn't be too bad, I don't know what else to do!"

Bill looked at his father significantly. Mr. Sanders cleared his throat.

"You know, David, that Bill has some associations with the Central Intelligence Agency..."

David nodded. He knew about Bill's association with the CIA, but he had never been curious about it.

"With your doctorate in psychology and your expertise in martial arts, you would be an attractive candidate for the CIA. Would you think about it?"

David was intrigued, and the idea appealed to him. He did not want to dwell on the pros and cons for fear that he would be stuck again.

On impulse he said, "I don't want to think about it, Mr. Sanders. The answer is yes."

David applied and was accepted. He was on a career path, and for the first time in his life, he had a purpose.

Still, he was unfulfilled. There were now people who cared for him, who loved him, who had given purpose to his life, but they were not "his." Not in the sense that he wanted to possess them but in the sense that he felt on the fringes and not part of their daily lives. Paradoxically, even though he knew that the Sanders family cared for him as much if not more than Master Kwang did, he felt more a part of Master Kwang's life. Indeed the do-jung and his students were the core of the old Korean's existence. He had felt a part of it and not on the fringes.

He remembered the master's final words to him: "Tang-Soo-Do makes life cleaner and better, but Tang-Soo-Do should not be all your life."

He had answered, "Thank you, Master. I will not forget."

And, indeed, he had not forgotten, and every month he would write a letter to the old man and share with him the highlights of his life. Sometimes, the old man would answer; more often, he would not. Yet, David knew that the bond was always there. It had been difficult to make Tang-Soo-Do just one part of his life and not the core of it. Over the years, however, it had happened. His involvement with Bill's family, his graduate school years, his work with the agency, then on his own, while not crowding Tang-Soo-Do out of his life, had assumed their proper place in it. Still, he always set aside two hours a day to practice the art which, in so many ways had kept him alive.

The day after accepting his new mission to Salonica was no different. In the empty conference room, which the Shoreham Hotel had allowed him to use, he went through all the basic combinations, kicks, forms, totally immersed in the fluid motions until he realized that the time was up. His plane would leave at 10 a.m.

Chapter 5

Steve Harper

It was spring in Fairfax, Virginia, approximately four years before Steve Harper met David Castro at the Mayflower Hotel in Washington D.C.

Harper was an ambitious man, tall, handsome, charming when he wanted to be. He and his wife, a strawberry blonde with a good figure and penetrating blue eyes, were in the large, exquisitely furnished living room of their home.

"Steve, let's go back to Richmond. We have a house there and you should not have any trouble finding a job that pays a hell of a lot more than you're making now."

"Dorothy, you don't understand."

She looked at him with sad, wistful eyes.

"What is there to understand? We are in debt up to our ears. We don't have a minute to ourselves, no time to spend with the children. They are not doing well in school."

He sighed in exasperation, but not at Dorothy. Indeed, he could well see her point; he also missed spending time with the children. He worried about Ned. No, he was not angry at her but at the whole damn mess.

"We can't quit now, Dorothy. It would be like letting my country down. Maybe it wouldn't be as easy as you say to get a good paying job in Richmond. I am not a young man, Dorothy. As for the children, it is true that we don't spend as much time as we should with them, but think of all the cultural opportunities available to them in Washington. Richmond is a dead city still full of prejudice. Is that what you want our children to learn?"

He was quite forceful in his arguments, but he felt like a fraud because he could not bring himself to share with her the real reason for his refusal to return to Richmond. All his life, as far back as he could remember, he

38

had wanted to be an ambassador. He had never shared that fantasy with Dorothy for fear of sounding childish or unrealistic. Indeed, he knew that he was not ambassador material. At any rate, he had never expected to retire to Richmond.

He did not enjoy arguing with Dorothy. He loved her very much, and he knew she was unhappy. The beginning of their union had truly been blissful. They both belonged to old Virginian families, both had gone to expensive private schools, and they graduated together from the University of Virginia. When he secured a position as a mid-level employee of the State Department, they moved to Fairfax, Virginia.

"Steve, do you remember our first small apartment when we arrived in Fairfax? We were so happy there."

He looked at her with some exasperation but also sharing in her wistfulness.

"I remember, my love, but things cannot always remain the same. For one thing, we had the children, and they needed space."

"I know, and I am so worried about them. Sheila wants to go to medical school and she has the talent for it. Thank God! Ned's therapist tells me that he is doing so well."

Their sixteen-year-old, Ned, had caused a car accident. He was not injured, but cocaine had been found in his car.

"It was," said Steve, "perhaps the worst experience in my life when the psychologist told us that some of his problems stemmed from our relationship. That I would have caused such pain to my son. I wanted to die."

Dorothy leaned over and held Steve's hand.

"I know, I felt that way too. But he's okay now."

Both Steve and Dorothy were honest and intelligent enough to realize that there was truth in the psychologist's statement that Ned had been adversely affected by the endemic tension in the household. They made a real effort to appear calmer and more peaceful in the presence of their children. Their efforts paid off. Ned made a remarkable adjustment, and the twins seemed as happy as normal teenagers could be. The real problem, however, did not go away. The attorney's fee and Ned's psychological treatment ate up whatever meager savings they had left. Neither Dorothy nor Steve wanted to turn to their parents for help. Both felt that their parents had worked hard enough and deserved a worry-free retirement. They borrowed money, more than they could ever repay, and they dipped into their retirement savings. They mortgaged their house. It was not enough; it was never enough.

✂

It was at about that time Steve and Von Eckardt met at a State Department function sponsored by the U.N. ambassador. It was a joint venture sponsored by the Department of Commerce and the State Department with the avowed goal of promoting face-to-face contacts between German and American businessmen.

Steve's wife was ravishing in a pale blue chiffon dress, which set off to perfection her naked shoulders and long aristocratic neck adorned by a gold medallion. How he still loved her, and how he missed the intimacy of the early years of their marriage. He sighed deeply. Those days would never be again.

"You look beautiful, my dear."

She glanced at him. Indeed, he no longer was the dashing figure she had married not so many years ago. His hair was thinning, his shoulders were bent, and there were lines of worry around his eyes.

She also sensed the loss of intimacy and missed terribly the easygoingness, openness, and sharing that had characterized the beginning of their relationship.

"Thank you, Steve. You look pretty good yourself."

Their home was elegant, their furniture a tasteful blend of the traditional and modern with a few antique pieces, such as a dish and a rocker that had belonged to Dorothy's mother. There were many pictures of their children, and their love for their children was the only remaining part of emotional contact.

"It is still early. How about a drink before we go?"

They sat side-by-side on a white leather sofa, a concession to comfort-oriented contemporary furniture. These few moments of togetherness were increasingly rare; they sensed their love for each other, but the words would not come.

It was he who broke the spell first.

"I think it is time. It wouldn't do to arrive late."

Their arrival at the ambassador's mansion went almost unnoticed. Some of his colleagues nodded, some wives gravitated toward Dorothy, always more popular than he was. A martini in hand, he sat on a marble bench along the wall of the reception hall and spotted Von Eckardt. He had seen him once before from a distance and knew a little about him. He knew that, while born and raised in Germany, Von Eckardt had become an American citizen. His holdings in Detroit and his fluent knowledge of German and English probably made him an invaluable asset to the promoters of the meeting. Von Eckardt looked at Steve, and their glances met. The man approached Steve's bench and bowed from the waist down, a stilted gesture that almost made Steve smile. *You can take the Prussian out of Prussia*, he thought, *but not Prussia out of the Prussian.*

"I am Dieter Von Eckardt. May I join you?"

"Of course," said Steve, without mustering much enthusiasm. He was intrigued but somehow did not like the man. "My name is Steve Harper." They sat in silence next to each other on the bench. Steve helped himself to another martini from a passing waiter. He wondered what the man wanted from him.

"These receptions can be boring," said Von Eckardt at last. "Yet, it is interesting to watch these people and wonder what they think."

Steve nodded. It was the right thing to say, but somehow, Steve's discomfort did not diminish. There was something repellant in Von Eckardt that Steve could not quite identify, perhaps his features, which moved very little, or his reptilian eyes. Yet, there was strength in the man. After the fourth martini, however, Steve's uneasiness evaporated a measure; he was lonely, and it was good to talk with someone.

Steve dimly realized that he had had more than his usual share of cocktails and that he was not altogether in control of himself, but somehow he felt a need to unburden, to share some of his pain and disillusionment. It was, he thought ruefully, like meeting a stranger on a cruise. You shared intimate details of your lives, safe in the knowledge that upon arrival at your destination, each would go his way and probably never meet again. What did it matter? He did not share state secrets but only his own personal anguish. He felt Von Eckardt could relate to what he was saying.

"You see, Mr. Harper, it was hard for Helga and me when we came from Germany after the war. The Nazis had taken everything we owned, and it was difficult to get used to a life of mediocrity, especially in a foreign country, especially after a life of affluence."

"Yes," said Steve, "you don't have to be in a foreign country. In fact, it can be even worse when everyone knows you and you have to maintain a façade behind which there is nothing."

Von Eckardt remained silent for a long moment. "It does not help relationships at home, either. Even the most loving wife eventually becomes bitter."

Steve was startled. It was as if the German had read his thoughts. "Yes, that is what happens, and it is so sad, and there is no way out."

"There was for me, Steve--you don't mind if I call you Steve, do you? I feel almost like an older brother to you. Anyway, there was a way out for me in the person of someone who had gone through the same trials as I did and offered me a partnership, which became the beginning and cornerstone of my present fortune. But I don't want to bother you with details. The point I want to make is that there is always hope. Anyway, I see that my wife is signaling to me, and I must go. It was a pleasure talking with you, Steve."

On the way back from the reception, Steve felt somewhat uneasy. The relief he had felt during his conversation with Von Eckardt had waned and been replaced by a vague sense of discomfort he could not understand. He did not share his experience with Dorothy, which surprised him. Indeed, except for classified matters pertaining to his work, he shared just about everything with his wife; he valued her judgment and insights, and besides, he enjoyed talking with her. Yet, he did not tell her about his conversation with Von Eckardt. After all, it did not matter. He would probably never see the man again.

It did not turn out that way. Approximately two weeks later, he received an invitation from Von Eckardt. His immediate reaction was to refuse, but he held it back. He was intrigued, he said to himself, but deep down, he knew there was more than mere curiosity that made him accept, some ill-defined, unformulated hope that some miracle would happen to help him overcome the terrible situation in which he found himself and, perhaps, beyond that hope, a wish that it would not be fulfilled and that he would never see Von Eckardt again.

The luncheon was pleasant. Von Eckardt had chosen a small French restaurant in Bethesda. The wine, an old Merlot, was good and the food quite passable. The prices were outrageous, and Steve delighted himself with the thought that Von Eckardt would pick up the tab. They talked about inconsequential things, and it was only toward the end of the meal that Von Eckardt broached the real reason for their meeting.

"I thought about our conversation when we first met, and I was deeply touched by your predicament, maybe because my wife and I went through almost similar experiences. I thought also that I may be able to do for you what my friend did for me many years ago."

"I thank you, Mr. Von Eckardt, but I truly do not believe that there is anything you can do for me."

As Steve was about to stand up, Von Eckardt put out a restraining hand.

"Please, at least hear me out."

"Okay," said Steve.

"You see, I come from an old Prussian family, and military service was a tradition with us. My father and I were appalled by what the Nazis were doing to our country, especially to the honor of our military. We, especially my father, stated our opinions a little too openly, and we had to pay for that mistake. My father was imprisoned and died after having spent one year in a concentration camp. The Nazis took our house, everything we owned, and I was drafted in the army as an enlisted man. A commission was out of the question considering my views. It was just as well. I managed to survive the war and the Russian front."

Von Eckardt stopped his narrative and stared at his glass as if he were lost in memories. Steve wanted to say something but did not know what. The words of Von Eckardt were poignant, but there was no emotion in them. It was as if he was reciting a script to which Steve could not relate. He simply nodded, and after a while, Von Eckardt continued.

"We had many friends, however, members of old Prussian aristocracy who shared my father's opinions but were more circumspect in expressing them. Many of them became officers, some reaching fairly high ranks in the Wehrmacht. After the war, many escaped and came to America, not always in a legal manner, as my wife and I did. They did well in this country. They became loyal, productive U.S. citizens under different names. They pay taxes, they have raised families, children who will make great contributions to this country. Yet, they live in mortal fear that, one day, they will be found out and their world will come apart. These people did their duty as officers of the German army, and if arrested, they will be made to pay for the sins of the Nazis."

Steve was interested in spite of himself.

"What does that have to do with me, Mr. Von Eckardt, and with you, for that matter?"

Von Eckardt remained silent for a long minute, then lit a cigarette. "I do not smoke often. In fact, I try to not smoke at all, but sometimes I can't help it." He waved away the smoke dismissively. "You see, many of these people are my friends, and many were friends of my father, and I want to help them. Now, this is where you come in. I know that your department does not deal with illegal aliens or war criminals, as many of these people have been mistakenly dubbed. On the other hand, you have connections and access to much classified information. You have the means of finding out who of these unfortunates is being investigated. If this information reaches them in a timely manner, they will be able to do what is necessary to protect their families. That is all I ask."

"What you are asking me is to betray my country, and I won't do it. Maybe you can, Mr. Von Eckardt. You came from an old Prussian family, but you are not an American yet. Good day, sir."

Steve was enraged. How dare Von Eckardt submit such a proposition to him? He was even more furious at himself. Von Eckardt must have seen something weak, something needy, something perhaps even vile in him to have asked him to do such a thing.

Back home that night, Steve avoided Dorothy. Somehow, he felt vaguely guilty and unclean, although he knew that he had done nothing wrong.

In fact, he had acted quite properly. Several times, Dorothy asked him if something was bothering him.

"You look upset, Steve, like preoccupied with something. Is there something wrong at the office? Are you all right?"

"No, yes... I mean, I am all right, and no, there is nothing wrong at the office. How was your day?"

She did not respond to his clumsy attempt at changing the conversation. "We went through a lot together, Steve," she said, "and one of the things that kept us going was that we always shared what was bothering us, and recently, that has not been so. You look absorbed, even distant, and that frightens me."

"Nothing is bothering me," he said, more sharply than he intended. "I can't make something up to please you."

Dorothy remained silent.

He was uneasy, embarrassed, thought some more of Von Eckardt. Steve knew he should report the man to the FBI through channels even though it would be Von Eckardt's word against his; but he did not.

Several weeks went by. Steve and Dorothy's financial situation kept deteriorating. They were still paying Ned's college tuition and were faced with the prospect of having to pay for Sheila's medical school. Sheila was brilliant and would make an outstanding physician. Medical schools, however, would cost a fortune, and it would be years before they could make a dent in their staggering debt.

It was then that he started thinking of Von Eckardt's proposition again. One night, he did not go to bed but stayed up in his study all night. He was under no illusions and knew exactly what Von Eckardt was asking. He did not, for a minute, buy Von Eckardt's story of belonging to an old Prussian family. He was probably in the pay of a Nazi organization which was trying to protect its own. It never occurred to Steve, however, that Von Eckardt might have been a Nazi himself. Could he do what Von Eckardt wanted? Yes, of course he could. He could easily access the information. Would he do it? The thought nauseated him, made him truly physically ill. On the other hand, there was no way Sheila could go to medical school even if she borrowed all the money necessary. He did not want his little girl to go through her first twenty years of professional life trying to get out from under this debt. He did not want her to go through what Dorothy and he had, were, and would continue to go through, probably until the end of their lives. After all, what was Von Eckardt asking for? It was not as if the information divulged would put his country at risk. He could be caught, it was true, but he did not believe he would be. The risks were minimal, and there would be no paper trail. On the other hand, how could he look at himself in the mirror, how could he look at Dorothy? Would she understand?

When dawn came, he shaved, showered, had a light breakfast and went to the office very early. From a pay phone, he called Von Eckardt in Detroit and arranged to meet in Washington that same evening. This was six weeks after their first meeting and four weeks after their luncheon.

&

Their meeting next had a totally different tenor.

They met in the same French restaurant in Bethesda, but this time Steve declined the wine. He was angry, felt dirty and powerless, and wanted to get the matter over as quickly as possible.

"I know what you want me to do, and I'll do it. Now you will hear my conditions."

Von Eckardt was taken aback by the blunt statement and wondered what had happened that made Harper change his mind so completely and so quickly. He said, tentatively, "Of course, Steve, I would not want you to do anything that you would not feel completely comfortable with. I wouldn't dream of asking you to do anything against your personal and professional values."

Steve's angry retort was convincing, indeed. "Cut the crap, Von Eckardt. I know what you want. I despise you, but I need money. I will give the names of German residents who came to the United States after the war and are under investigation. In exchange, you will mail every month six thousand dollars in cash to a mail box. Is that agreeable?"

Von Eckardt thought for a long moment. This could be an entrapment, yet all his instincts told him that Steve's proposal was genuine. His efforts at not leaving a paper or bank trail would work in each man's favor. He did not like Steve's crude way of stripping the deal from acceptable rationalizations. He would accept it but made a last ditch attempt at outguessing Steve.

"I will give you an address where you can send the information."

"No, that won't do at all. You will give me a telephone number and I will call the information, my friend. This way, it cannot be traced back to me."

Von Eckardt was more reassured.

"Okay," he said, and the deal was concluded.

&

Steve Harper and Von Eckardt had not met since that day almost four years ago, but their understanding was still in full force.

Steve's financial situation had vastly improved. Debts had been paid off, and money was set aside for Ned's college tuition and Sheila's medical school. While under less immediate pressure, Steve was not happy, and his relationship with Dorothy had not improved.

Paradoxically, their estrangement worsened when their financial situation started to ameliorate. She had wondered about the origin of the extra money, but he would remain evasive and never answered her questions directly. Then, the suspicions began, but they were ill-formed and vague. What would he have done wrong, he who was honor incarnate? Still, why would he not answer her questions? Eventually, she stopped asking, but the damage was done, and the gap between them increased. He was still the same attentive, solicitous husband, but something was missing, and they both knew it.

A few days later, he found a telephone message on his desk summoning him to his department head's office. His initial reaction was one of sheer panic.

"Georgia," he almost screamed. His secretary, a middle-aged woman with kind features and hair drawn back in a severe bun, showed her head through the door, surprised at his unusually sharp tone.

"Who brought this message in?"

"Nobody. I took it on the telephone. Why, is there something wrong?"

"No, no, of course not." He tried to control his furiously beating heart. "Who did you talk to? The boss himself?"

"No, his secretary."

"Did she say anything else?"

"No, just to be there at 10:30 sharp."

It was 10:15. There was not much time left. He tried to calm himself down. He fleetingly thought of running away, but he knew that it would be the most stupid thing to do. He pulled himself together and resolutely walked to the department head's office. There were two men sitting around the table, and his boss made the introductions.

"This is Steve Harper, one of my most valuable colleagues. Steve, this is Tom Scorcese, FBI, and Bill Sanders, CIA."

They shook hands all around, then helped themselves to coffee ready on the credenza and settled around the table.

"All right," said the department head, opening a file in front of him on the table. "Have any of you heard of a Detroit millionaire, naturalized German, by the name of Dieter Von Eckardt?"

Steve's legs shook, and his face drained of all color, so much so that his superior noticed it.

"Steve, are you all right?"

"I am fine. Just the beginning of a migraine headache. You know, it happens to me sometimes. And yes, I met Von Eckardt at a U.N. function, but hardly remember him."

As the migraine part happened to be true, Steve' superior threw him a sympathetic glance and continued.

"We have received word from the Mossad that Von Eckardt is a wanted criminal of war named Colonel Richter. The evidence, however, is hidden somewhere in Greece, and a CIA contract agent is going to retrieve it. This is strictly a CIA operation, but I need you, Steve, to be on top of things in the unlikely event there are repercussions from the Greek government. I very much doubt that there will be, but if it happens, you will handle such eventuality, Steve, with your usual savoir faire. Mr. Scorcese, Bill Sanders will keep you abreast of any developments in the case. If Von Eckardt, or Richter, has engaged in any shenanigans within the continental USA, that is when you come in. Now, Sanders will brief you on the details. Any questions?"

There were none.

The briefing lasted no more than twenty minutes, and as soon as it was over, Steve left the building precipitously. His heart was still beating fast and his legs were still shaking. He badly needed a drink but decided against it. He needed a clear head to plan his next step.

He walked around the area for a while, found a deserted park, and sat on a bench. He knew that a piece of valuable information had fallen in his lap, but he did not know how to use it. He could not blackmail Richter. In the first place, he was afraid for his life. Furthermore, as soon as the CIA found the evidence against Richter, the information would be worthless. He could sell it to Richter, but what would he ask for in exchange? Money? The mere idea was repulsive. And then the answer came to him. He would buy his freedom. Richter would never allow their partnership to be dissolved as long as he needed Harper's information. Steve knew that he had reached the end of his rope. He no longer could go on. He would buy the dissolution of his contract with the information he had. He would buy his freedom.

They met at the same French restaurant in Bethesda.

"What a pleasure to see you, Mr. Harper. To be honest, your call surprised me. Please tell me, can I do anything for you?"

Steve did not beat around the bush; his heart was pounding, and he felt as if he had drunk gallons of coffee. It was a last sell out, but then he could be free, and the nightmare he had been living during the past four years would be over at last. He would never be able to look at himself in the mirror; he would never share with Dorothy what had happened, but at least it would be over and the terrible weight he carried around, the horrible anxiety he felt every time he obtained bits of information he had to impart to Von Eckardt would be lifted. Who knows, perhaps someday he and Dorothy would become close again once the stress was gone.

"Von Eckardt, or should I say Colonel Richter, I know who you are at last, and I must say that you have played your role quite well, you proud descendant of an aristocratic Prussian family and victim of Nazi persecutions. You are slime, you know. Not that I am much better than you. At least I have no illusions. I know what I have become."

Von Eckardt felt his head spinning; he was glad he was seated, otherwise he would have lost his balance and fallen on the restaurant floor. He could not talk. The shock of hearing his real name hurled at him was such that, for what seemed to him an eternity but was no longer than a few seconds, he was unable to think. Yet, his face remained expressionless and revealed nothing of the feeling that he was tottering on the edge of destruction.

"Steve," he said, and he sounded truly amazed, "What, in God's name are you saying? Where did you hear such fairy tales?"

"This won't wash, Colonel Richter. I can assure you that my sources do not favor fairy tales."

By that time, Von Eckardt had regained his composure, but his fear was as intense as ever.

"Mr. Harper," he said, and his voice was low and ominous, "Mr. Harper, if what you say is true, you must realize that this would be a cruel blow to my family. You realize that I cannot allow such drivel to be propagated."

"Are you threatening me?" countered Steve. His voice was steady and he did not sound frightened at all. He deliberately poured himself a glass of the expensive Chateauneuf du Pape which he had ordered.

"If you are," he continued, "it would not be wise at all."

The German chose to disregard the last exchange.

Steve almost laughed. "You understand now why it was foolish to threaten me. The FBI and CIA know. The Mossad also knows, and they are in the process of gathering evidence. I can tell you exactly what they plan to do, and I will--under one condition."

"And that is?"

"Our deal is off, off for good and forever. No more information, no more money. We'll go our separate ways and will never intersect again. I want no money, nothing from you. I just want out. And one more thing. Knowing what I know of you, you will, of course, make sure that the evidence is never collected. You must know that I have carefully kept all the envelopes which you mailed to me over the years. I would be very surprised if your prints did not appear on at least some of them. The dates of monthly six thousand dollar deposits coincide pretty well with the dates on the envelopes. Furthermore, I have written a long narrative of our deal, all the information passed on to you. All this is in a sealed enveloped which I gave to my attorney with instructions which you can easily imagine. Live your life in peace, Richter, and let me live mine. What will it be?"

The German remained silent for a long while. After all, Harper was not so much of a fool as he had believed him to be, and, by God, he was not greedy. Harper could have taken him for a pretty penny. Indeed, he would have paid a good deal of money for the information which Steve possessed. Why not, after all? He bore no ill will toward the American. Besides, after this, he could be of no use to him.

"All right," he said brusquely. "Tell me what you know."

Steve cleared his throat, drank a glass of water, ordered a cognac, and began.

"I must say, you really fooled me. I truly thought that you were only after a buck or two in trying to sell information to Nazi bigwigs and help them escape their just due. I never dreamed that you were one of them and that your primary motivation was self-protection. Anyway, it really does not matter, and here is the story. The State Department and the Department of Justice know or at least suspect your true identity. They need, however, concrete evidence, and they know how to get it. It seems that in Salonica there was an old Jewish historian who painstakingly recorded and documented what you Nazis did there. They expect that the name Colonel Richter will figure prominently in that old gentleman's memoirs with accompanying evidence." Harper paused to let that information sink in before continuing. "The problem is that he died quite unexpectedly, and no one knows the whereabouts of the old man's manuscript, except maybe a well-known lawyer in Rome, who, at that time, was an Italian officer stationed in Salonica and who had befriended doctor whatever-his-name-was.

"The State Department and the FBI want this manuscript and asked for the CIA's help. The CIA is reluctant to become involved because of possible international repercussions, and, to make a long story short, they enlisted the help of a former CIA agent who is now freelancing. His name is David Castro." Harper slid a slip of paper across the table to Richter. "Here are his and the Italian lawyer's names and how they plan to meet. And now, good-bye forever, *Von Eckardt*." Harper spat the German's name from his lips and glared at him.

For a long time, taking in the sharp triangular face, the opaque blue eyes which revealed nothing, Steve stared at this man, a symbol, at the same time, of deliverance and shame. He then rose and walked away without a backward glance. He thought he would feel elated, but he didn't. He did, in fact, feel a sense of relief. Yet, at the same time, he hunched his shoulders; he could no longer walk straight. He had just sentenced a man to death, for he was under no illusion as to what would happen to Castro. Would he ever be able to live with himself? He kept walking along the wide sidewalks, oblivious to traffic, oblivious to sounds and sights, lost in his own personal despair. His life was like a long, dark tunnel.

Steve Harper never saw Colonel Richter again.

Chapter 6

Johann Richter, Alias Von Eckardt

The big suburban ranch-style house on the outskirts of Detroit, with its tennis courts and covered swimming pool, conveyed an impression of arrogant prosperity in an economically depressed area. Johann Richter sat in his very large, very masculine office with its deep leather chairs and immense desk and marveled at the speed and efficiency of modern communications. At noon, he was having lunch with Steve Harper in Bethesda; at 3:30, he was back at his desk.

He thought with mixed feelings about his arrangement with the American. On one hand, it was a shame to lose such a valuable source of information; on the other, he doubted that the man could be of much help in the future. Besides, the monthly payments were beginning to mount up, even though part of the money was provided to him by other sources better left unnamed. He looked around him with a pleased expression. Richter had done well, but not well enough. He could have been a millionaire many times over and would not have worked as hard had he kept the treasure he had stolen during his army career. He winced at the word "stolen." He had not stolen it. The treasure belonged to the Third Reich, and since the Third Reich was no longer, it belonged to him. Somewhere, hidden, were tens of millions of dollars in gold, diamonds, and jewels. For the past twenty-five years, he had not even searched for them because he had no leads, did not even know how or where to begin.

He stood up and walked toward a mirror attached to a door. He was nearly sixty-five, still a handsome man, still standing tall and straight. A military bearing never disappears. True, true, he was balding at the top, a little bulging at the middle. Ah! But that SS uniform fit him well in the old days. As he did more often these days, Richter fell into a reverie of his glory days in proud servitude of the Third Reich.

છ⁄૭

Most of all, he remembered Salonica, a beautiful city, a city of white and pink homes and large downtown avenues, dominated by a majestic white tower, remnant of Venetian conquerors, and graced by beautiful beaches and an incredibly turquoise sea. It was also a city gripped by fear. After one year of German occupation, the Nuremberg laws were being applied in all their harshness. One fourth of the city's population, the entire Jewish community, had been segregated in a designated ghetto. Fine old homes had been evacuated, their occupants leaving with whatever belongings they could carry with them.

It was then that he, SS Colonel Richter, had been transferred to Salonica. As an assistant to the chief of the Gestapo, his main duties were to manage all legal and logistical aspects of confiscated Jewish businesses, duties of which he acquitted himself admirably well to the greatest glory of the Fatherland's coffers. But what SS Colonel Richter really enjoyed was to prowl through the beautiful abandoned homes immediately after the eviction of their occupants. He would get out of his staff car--immaculate in his black uniform, polished black boots, and silver insignia--followed by four or five of his henchmen. He liked to think of himself as the vulture, a huge bird of prey falling upon its unsuspecting victims. He would go through the abandoned homes, discard most items, and select for himself what was rare and precious: Oriental carpets, gold coins, jewelry, diamonds, and pearls. He had become something of an expert, and, in his rare moments of honesty, he allowed himself to feel awed and somewhat intimidated. In his small apartment in Bavaria, with its smell of sauerkraut and cheap tobacco, he had never dreamed that such beauty even existed.

He stood up, moved to the bay window, glass in hand, and looked at the manicured lawn and tennis courts. He did not like to think of his childhood, and when he did, he had an unreasonable fear that someday, he would be poor again. He felt the need to look at the tangible signs of his present wealth. He sighed, returned to his desk, and refilled his glass.

Richter had no recollection of his father, who had died shortly after the end of World War I. His mother, a strong woman both physically and psychologically, managed to raise her two children, Johann and his sister Henge. She would clean the homes of wealthy people, many of them Jews. She liked the people she worked for, and they liked her, often helping her at difficult times. Johann grew up aware of his mediocrity and hated them. Mrs. Richter could not understand why he railed vehemently against her Jewish employers who, over the years, had been so kind and generous to her.

"It makes me sick, Mother. It makes me sick to know that you are working for these people, parasites who suck the blood of the German people."

"Johann, how can you say that? Dr. Rosenbloom is a physician, and besides, half his patients, good German people, are too poor to pay him, so he doesn't charge them."

"Yeah! And he probably poisons the other half."

Sometimes she would be infuriated. "Jews may be wealthy, but they work very hard for their money. Look at you. You are close to twenty and do nothing but loaf around, drink beer, and smoke cigarettes. If it were not for the Jews who hire me and whom you despise, there would be no food on the table. You are the spitting image of your father."

The last comment would always rouse his anger and he would leave, slamming the door. He knew that she was right, of course, but he hated being compared to his father, whom he despised almost as much as he despised his mother's Jewish employers.

The advent of the Nazi party became an answer to hopes that had withered and almost died. He loved uniforms and had a nice presence and absolutely no scruples. He found a home in the SS and swiftly rose through the ranks.

He met his wife, Ingrid, a statuesque blonde, at a party meeting and was deeply impressed by her Aryan looks, aristocratic demeanor, and, of course, party connections. The fact that she doubled in size within two years of their marriage did not diminish his ardor. In fact, he was truly fond of her and sexually aroused by her physical attributes. Ingrid, like his mother, was a physically and psychologically strong woman. The resemblance, however, stopped there. Whereas his mother was a gentle, selfless person, Ingrid was ferociously ambitious and could be harsh and cruel. Yet, somehow, the two of them were devoted to each other, although from the beginning of their union, they had no illusions about each other.

Richter was in Yugoslavia when he had been promoted to Standartenfuehrer (Full Colonel) of the SS. His stay in Yugoslavia had been profitable, and it was there that he had made the acquaintance of Otto Streicher. Quickly after his promotion, he had been transferred to Salonica. In Salonica, at last, he was getting his due and amassing a fortune. He enjoyed exploring sections of the ghetto where, like a giant knife slicing a cake, the SS would evacuate several blocks of apartment houses and form a convoy for deportation to Auschwitz. The pickings were often more substantial than from the big homes as the Jews were not allowed to take baggage with them. Oftentimes after what he called his "inspection," he would stand by with a smile of disdain and watch the SS turn the apartments over to the Greek populace. They were like maggots, scarcely better than the Jews who preceded them. It was funny about the Jews; he didn't really hate them as he did at one time. Unlike some of his fellow SS, he wasn't so terribly bent on their annihilation. To him they were just non-people. He would have laughed at the suggested possibility that they could feel pain or anger or sadness. Such occurrences could not even enter his mind. In fact, he felt much the same way about Greeks, with some exceptions, of course.

One such exception was Athanassopoulos. What a shrewd bastard! He had asked for an audience shortly after Richter had opened his office. The fellow's arrogance had so surprised Richter that he had agreed to see him simply out of curiosity, and very quickly each had seen in the other a kindred soul.

He remembered with amusement his first interview with Athanassopoulos. He had him ushered into his office, and, as he had seen Himmler do once, he kept studying some documents on his desk and did not look up for five good minutes. When he did, he saw a tall, lanky fellow in his early forties with a lock of jet black hair on his forehead and a small mustache which made him look like Adolph Hitler. The mere thought was desecration. The man wore old but elegant clothes; he did not avert his eyes. In fact, he looked at him directly, with a faint sneer on his face.

His apparent lack of fear disconcerted Richter, who asked him, "What do you want?"

Athanassopoulos did not appear the least upset at Richter's tone. "Why, Herr Standartenfuehrer," he replied in flawless German, "I have a business proposition for you."

Richter was somewhat mystified by the Greek's use of German. In addition, his curiosity was aroused, and instead of throwing the rascal out, he asked, "What business could you and I possibly have in common?"

Athanassopoulos took a pack of cigarettes out of his pocket. "With your permission, Herr Standartenfuehrer." And without waiting for an answer, he lit his cigarette with a magnificent golden lighter while offering the pack to Richter. Richter declined, but he could not help but stare at the lighter in obvious admiration.

"Yes," said Athanassopoulos negligently, showing the lighter with a flourish as he followed Richter's glance. "Yes, I see you have an eye for beautiful things. This was given to me by a British officer as he was leaving Greece for England. I am glad you like it."

"State your business," interrupted Richter impatiently. "You have three minutes and then my men will throw you out."

"That is all I need." Athanassopoulos did not appear the least perturbed. "You love beautiful things and so do I. You have access to them, but you cannot keep them. I know how to keep them, but I have no access to them. We complement each other. Shall I go on?"

Richter was appalled at the man's audacity, yet intrigued in spite of himself. "Yes."

Athanassopoulos seemed to pull himself together. He abandoned his bantering tone, and his voice became serious.

"You are the SS officer in charge of disposing of Jewish properties. This is common knowledge. It is also common knowledge that many, if not all, of the Jewish families have lived in Salonica for generations, and over the years, they amassed fabulous quantities of precious heirlooms, gold, silver, diamonds, not counting priceless rugs and furniture. Your job is to see to it that all these items are shipped back to Germany. In the process, some of these are diverted to high-ranking SS officers, and you keep a few for yourself. Please do not be angry. I am not being judgmental. As a matter of fact, I would do the same thing, only, unlike you, I would not do it in an amateurish fashion but on a grand scale."

Athanassopoulous paused to take a drag of his cigarette before continuing. "Listen, there is no way on earth that the Reich's authorities can know the nature and extent of the loot. They have to rely entirely on the information that you provide. You can, theoretically, divert as much as half of what your men confiscate, but you do not have the means to divert and store your part. This is where I come in. I will provide the *logistical support*, as you military people might say. My men and I will appropriate--or misappropriate, if you prefer--the items that you will designate and store them in a safe place known to only you and me. When the war is over and things quiet down, we shall dispose of the merchandise and share the profits according to a formula that will have to be mutually satisfactory. Now, Herr Standartenfuehrer, if my proposition appeals to you, we can talk further, if not, you can place me under arrest. By the way, I still have ten seconds left of my three minutes."

Richter did not place Athanassopoulos under arrest, and a strange friendship developed between the two men. Richter despised Athanassopoulos. Athanassopoulos thought that Richter was a pompous idiot, without vision and initiative. Yet they constantly sought each other's company. In truth, they were alike in many ways, except that Athanassopoulos did not have the streak of cruelty that characterized Richter.

Thus it was that Athanassopoulos warehoused and disposed of Richter's loot. Much of it was magnanimously offered as gifts to fellow SS officers; a great many items had been shipped to Germany in care of Mrs. Richter, the young 100 percent Aryan woman with heavy blond tresses, heavy breasts, and a heavy posterior. The bulk of the merchandise, however, had remained in Salonica to be disposed of at a more propitious time. It could have been sent back to Germany, but then he would have had to share with higher ranking SS officers, and he was not willing to do so. Only Goering could afford to keep for himself whatever he confiscated. Not that he, Richter, was greedy of course. But he was doing all the work and deserved his due. He could wait until the end of the war.

The war, however, had not ended as expected, and he had escaped from Salonica a step ahead of the partisans. The humiliation of that day still rankled twenty-some years later. He still could not believe that the mightiest military force ever assembled, the army of the Third Reich, had been routed by ragtag bands of partisans.

Richter came out of his reverie and drained his glass. Salonica had been good to him, but that was the past. The present was giving him a second opportunity, and he was not about to let it go by. He took a pencil and a pad from his desk and tried to remember the events that transpired after his hasty departure from Salonica.

Athanassopoulos was left in charge of the treasure, but that idiot had managed to let himself be captured, then executed. Fortunately, he had told no one about the pillaged Jewish property, mainly because no one knew of it, and therefore, no one asked about it. The Greek had hidden the loot well, and in spite of all his efforts and many investigations, Richter was now no further advanced as to its whereabouts than he was when he had left Salonica many years ago.

Athanassopoulos had no wife, no relatives nor friends. He had left no papers or documents of any kind. Two days before his execution, he had a long conversation with a Jewish historian. Now what the hell would Athanassopoulos want to talk to a Jew for? Anyway, that old bastard had died five months later on his way to Israel. Like Athanassopoulos, the Jewish professor had no kin. His whole family had been killed at Auschwitz.

Sometimes, Richter thought ruefully, *sometimes, we SS do our work too well. We could have let him have a son or a nephew with whom he could have shared Athanassopoulos in extremis communications.* The death of the old Jew had severed the last link to Athanassopoulos and therefore to the treasure. That was all he knew, and he had given up all hope of ever recovering the treasure.

And now, now after so many, many years, the past was resuscitating, and Richter was getting his second chance. He wouldn't even have to do anything about it. Those idiots at the State Department would do all the work, and their agent, whoever he may be, would get the Jewish professor's documents for him--provided they existed, and Richter was confident they did.

He kept doodling on his pad. His first active step was to get the documents from the State Department's man. That should prove no problem. The P.L.O. would gladly do this for him; he had pumped enough money into their terroristic efforts, the little brown monkeys. My God! To let themselves be made fools of by Jews. Maybe, as a race, Arabs are even lower than Jews in the phylogenetic scale? After all, both are Semitic people, aren't they? The P.L.O. may be used to take the papers from the State Department's man, but under no circumstances must they be allowed to look at them. If, as he believed, the documents contained any indications at all as to the whereabouts of the treasure, the P.L.O. would certainly take advantage of that discovery. They were stupid, but not that stupid. His next step was to prevent this from happening, and that was where Streicher would come in. He stopped writing, refilled his glass, and was swept again by memories.

Good old Streicher! Now that was a man, a real German, and devoted to Richter. True, he was a little violent at times, but if the situation called for violence, every good German should rise up to the circumstance. Ex-Gestapo officer, ex-police inspector in Hamburg, recent killer-for-hire, Streicher had always carried out his assignments to perfection, and Richter had often used him to their mutual satisfaction. In his very rare moments of honesty, the former SS colonel knew that he was afraid of Streicher; he also knew that he was jealous of him, jealous of his physical strength, his fearlessness, even his ability to kill without hesitation. Perhaps, he envied his ability to kill more than his other qualities. Of course, there was a big difference in age. Streicher was twenty-three and he was thirty-five in 1940 when the war had started twenty-eight years ago. Yet, in the deep recesses of his mind, he knew that age had nothing to do with it. Streicher was a strong man, and he... well, enough of this nonsense. Streicher always obeyed him, always respected him, and recognized his superior intellect. Streicher would take care of the P.L.O.

‿

First things first. He had to contact the P.L.O. and had to do it now.

Richter drove the small, battered, bluish-gray Volkswagen out of the side garage. Fortunately, there was still some gas in the tank. The VW was the first car he had purchased in America, and although he now drove an expensive Mercedes, he had never sold the little car. It was his good luck charm, and he felt a sentimental attachment to it, and occasionally, very rarely, he drove it around. The Volkswagen was handy for the kind of business he had to transact tonight. It would not do for his black Mercedes to be seen in front or even near the Baghdad Café.

He drove for a good forty-five minutes through some of the poorest streets of Detroit and stopped in front of a rather seedy place where a moribund neon light indicated *T e Bag dad Ca e*. The place was smoky and small, with a pronounced aroma of shish-kebab and manned by two waiters with soiled aprons and distinct Middle Eastern features. The lady at the counter walked toward him, stopped as she recognized his features, then discreetly motioned for him to follow.

They went through a small, dark antechamber, then through another door, and he stepped into an altogether different world. It was a windowless but large room with a high ceiling and very thick beige carpet which muted the sound of his steps. The walls were wood paneled and bookcases filled with what appeared to be law books lined two of them. The other two displayed what seemed to be an original Picasso and an original Cezanne. Someday, he would have to look at them closer and more carefully.

In the center of the room was a sculpted coffee table surrounded by four comfortable leather chairs. Against one of the walls was a huge desk with a leather top and two telephones. There was no clutter on the desk. Two straight-backed chairs stood in front of the desk. There was a faint scent of cigar smoke and expensive after-shave. The whole place conveyed a feeling of luxury and peace. The man behind the desk stood up and rushed to meet him with an extended hand and a friendly smile. Short, well-dressed, if slightly rumpled, with thick glasses, he looked like a college professor and not at all like a business man, even less like a P.L.O. agent.

"Mr. Von Eckardt, what an unexpected pleasure. Please do sit down. To what do I owe this visit?"

Richter sat on one of the leather chairs and accepted a glass of fine cognac. "Mr. Zaccaria, it is good to see you. I came here because I need a favor."

Zaccaria, Richter knew, was born and raised in Lebanon to well-to-do parents. He had gone to school in France and eventually had graduated from the Sorbonne. He prided himself in having shed many of what he thought were uncivilized Arabic customs, one of them being the habit of spending inordinate amounts of time inquiring about one's health and family rather than getting straight to the point. Ibrahim liked to go straight to the point.

"Of course, Mr. Von Eckardt, and what can I do for you?"

Richter paused for a few seconds. How much could he tell the man? He had collaborated with him several times but did not trust him.

"Well, Mr. Zaccaria, the favor I need is not relevant to your cause, and I know you have only a limited number of agents. On the other hand, I have come through for you several times, and I know how to be generous."

Zaccaria waved a hand dismissively. "Money is unimportant. Please tell me what you need done."

Richter stretched back in his chair and swallowed a sip of cognac.

"Well then, a Jewish former CIA agent is on his way to Athens to bring back certain World War II documents. These documents are of interest to no one except some of my old war comrades. It is vital that they don't fall into the hands of the Jews, who may use them to further besmear my country. I will give you the name of the agent, the name of his contact, and the date, time, and place of their meeting. I want you people to get the documents and return them to me. It is a rather easy mission."

Zaccaria was devoured with curiosity. He was certain there was much more to the documents than the German was saying. He was no less certain that Von Eckardt would tell him no more than what he had already volunteered. But it didn't matter. The documents would be in his agents' hands for a short time. That is all that was needed.

"Very well, Mr. Von Eckardt, my organization will do this for you in recognition of your good services. Now, while we shall not charge you anything, as I said earlier, we shall need some operational funds, say around $10,000...?"

Richter remained impassive. "Very well, cash will be delivered to you through the usual channel."

Back in his study, Richter was pleased with himself. He knew, of course, that Zaccaria would instruct his agents to duplicate the documents, and that would not do. His next immediate step would be to contact Streicher.

Still, Richter was not completely satisfied. He weighed options. Perhaps he did not need the P.L.O.; perhaps he could have Streicher steal the documents himself and bring them directly to him. This would eliminate the P.L.O. intermediary and save him money to boot. Yet, he did not feel comfortable with that decision. In the unlikely event that Streicher failed and was arrested, he was a link to Richter. He admired Streicher's strength, respected and sometimes envied his ruthlessness, but did not think highly of his loyalty. Should he be arrested and in possession of documents linking Streicher to him, he would not put it past Streicher to strike a deal at his expense. The odds that he would be apprehended while taking the documents away from the P.L.O. were much lower, practically nonexistent. Indeed, a novice, usually untrained Palestinian agent would be much more vulnerable than a trained, experienced CIA operative, and certainly less likely to sound the alarm. Of course, the Palestinian could be arrested in the attempt, but they could not implicate Richter. Indeed, they did not know of him. Only high-ranking P.L.O. officials, and only very few at that, knew who he was. Well, that is how it was going to be. The P.L.O. would take the documents from the American, then Streicher would take care of the P.L.O. people. He could count on Streicher.

He jotted a few more notes on his pad and felt satisfied with himself. The Arabs first, then Streicher. His plan needed some finishing touches, but it was logical and would work.

He poured himself another generous dose of cognac. He had acquired a taste for cognac during the war when the German army had misappropriated all the fine things that France had to offer. After the war, he had almost forgotten the taste of good cognac.

Those were hard days, indeed. He gritted his teeth at the memory of how he had to discard his Nazi uniforms and had never been able to wear them again. It was a miracle, indeed, that he had not been captured and had been able to join Ingrid in Berlin. Their home had been bombed and destroyed, all their belongings lost. Her mother had been killed in an air raid, and his sister had never been heard from again. He and Ingrid had to start over again, and he had to admit to himself that if it were not for his wife's indomitable strength, he never would have made it. They flew from Berlin to Munich after they changed their name from Richter to Von Eckardt. Thank God, now he could afford just about anything he wanted.

His thoughts took a different direction. How, in God's name, had they found who he really was? His change of identity and emigration to America had been taken care of by an underground fraternal organization of former SS officers, and he knew how thorough and efficient they were, leaving nothing to chance and no loose ends. Besides, he seriously doubted that any security service would have expended the necessary effort, manpower, and money to track him down except, except... the Jews, of course, the Mossad. Too bad the war ended so soon before they could all be exterminated. Well, he and his brother SS had done their best. And now, so many years later, things were falling into place, thanks to his friend Steve Harper. Whatever evidence existed against him would be destroyed, and, in the process, he would recover the fortune which that idiot Athanassopoulos had lost when he allowed himself to be arrested and executed. There was justice in this world.

Chapter 7

The Trial

Upon his arrival in Athens, David Castro checked in at the modest Athenean Hotel after canceling the reservations which his friend had made for him at the Grande Bretagne. He felt that he would be too conspicuous at the most expensive hotel in Athens and preferred the anonymity of a smaller place. He immediately called Attorney Venchiarutti to set up an appointment. This proved to be harder than he had expected. Apparently, Venchiarutti was well known at the Grande Bretagne, and his privacy was jealously guarded.

"I am sorry, Sir, Mr. Venchiarutti has left orders not to be disturbed."

The desk clerk hung up, and David immediately redialed, and this time there was steel in his voice.

"Please do not hang up on me again or I'll have to go there in person, and that would not be a pleasant experience."

Duly impressed, the desk clerk stammered, "If you would leave me your name and number, I will call Mr. Venchiarutti, and if he wishes to talk to you, I will call you right back."

"Very well then, I am at the Hotel Athenean, and you can easily find the number. As for my name, just tell Mr. Venchiarutti that I come from the United States. I shall wait for five minutes and no longer."

The man called back within three minutes, and his voice held a tone of deference and respect that was not there before.

"I am sorry, I did not know. Mr. Venchiarutti will see you in the hotel bar in approximately thirty minutes."

David did not ask the desk clerk what it was that he didn't know and had so rapidly found out. He chuckled with a hint of disgust at how easy a little bit of assertiveness could overcome most bureaucrats.

The Athenean was within walking distance from the Grande Bretagne. The Grande Bretagne was on Syntagma Square, and the Hotel Athenean was on a small adjacent street. He arrived a few minutes early but was expected and directed to a table away from the noise of the bar customers. Venchiarutti arrived five minutes later, introduced himself, and both men shook hands.

David liked the old man. Tall, spry, even though he was nearing seventy, snow white wavy hair, and a scar bisecting his forehead gave him the roguish appearance of a pirate belied by kindly, twinkling blue eyes.

"Your company informed me that you would be calling, young man, but gave me absolutely no clue as to what your visit is all about. Normally, I would not have seen you outside of my office, but the request was supported by my old friend, the former ambassador to Rome, Henry Johnson. What can I do for you?"

David had given much thought to how he would have introduced the matter to Attorney Venchiarutti and had discarded one alternative after the other. Somehow, the idea of lying to this patrician old man seemed repugnant to him, and impulsively, he decided on the most open and direct approach.

"Sir, I represent certain parties in my country vitally interested in gathering data necessary to convict an ex-high-ranking Gestapo officer, Johann Richter. The man was in Salonica, Greece from 1942 to 1945 and is believed to be presently living in Detroit under the name of Dieter Von Eckardt. The evidence against him, however, is strictly circumstantial, and although we are convinced that Richter and Von Eckardt are one and the same, the evidence is not enough to convict him in a court of law. We learned that you may possibly lead us to harder evidence."

"And how would I do that, young fellow?"

"Well, Sir, according to our information, there was a Jewish historian in Salonica who survived by hiding out in the Italian Consulate. It is said that Professor Assael chronicled the events of these days as they related to the fate of the Jewish community, and he was able to document most of what happened. Assael, however, died shortly after the war ended, and his papers were never found. Our sources also told us that Professor Assael was very close to the man who saved his life and the lives of many more Jews at the risk of his own. That man is the only person still alive who would know the hiding place of Dr. Assael's papers. His name was Captain Francesco Venchiarutti, and he is today a jurist of international renown, advisor to prime ministers and international corporations."

"I am afraid your information--"

"That's not all," interrupted David, "but the rest of the story is personal and does not concern my employers. If you would do me the honor of hearing me out, I shall share it with you."

David talked for a long time. The words, halting at first, came more freely as he shared with the old Italian the memories which had flooded him during the past few days, memories which he had shared only with Bill, Dr. Rosen, and, sometimes, with Master Kwang. Somehow, it felt right and not like an intrusion. Venchiarutti was a righteous Gentile in David's eyes, the noblest kind of person. He had been willing to sacrifice his life for the sake of humanity, to die a death of dishonor and torture in order to save the lives of fellow men and women. He had earned the right to enter David's forbidden world. He told the old man about his childhood, about his mother's love of her home, about the crumbling of his world, the fears, the sadness, the loneliness, the anger. He did not tell him about Auschwitz; he did not trust himself. It didn't matter; the old man knew.

When David stopped talking, the two men remained silent for a while, then Attorney Venchiarutti said, "I need some time to myself. I need to think about it." He called the waiter and then asked David, "What will you have?"

"Just coffee."

"Take your time and give me about thirty minutes, then come up to my suite, 1620. Please don't get up," he continued, as David tried to get off his chair.

∽

Back in his suite, the elderly Italian splashed some water on his face and sat in a comfortable chair on his balcony overlooking the bustling Syntagma Square. David's words had re-awakened much of what Venchiarutti had thought was buried in the recesses of his mind. It had all happened so long ago. His convalescence at the Italian military hospital in Salonica had only lasted a few days. The German's bullet had merely creased the side of his skull, and his recovery was quick and complete. He was awarded a week's leave, which he had spent with his family in Rome, and was informed that at the end of his leave he would return to Salonica as Military Attaché to the Italian Consul General.

The reunion was not altogether satisfactory. When he squeezed Stella and Bruno against his heart, he thought that he would die of happiness. His first night in their magnificent bed, which they had inherited from Stella's grandparents, was restless; the mattress was too soft, and he could not breathe. In a way that he could not understand, he longed for the mountain tops of

Mavropotamos. Later that morning, he was shocked to see the dark circles under Stella's eyes and how thin Bruno was. He asked no questions, knowing full well what the answer would be.

That afternoon, they called on his parents. His mother had not changed, but his father had aged considerably. The fire of old was still in his eyes, but he no longer stood erect, and his head was all white. He hugged his son almost violently, as if he didn't want to let go of him. After a lunch of pasta, meager fare for the Venchiarutti's, he and Stella went for a walk in the park while his parents watched over Bruno, and they sat on the old stone bench. He looked at her, and her eyes were full of infinite sadness.

He held her for a while. "Tell me, Stella. I can guess most of it, but tell me, anyway."

She trembled slightly in his arms. "It's the fear, Francesco. It is everywhere. The fascists sense the end coming, and they are like wild animals lashing out at everything and everyone."

"Have they bothered you?"

"No, not yet. They don't dare, but it won't be long. Your father, may God bless him, is not one for keeping opinions to himself, and while most everyone respects him for that, he has not endeared himself to the fascists."

"Bruno is thin and so are you."

Her smile was as radiant as ever. "When you come back to stay, it won't take us long to get fat again."

"I'll talk to Dad..."

"No, please don't," she interrupted. "All he has left is his pride and self-respect. It would kill him not to be able to say what is in his heart."

He looked at her in adoration. She was indeed "the woman," and all he could say was, "I love you." She squeezed his hand.

"Let's go back. They will wonder what happened to us," she said.

His second leave-taking was infinitely worse than the first. When he had left the first time, they were afraid for him, and he had tried to reassure them. This time, he was afraid for his loved ones, but they could not reassure him. He hugged and kissed them one by one, held his father's white head, lingered in a long embrace with Stella and Bruno, then got in the staff car, which they had sent for him.

"Andiamo." He did not look through the rear window.

He boarded an Italian naval vessel in Bari and reached Salonica on a clear, beautiful spring morning. The White Tower loomed majestically and along a quay, rows of white, yellow, and pink homes looked inviting and friendly. Small sailboats were criss-crossing the bay. The picture was idyllic, and for a moment, he thought ruefully, *Wouldn't it be nice to finish the war in a place like this? I could even bring Stella and Bruno here.* But he knew that this could not be. He could never have his family live in a German-occupied city. To live with the "fascists" in Rome was bad enough.

An Italian military staff car drove him to the consulate, and an affable, matronly lady who, he found out later, would be his secretary led him to his quarter, an airy, well-furnished room with an attendant studio and a marble bath, a far cry from his spartan room in Mavropotamos. Mavropotamos... He wondered how many of those poor people had survived the massacre--if any.

"Commandatore Castruccio, the Consul General, will see you in an hour. I shall take you to his office."

It took Venchiarutti less than an hour to unpack, shower, and get into a dress uniform. He was looking outside the window into a beautiful courtyard, which somehow reminded him of his parents' garden in Rome, when his secretary knocked at the door and informed him that the commandatore was ready for him. He was mildly curious to meet the man who, for an indefinite period of time, would certainly affect his destiny.

He was instantly put at ease by a warm smile and a casual gesture which waived aside his attempt at a snappy military salute. Castruccio was a commanding figure, a big man, not fat, but tall and muscular. His hair was turning gray, and his mustache, jutting jaw, and piercing dark eyes, gave him a ferocious look tempered by his friendly, casual manner. He courteously stood up, came from behind the desk and extended his hand.

"Welcome, Venchiarutti. Please sit down. I know of your father in Rome."

Venchiarutti had a lopsided smile and replied, "Then you know that he is not held in high respect by our leaders."

"Yes, I know, and that is why, among many other reasons, I like your father."

Venchiarutti marveled at the man's candor yet remained on his guard. Was he expressing his true opinions, or was he setting a trap for him? Later he would learn that Castruccio made no secret of his profound dislike for the fascists and, especially, their German allies. In fact, everyone thought that it was a miracle he had survived in his diplomatic post for so long. Venchiarutti remained non-committal.

"I hope that I will not disappoint you, Mr. Consul General," Venchiarutti said.

"I am sure that you will not. By the way, are you satisfied with your accommodation?" And without waiting for an answer, Castruccio continued. "You were assigned to this consulate as a military attaché, Captain Venchiarutti. While this is your formal title, your duties will, however, be of a different and special nature. They will be dangerous and may jeopardize your military career. So, I am not willing to order you to perform them. After I explain what I expect of you, please feel free to say no."

Intrigued, Venchiarutti leaned forward in his chair. At the same time, he could not help a smile.

"My military career, Mr. Consul General, will end the same day this accursed war is over. I have no ambitions in that area."

"Very well then. You know, of course, that the Germans have embarked on a program of persecution of European Jewry. What you may not know, however, is the extent to which this program goes. Their intent is, no more, no less, to exterminate, I mean to massacre outright an entire people. They are being deported to concentration camps in Germany and Poland. These camps are, in reality, death factories. Upon arrival, deportees are led to gas chambers and killed outright."

Venchiarutti listened intently as a wave of nausea engulfed him. He could not doubt the veracity of the consul general's statement. Yet, there was something so monstrous, so terribly inhumane about what he was hearing that his mind rejected it. If this were true, Mavropotamos paled in comparison.

He stammered, "Are you sure?"

Castruccio nodded, "Yes, I know. I had exactly the same reaction. It is inconceivable that a civilized nation can engage in genocide. I feel a deep shame that our nation is an ally of these monsters."

"What do you want me to do?"

"I was getting to that. As you may know, Salonica is home to a fairly large, prosperous colony of Italian Jews. It is our job to protect them and repatriate them to Italy. The Germans snort and stomp, but there is nothing much they can do about it. I have also made it my duty to rescue as many non-Italian Jews as this consulate is able to. This is not a small operation. It entails forged passports, ID cards, and train tickets to Athens. In addition, many of these unfortunates come to the consulate as a haven. We accept as many as the consulate can absorb and then some. The Germans, of course, know of our activities, but the consulate is off-limits to them. The real problem is to get these people in and out of the area without alerting the Gestapo. To this you must add the logistics of housing and feeding our guests, the forging of passports and ID cards. Captain Venchiarutti, that is what I want you to do. How do you feel about it?"

Thus began for Venchiarutti one of the most exciting periods of his life. The thrill of the danger, the shared fear with the people he rescued was matched by his satisfaction at outwitting the Germans and the profoundly rewarding gratitude of those whose lives he saved. He became quite close to Commandatore Castruccio and learned to appreciate the kindness and humanness hidden under his gruffness. The highlight of that period of his life was the friendship he developed with the old Jewish historian Professor Assael. Assael had taken refuge in the consulate in the early days of the German occupation and had doggedly refused to escape to Athens, which was occupied by the Italian army and safe for Jews.

"Someday, Francesco," Assael said to him once, "someday we'll all be free again, and when this happens, people in other countries will not believe that all this has happened. They will not believe that the nation that produced Schiller, Goethe, and Beethoven stooped to the level of jungle animals, even below that level. Jungle animals kill for food while they kill for thrills. Someone has to write about what happened and document these happenings. This someone will be me. It is a self-appointed mission, and I consider it sacred,"

They would spend hours talking together. Venchiarutti was a learned man, but Professor Assael's knowledge was encyclopedic. The young man would never tire of listening to the old man and once jokingly told him, "We are like Edmond Dantes and the Abbas Faria."

Professor Assael did not smile at the comparison. Instead, he looked at Venchiarutti very seriously and said, "You are quite right, except that any German-occupied city is a more formidable fortress than the Chateau d'If."

Shortly before Lt. Venchiarutti--by then Captain Venchiarutti--was rotated to Rome, Professor Assael took him by the hand and led him to a small bare room which, with its white-washed walls and flagstone floors, looked very much like a monastic cell.

The old man kneeled by the corner of the room and with some difficulty removed the cornerstone. Underneath that stone was an empty space. The old man looked up at Venchiarutti.

"If anything happens to me and I don't survive this war, you will find all my writings here. Make good use of them."

A few days later, Captain Venchiarutti departed and never saw the old man again. He learned through Italian consular sources that Professor Assael had died in an accident one year after the end of the war. Venchiarutti had felt profoundly sad upon learning of his death and had always assumed that his old friend had taken his chronicles with him. Apparently, he had not done so, and the documents were still hidden in the small white-washed cell. It was time they saw the light and that good use be made of them. It was time the guilty be punished and the victims rewarded.

℮℈

There was a knock, and Mr. Venchiarutti opened the door and motioned to David to enter.

"Please sit down, David. I believe that I can call you David? I believe I know the parties you represent. I also realize you will not admit it. It does not matter. For reasons also of my own, and which I shall share with you, perhaps at a later time, I will help you, but now I wish to be alone. We can have breakfast tomorrow at eight in my suite and discuss the details of our collaboration."

David nodded, stood up, bowed slightly, and left. He felt no elation or feeling of success, perhaps just a sense of peace. The old gentleman and he had understood each other.

The old magic of Athenian nights was still present in spite of the noise, the tourists, and the gasoline fumes. Instead of returning to his hotel, David walked through Syntagma Square, past the Royal Gardens (renamed Gardens of the People), and walked a steep hill leading to Kolonaki. Kolonaki, at one time, was a rather exclusive suburb of Athens, and it still maintained some of its old dignity. A former girlfriend, who, many years ago, had somewhat influenced his life, lived in Kolonaki. He wondered what had happened to her but had no real desire to find out. Yet, it felt good to walk through the dark, peaceful, almost deserted streets. A heady wine of adolescence, good yet fleeting memories. He sighed, turned around, and returned to his hotel.

The hall was deserted as he got off the ornate elevator and turned left to enter his room. The almost invisible thread he had placed a few inches from the ground between the doorjamb and the wall was gone. He made it a practice never to lock the door when he left his hotel room, always wanting to know if someone had tried to come in, and he would always leave the light on. He did not hesitate, opened the door in a fluid motion, and entered rapidly. His right leg shot out in a back kick aimed at approximately the height of an average man's chest. The dull thud and the groan of pain told him that he had calculated his distance well. The second intruder was facing him, a gun in his right hand. David's left hand fingers went rigidly straight and with lightning speed made a semi-circle from right to left, deflected the man's gun, and hit the side of his wrist. There was no need to follow through; the gun had clattered to the floor, and the man was holding his right hand with his left. That wrist, David thought, would hurt for a few days even if there were no bones broken.

David's voice was very calm, almost gentle, but with an icy, threatening quality to the gentleness. "You will tell me who you are and what you were doing in my room, then I shall decide whether to let you go, turn you over to the police, or dispose of you myself. Now talk."

To David's surprise, the man with the gun paid no attention to him but, instead, walked over to his unconscious companion, knelt, and without a word started ministering to him. David reached for the additional overhead light and, curiously, had his first good look at the two intruders. The man lying on the floor, still unconscious from David's back kick, was a handsome, dark-haired youth, probably in his twenties, wearing youth's international uniform: T-shirt, blue jeans, and sneakers. The other fellow was a much more commanding figure, a big man, as tall as David but somewhat heavier. Splendidly built, he wore a dark, striped shirt without a collar, the kind favored by Greek villagers, riding breeches, and boots. His luxurious mustache, black tinged with silver, gave him a ferocious look, and the man brought to David's mind the image of the legendary *Pallikari*, the swashbuckling heroes of the Greek revolution. The man looked up at him, and David saw there was no fear in the piercing black eyes, no arrogance either, pride, maybe, and determination. David walked over to the wet bar, filled a glass with ice and a liberal dose of whiskey and handed it to the older man.

"He will be all right. I held my kick back," David said. Indeed, the youth soon opened his eyes, massaging his hurting and bruised chest.

"All right," said David, somewhat impatiently. "I want answers, and I want them now."

The two intruders looked at him, and the older man spoke for the first time. "Do not waste your time, you will learn nothing from us."

David sighed in disgust. He had persuaded recalcitrant adversaries to talk before but never relished the task. Besides, there was something about his two captives, especially the older man, that made him even more reluctant to use violence. The directness of his stare, maybe the unafraid look. He could try to intimidate the youth, but something told him that he would not get very far. *Well*, he thought, *I have followed my intuitions more than once and it usually paid off.*

With a last glance at the two men, he simply opened the door and said, "You are free to go." The young man, in spite of his bruised chest, stood up immediately and moved toward the door. The older man, the *Pallikari*, lingered on, however, for a few seconds. He stared at David with a half-smile, which David could not decipher. It was neither hostility nor defiance, perhaps a mixture of understanding and appreciation. As the two men closed the door behind them, David, with quick and precise gestures, pulled a pair of tennis shoes from the closet, put them on, and opened the door. The hallway was deserted, but an elevator was waiting. The two men had not gone far, and David's gamble had paid off. They were walking and not riding in a car. To follow was child's play, and twenty minutes later, the two men entered a small house on the outskirts of the Plaka at the foot of the Acropolis. David carefully noted the address. He now had the beginning of a thread and could follow through in the morning.

❧

Back in his hotel room, lying on his bed and nursing his glass of *ouzo* on the rocks, David reviewed the events of the past hour. He could not get the *Pallikari* off his mind. The ice cubes melting fast in his glass, clouding the clear drink with the licorice scent, as always brought him visions of sunshine, vineyards on the outskirts of Salonica, bread and feta cheese, plaintive *bouzouki* music, peaceful evenings and quiet conversations under huge oak trees, and long, long before that, in the dim recesses of his childhood memories, Youssef. Yes, Youssef, his *kavass* with his bushy, gray moustache always scented with *ouzo*. Of course, that was who the *Pallikari* had brought back from the dead. Youssef who, in a little boy's life, was a very short step below his father and two very short steps below God! In these bygone days, it was customary for well-to-do families in Salonica--barely independent from Turkey, but still under the influence of Turkish customs--to hire a *kavass* for the children, a combination of teacher, male nanny, and bodyguard. Youssef was a retired policeman, but in the little boy's imagination, he was that and much more: a dashing, romantic, huge figure in scuffed boots, riding breeches, and wide leather belt. He squealed in frightened delight when Youssef would roar at him or throw him way up in the air, and on late evenings when his parents would go out at night, he would fall asleep listening to the terrifying and marvelous stories of Youssef chasing bandits and Turks through dark and foreboding mountains or rock in the giant's arms to the melancholy sound of a Sephardic melody. Only his father's arms offered a comparable safety and warmth. Tomorrow, David thought, as he drifted into sleep, he would look him up.

❧

May 9, 1976

Attorney Venchiarutti's suite was luxurious indeed, and in his silky morning robe, the old gentleman offered a picture of undeniable distinction. The breakfast table had been set up on the terrace, and he affably motioned David to a chair.

"I must apologize, David, I was a little curt last night. The memories which you shared with me brought back a period of my life which I believed forgotten. Of course, it is not so."

David waved the apology aside. "There is no need to apologize, Sir. I knew exactly what was happening."

"Thank you, David. You see, our lives have overlapped at one time before, even though there is such a difference in age between us, and it is because of what we share that I shall help you and your people. Now let us breakfast and talk about specifics later."

"One moment, Sir," said David. "To your knowledge, do you have any enemies in Athens, anyone who may have been following you?"

Venchiarutti's expression was of genuine puzzlement. "No, no one that I know, and if it weren't a rather naive statement, I would be tempted to say that I don't have an enemy in the world. Why do you ask?"

David related to him the incident of the night before, but it seemed to have no meaning for the Italian aristocrat. He stood up and took a couple of steps toward the entrance to his suite.

"Only once in my life did I associate with people like those you describe, but that was over twenty-five years ago, and if anything, they would feel friendship and not animosity toward me."

As he said those last words, Venchiarutti seemed to lose his balance. David tried to get up and assist him, but his own knees were wobbly. The room started spinning and he tried desperately not to lose consciousness without avail.

&

Consciousness returned gradually, and David shivered. How could he feel cold in May in Athens? Voices floated around him, and one voice in particular sounded familiar. He had heard it before but couldn't remember where or when.

David was debating whether to open his eyes or not when the decision was made for him by a rough voice saying in Greek, "Wake up, American, wake up and look," and a boot which nudged him not gently at all in the ribs.

His right hand shot out, almost reflexively, grabbed an ankle, and jerked. Like a big cat, he was on his feet, crouched and ready to strike. What he saw, however, left him breathless, and he stopped while the man who had kicked him picked himself off the ground. It was a large mountain meadow and what had seemed like daylight through his closed eyelids was the light of dozens of resin torches attached to poles firmly planted on the ground. Men, women, and children lined the meadow like an arena and there were several men sitting at what seemed to be a head table. The flickering lights of the torches distorted features in that apocalyptic scene, but David was sure that one of the men sitting at the head table was the *Pallikari*. Of course, his was the voice that had sounded so familiar.

"Bring the American closer."

David was covered by four men carrying what in the semi-darkness looked to be Uzi submachine guns. He slowly approached the head table, and there he saw Venchiarutti. The Italian was seated in a straight-backed chair, his hands tied behind his back and his feet bound together. Even in this humiliating posture, the old man kept his erect bearing, his air of dignity, and by his mere presence he dominated the scene. For a fleeting second, David had the fantasy that he was witnessing an epic duel between two giants, the patrician old man and the tough mountaineer.

"We wanted you here, American, so that you can tell the world that this is a just trial and we are not murderers. You are an honest man, and you will not lie." David silently nodded, and the *Pallikari* went on. "This, my friends, is the last scene of a drama which began on a cold night of December, 1942. Many of you were here, in this village of Mavropotamos. Some of you were children, some of you were not even born. I, myself, was a young man, barely eighteen years old. Our village, at that time, was occupied by a small Italian garrison commanded by an officer called Francesco Venchiarutti. Lieutenant Francesco Venchiarutti, a name etched in hate in the hearts and minds of every one of us here, a name synonymous with infamy. We did not like the invaders, but we were a peaceful people and caused them no trouble. Then, the andartes, the partisans, killed two German soldiers, and a German detachment came to our small village. The orders for the destruction of our homes, for the incarceration of the population which was to have been followed by execution, these orders bore the signature of Lieutenant Francesco Venchiarutti. Venchiarutti, we looked for you for many, many years. We never gave up, and a few years ago we found you, an internationally respected jurist, a mass murderer. We could have killed you easily, but we are not assassins, and we waited for the opportunity to bring you here for trial at the scene of your crime. Venchiarutti, for your crime against humankind, for the betrayal of your own uniform, for the tears and pain for which you are responsible, we shall judge you here. Do you have anything to say in your defense?"

David looked at the Italian lawyer and was puzzled. He could read no guilt, no shame, nor fear on the old gentleman's face but rather an ineffable gentleness and peace. David could have sworn that there was love in the way Venchiarutti looked at the formidable Greek.

"Yes, I have only one question. Why were you not killed?"

"Because on that night, on that fateful night, a stranger, an angel of mercy, an emissary of God, let us escape. We looked and looked for years and never found him. He opened the door of the barn where the soldiers had locked us up. I still remember his shadow in the dark, and I remember every word he said. He opened the door and he said..."

"And he said," interrupted Venchiarutti, his voice suddenly loud but choked with emotion, "...and he said, 'I took care of the sentries. Hurry up into the mountains. May God be with you.'"

It was as if the meadow and the people had suddenly been turned to stone. The silence almost hurt, the resin torches had dimmed, and the wind no longer moaned through the pine trees. The *Pallikari* stood up, his steps heavy, his gait like that of a drunken man. With a violent gesture, he pulled a dagger from a sheath on his wide belt, walked toward the prisoner, cut the ropes binding his wrists, and knelt and freed his feet. He did not stand but remained kneeling, sobs wracking his muscular body and echoing through the meadows, like the pain and anguish of primeval man. With infinite gentleness, Venchiarutti put his hands on the shoulders of the younger man, slowly helped him up, and the two men, the old patrician lawyer from Rome and the tall *Pallikari* from the mountains of Greece, threw their arms around each other in the age old gesture of friendship, love, and forgiveness. The meadow came back to life, and the people cried and laughed and hugged each other, and the flame of the torches shot up again, and the wind sang in the pine trees.

❧

Much later that night, the three of them--David, Francesco Venchiarutti, and Mihali Diamantopoulos, the *Pallikari,* sat under a huge oak tree in the village square and sipped a last glass of *ouzo.* The lambs had been slaughtered, roasted on a spit, and eaten. The villagers had gone to sleep.

"Perhaps the first really peaceful night since December 1942," said Mihali.

David and Mihali turned to the older man, and Venchiarutti sighed, looking at the cloudy liquid in his glass.

"It was so long ago. Anyway, after you disappeared through the rocks, I realized that I wasn't such a great hero after all, and my legs were shaking so much I couldn't walk. Apparently, one of the German sentries must have come to, and he saw me in the dark. If his shot had been aimed a little better, I wouldn't have been here tonight. Fortunately, I lost my balance and fell down a ravine. The Germans found me two days later, and somehow it never occurred to them that I had been the one who had opened the door of the barn. They were convinced that it had been the work of the partisans and that I had been shot by them in the line of duty while making my rounds."

He paused for a while, a twinkle in his eyes. "Come to think of it, I was pretty proud of my accomplishment. I remember thinking that night that during those four years of war, I proved my valor by knocking two men out with a chuck of wood, and they were my allies."

David chuckled, and Mihali laughed outright.

"Anyway, I was quite content to let them think what they wanted. More than anything, I wanted to be as far away from them as possible. I convalesced in a hospital in Athens, then after a short leave I was assigned to the Italian Consulate in Salonica, a semi-military, semi-diplomatic post. It is there that I had the good fortune of meeting Professor Assael. He was a fine old man, David, a man of wisdom, of knowledge, and a man of mercy. Yes, I will help you. I think he would have wanted it that way."

David caught Mihali's questioning glance and knew it was his turn. In a few concise statements, he broadly outlined his mission, but he made no mention of his personal interest in achieving his goals. It was getting into the wee hours of the morning, and David felt an extreme lassitude which, no doubt, was shared by the two older men. But Mihali and Venchiarutti were insatiable in wanting to know more about each other, about that period of time during which their lives had overlapped.

"Tell me, Mihali, what happened to the village after I was shot?"

It was getting quite late. The torches and the last fires had been extinguished, but there were so many stars in the beautiful Greek sky. It was so peaceful, yet David had a sense of poignancy. The mountains, now silent, had seen so much pain, so much fear, so much despair. David felt like an intruder between these two men, who had seen so much. He wanted to leave, but he was afraid to move. It was as if even a slight motion could disrupt the magic of the moment and the total harmony between Mihali and Francesco.

Mihali pulled a pipe from the depths of the side pocket of his breeches, emptied the plug by knocking the pipe against the heel of his boot, refilled the pipe with fresh tobacco, tapped it carefully, and lit it with a Zippo lighter.

"A gift from my daughter," he said to no one in particular. He fell silent again, and after a few moments, he sighed deeply and spoke.

"Indeed, these are painful memories. The sentry's shot awakened the German garrison, and they took after us. Most of the women and children escaped, but many men died when they attempted to make a diversion by drawing the Germans' attention to them. Those of us who survived joined the partisans. The village was, of course, razed to the ground, and we rebuilt it after the war ended. As for me, I was obsessed, like so many of my friends, with the desire to find you. As you know, every order in the village, even before those two Germans were killed and the SS column arrived, had been signed by you. You were our only target."

It was at that moment David stood up and stretched. "It is past my bedtime, and I will leave you two to your memories."

Mihali looked at him with such a surprised look on his face that David felt both amused and embarrassed.

David sat down again. "Well, I do want to hear the end of it. You'll just have to wake me up in the morning if I oversleep."

"As for me," continued Mihali, "I joined the army, rose swiftly through the ranks, and fought during the Civil War, although more than once my sympathies were with the other side. I was not political enough, and a few years ago, I was gently nudged out with the rank of Colonel. Since then, I looked for you. By Greek standards, I am a well-off man. My father left me considerable property around Mavropotamos, and it was managed well, and I was able to save quite a bit of money during my army career. We were able to locate you in Rome but unable to get close enough to you to kidnap you."

"Kidnap me!" exclaimed Francesco.

"Of course, what the hell do you think we did yesterday?"

"That is true, but I never thought of it that way," said Francesco sheepishly.

Mihali shook his head in mock disgust. "These lawyers. Anyway, this convention of jurists in Athens was a once-in-a-lifetime opportunity. We monitored every one of your steps, and then David came on the scene. We didn't know what to make of him. We knew that you granted very few and usually very brief interviews, and yet you spent an entire afternoon with him. It could have been a coincidence, but we were not about to take chances, not after all these years. So, we followed you, David, my nephew Yanni and I, or rather we preceded you and waited for you. We waited for you, planning to question you and find out what you all about. Well, it didn't quite turn out that way. Where the hell did you learn to fight? My damn wrist still hurts. Don't ask me why, but somehow I knew you would let us go." He chuckled. "We also knew that you had followed us, but it didn't matter. Our hand was forced, and we had decided to take you with Francesco."

"The waiter," interrupted David. "The hotel waiter, right?"

"Yes, he was one of us, and a few knock-out drops were not hard to find. The most difficult part was to get you out of the hotel. You are both pretty big men, but somehow we managed, and here we are."

"What will you do now, Mihali?" asked Francesco. "Are you married? Do you have children?"

"I was married," answered the *Pallikari*. "A good and beautiful woman, but she died of cancer many years ago. We have a daughter, twenty-two years old, and she is studying to become a doctor in Philadelphia." Mihali smiled at David's somewhat astonished expression. "Well, you see, Mavropotamos is not as isolated as it was twenty-five years ago. In fact, I have been to America several times, and I don't always wear boots and riding breeches. All kidding aside, I don't know what I am going to do. Mavropotamos' peaceful life is not for me."

A hush fell for several minutes, then Mihali spoke again. "David, you realize, of course, that your mission may not be as simple as it appears. Those Nazi bigwigs have a well-organized intelligence network, and if they find out about your plans, they will try very hard to stop you. Have you thought of that?"

David nodded. "Of course. All I can do is be alert and face things as they come."

"Look, I am alone with obligations to no one. I know Salonica well and still have many friends there from my army days. Let me come with you. I might be of help," Mihali suggested.

The offer was tempting, indeed. Venchiarutti had no other urgent obligations, and much to David's relief, he had offered to accompany him to the hiding place of Professor Assael's papers in what had been the Italian consulate. Neither he nor David had been in Salonica in twenty-five years, and the city must have changed considerably. Besides, David was only a child when he and his family had been arrested. Mihali, with his knowledge of the city and possible official connections, could really come in handy and provide excellent cover if need be. Trust was not a question. David and the Italian looked at each other, nodded, and the three men shook hands. Dawn was tingeing the sky with a thin yellow line. It was time for a few hours of sleep.

Chapter 8

Hans Knoppel alias Otto Streicher

While David, Mihali, and Francesco Venchiarutti were forging new friendships, at about the same time, half a world away in New York City, a big man lay half-naked on the bed of a cheap hotel room. The man's name was Hans Knoppel. At one time, long ago, it had been Otto Streicher, a name better buried and forgotten.

The neon lights of the building across the street wove crazy patterns through the half-closed Venetian blinds. The man stared at the ceiling, a lit cigarette in his right hand. He loved New York, a sordid, ugly, dirty megalopolis but vibrant and alive, in perfect harmony with his enormous appetites and zest for the seamy side of life. He did not relish the idea of staying in his hotel room until time came to fly to Detroit, but Richter's instructions had been strict and specific. He was to show himself as little as possible, and then only at night. Not that he gave a damn about Richter's instructions; the old fart was a fraud, a windbag calling himself Von Eckardt nowadays. But he knew that to draw attention to himself was unwise. The good days were gone.

Once upon a time, American authorities would close their eyes to the fact that one had been a Nazi and fall all over themselves to make things easy if one would only supply some knowledge of Russian intelligence; those days were gone. It had been fun while it lasted, but now he had to be careful. His passport was pretty solid but one never could tell with American immigration authorities; they could be tough, almost as efficient as the Gestapo was thirty years ago when he had been chosen to join it. Too much was riding on his not ever being recognized.

Streicher was dead, shot by Yugoslavian partisans, and no connection should ever be made with Hans Knoppel, head of a somewhat shady but effective and discreet private investigative firm in Munich. Besides, there was much money involved in the caper, whatever it might turn out to be. One must give the devil his due; Richter was indeed a fraud, but he knew how to make money and how to part with it. He wondered what it was all about this time. The last time, two years ago, his mission had been to escort two former SS officers to Argentina. The pay had been good, and there had been no trouble. Richter had been afraid that the Israelis might attempt to kidnap them, but everything had gone smoothly.

Maybe this would be equally easy so that he could return to Munich as soon as possible. No matter; he put up with Richter because he paid well and on time, and Richter put up with him because he was efficient and asked no questions. The pompous ass fancied himself a judge of characters and took himself so seriously. Streicher remembered Richter in Belgrade twenty-six years ago, immaculate in his black uniform and black riding boots, visiting the cells in Gestapo headquarters where prisoners were being interrogated. He never stayed very long, afraid that blood would stain his shiny boots. The truth was that he had no stomach for what was going on. All these high ranking Nazis were alike, all show and no substance. Take their uniforms and boots away and they fell flat on their aristocratic asses. They knew how to give orders, all right, and let others do their dirty work. Others like him, Streicher, strong people, real people. But then, he had gone to a good school, a good school of hard knocks.

❧

The smoke of his cigarette drifted toward the ceiling, taking weird shapes, almost like shapes of people he knew. He did not like to dwell on the past. He did not like bitter, ugly memories, but sometimes they intruded against his will, especially when he was alone, like tonight. He remembered the voice of his father.

"Otto, where are you going? I don't want you out with these thugs. Stay home and help your mother."

"Yes, father."

The old man would soon fall asleep by the radio. Otto Streicher had learned long ago that it did not pay to argue with his father. The old man's opinions never wavered, never changed, and where did they get him--a dingy small, cold apartment shared by four members of the family in a decaying high-rise permeated by the smell of sauerkraut and sausages. For a long time after he had left his family, sauerkraut would turn his stomach, and he had forced himself to eat it again at party meetings so as not to look conspicuous. Eventually, he had reacquired a taste for it.

Even as an adolescent, Otto Streicher felt he was different. He wanted things, he wanted money; especially, he wanted women. The year was 1930, and Otto was sixteen. In those days, money was plentiful but worthless and to roll a drunk, snatch a purse, or mug an old lady did not really pay off. By the time he and his friends would spend the money, its value had evaporated. Like angry predators, they would hang around street corners, bitter, cynical, reading magazines coming from France, England, particularly America, and dreaming of fast cars, beautiful women and imitating their vision of the tough American gangster. Then the Nazis came, and young Otto saw his opportunity. Curiously, unlike his friends, he did not fall for Nazi propaganda, and uniforms never impressed him. He was, however, quick to see the potential for power, and power was what he needed to satisfy his zest for life and his enormous capacity for sensual and physical pleasures.

He liked to work quietly and unobtrusively and had gravitated toward the local police at first, then toward the shadowy world of the Gestapo. His first two or three years with the Gestapo were not as easy as he had expected. The discipline was stricter than anything he had ever experienced. The work was boring, involving long, tedious shadowing of suspected criminals or enemies of the state. An interminable amount of paperwork, which he hated, made matters even worse, yet he persevered, and halfway through his third year, he got his big break. He had arrested a vagrant simply because he didn't like his looks. This arrest turned out to be the turning point in Streicher's career. The vagrant was none other than a wanted agent for the French. The Gestapo had no fingerprints of the man and no reason to interrogate a vagrant in depth. He was, however, recognized by a visiting colleague from Munich. Streicher then took the biggest risk of his life. He prevailed upon the head of his department to turn the vagrant loose and allow him, Streicher, to follow him, together with a picked team. The gamble paid off, and Streicher received credit for the arrest of the whole cell.

This stroke of luck brought him to the attention of Haschka, the departmental Gestapo chief. Streicher would never forget this interview. He had never seen the boss but had heard some rather terrifying things about him. He was surprised by his appearance. The man looked more like a bank clerk than a Gestapo bigwig with a formidable reputation. But Streicher was no fool. Hitler and Himmler were no imposing figures--and he knew he had better keep such thoughts to himself. He was, therefore, properly respectful and soon found out that Haschka's reputation was well-deserved. Not only was he completely ruthless, but his organizational skills were without compare. Haschka was no less quick to recognize admirable qualities in his subordinates. Streicher's total lack of scruples matched his analytic skills and his willingness to undertake any task no matter how distasteful.

From then on, Streicher's career was on a roll, and he had quickly risen to the top. He had power, money. He was feared. Power and money were not important *per se* but only as a means to an end. The end for Streicher was the satisfaction of his sensual and sexual appetites.

He had quickly acquired a taste for fine food, for beautiful things, and an aversion to poverty.

In the late thirties, he had bought his parents a new house, a beautiful small cottage in the outskirts of Hamburg, set in flowers as a precious jewel in a bed of velvet, far away from the squalor of the inner city, the garbage-littered hallways of the high rise and the sickening smell of sausage and sauerkraut. It was to be a surprise, and the sour memory of that day still made him gag. The old man had refused to move. He was vaguely aware of his son's affiliations with the Nazis and bitterly disapproved of them. To him, the Nazis were a rabble not worthy of being called German, a blotch upon the fine traditions of an old country. A long time ago, he had finally given up trying to guide and discipline his son. Young Otto would not defy him but smugly say, "Yes, Father," and keep doing what he wanted. As Otto grew older, he wouldn't even bother to acknowledge his father's comments and totally ignored him.

"Where did you get the money to buy this house, son?"

"Would it make any difference? Don't you want to live in a place where it smells good, where the air is clean?"

The old man looked at him with steely eyes. "No, not if the money is dirty money. You and your friends terrorize people, make a mockery of the name of Germany. Gestapo! Ha! We were proud of our police, now we are afraid."

"Papa, before you say 'No,' look at Mother, look at your wife."

The father turned around and glanced at the old woman. She was sitting in a corner, silent, long-suffering, pretty much resigned to what the men would decide. She was, indeed, emaciated, he thought, so tired. He felt a wave of tenderness, some guilt, perhaps. He had not been much of a husband all these years.

He squared his shoulders and turned to his son. "No, your mother and I worked for everything we have had. We never begged, we never stole."

Streicher felt a wave of fury engulf him. "All right then, stay in your stinking hole, die in this filth with your stupid pride. See Mother die also." He left and slammed the door behind him.

Streicher never saw his parents after that day.

The old man had died shortly after the end of the war, preceding his wife by a few months, both believing that their son had been killed in action. Otto felt vaguely sorry for his mother; he would have liked to have seen her before she had died. He chuckled at the thought that his fake death had robbed his father of the opportunity to tell him, "I told you so."

The late thirties and the war years had been good to Otto. In those days, ranking Gestapo officers reigned supreme, and he was able to satisfy his unabashed thirst for power and women, especially women. He sometimes fleetingly wondered at how he handled them. Introspection was not his strong suit. Yet, sometimes he was puzzled. He remembered with a vague uneasiness a time long, long ago; he was seventeen, maybe eighteen. He had met Katya, a dark-haired, frail child of sixteen with the most beautiful blue eyes, and she was the only person ever in the presence of whom he had felt at complete peace. They had liked each other and spent hours talking together, going on picnics in the countryside. She was a part of his life which he had never shared with his ruffian friends. Incredible as it may sound, nobody ever found out about Katya. And then, one day, at the end of a picnic in the wood, as night was falling, she offered herself to him. He made love to her in a clumsy, awkward manner, then, not knowing why, he just walked away. He never saw Katya again.

His thirst for sexual encounters became almost an obsession, but there was never anything gentle or tender in his lovemaking. It was the satisfaction of an animal need, and when spent, he would move away, irritated, almost nauseated at the sight of his naked partner.

☙

Otto Streicher checked his watch. It would soon be time to shower, get dressed, and catch a cab to the airport. He stood up and looked at his body in the mirror with a smug sense of satisfaction. He was a massive man with bulging muscles and, at fifty-three, he felt at the peak of his physical strength. He exuded a sense of raw and brutal power that attracted some women and intimidated most men, and during his years with the Gestapo, he had learned to take advantage of that strength. There was no known way to kill a man with which he was not familiar, and he thought with pride that there were very few things that frightened him. In fact, he couldn't think of any.

The flight to Detroit left at 10:00 p.m.; he still had some time left, and the memories were crowding him at the thought of seeing Richter again. He had met Richter for the first time in Belgrade in '40 or '41. He could not remember the exact year, but he surely remembered the meeting rather vividly. Two SS soldiers had been found killed in an alley, and the Gestapo was investigating their deaths. Otto had visited Richter's office, and he remembered with amusement the contrast between his own rumpled civilian suit and Richter's resplendent SS uniform in black and silver. He remembered Richter's initial contemptuous glance which had quickly changed to a vague uneasiness.

In those days, not even a high ranking officer of the SS could afford to look down with impunity upon a Gestapo investigator, and Otto's attitude, a carefully calibrated mixture of deference and arrogance, was perfectly designed to make Richter feel both pleased and intimidated. Richter was everything Otto Streicher loathed, a low middle class failure, without the courage of whatever few convictions he might have had but with an imbued sense of self-importance and an enormous concern with what was proper. Whether or not it was right mattered not at all. Otto's father was also a failure but, unlike Richter, was unbending in his beliefs in what was right or wrong. Richter had an uncanny ability to take advantage of every opportunity and transform failure into success. Nazi Germany was then an ideal environment for people like Richter. Otto could relate to him better than to his own father. Both he and Richter were opportunists, both lacked scruples, and both were ferociously self-centered. The big difference was that Otto saw himself as he was, had no illusions, and, except in his relationship with women, was pretty much at peace with the way he was. Richter, on the other hand, thought of himself as a noble, dashing, swashbuckling figure and wanted others to see him in that same way. That made him so easy to manipulate.

Their first meeting had ended to everyone's satisfaction. The death of the two soldiers, a sordid affair involving prostitutes and drugs, was quickly classified as the result of a hooligan attack, and a few hostages were summarily executed in retaliation. This had left both Otto and Richter conveniently off the hook, and their relationship, started under such propitious auspices, had been strengthened over time. Favors were exchanged back and forth, then Richter was transferred to Salonica, and Otto Streicher did not see him again until after the war.

In fact, it was in Munich in December 1946, a year and a half after the end of the war, that he saw Richter again.

Black, irregular letters on the door spelled *Hans Knoppel - Private Investigations.* It was a cold, damp December night, and rain, mixed with snow, pelted the few passers-by who walked hurriedly, holding the collar of short leather jackets or threadbare overcoats. The dark street, punctuated by piles of rubble, reflected the soul of Germany less than two years after the end of the war: seamy, hiding in the dark, as if ashamed to be seen in the daylight. The office was small, dusty, and smelled of stale cigars. A naked bulb projected dancing shadows on the walls. There was an old desk, a small file cabinet, and two chairs, the bare essentials.

The man behind the desk looked as if he had come out of a Humphrey Bogart movie. He was a big man, beefy but not fat, conveying an impression of rock-like solidity. His hat was pushed back, his tie loosened up, and, in the semi-darkness, he smoked a cigar. He hardly moved when the door opened and a man walked in. Otto Streicher was barely able to conceal his surprise. In spite of the cheap suit and the leather coat a size too small, the sneer and the arrogant bearing were unmistakable.

Streicher's first thought was: *Johann Richter, the old bastard made it after all.*

"Hello, Otto."

"Hello, Johann. It has been a long time."

The resounding titles were gone the way of the black and silver uniforms and the immaculate boots. Otto Streicher slowly opened the top right-hand drawer of his desk. His right hand gently caressed the Luger in the drawer, and the gesture was not lost on Johann Richter, former colonel of the SS.

"No need for that, Mr. *Knoppel*. I know that Otto Streicher is dead, killed by the partisans in Yugoslavia, wasn't he? So was SS Colonel Johann Richter."

The big man behind the desk allowed himself a sardonic smile.

"And who, may I ask, carries on the tradition?"

The visitor stiffly bowed from the waist. "Permit me to introduce myself. Dieter Von Eckardt, Import-Export."

The big man closed the desk drawer, a gesture elegant in its simplicity. He stood up and from the small file cabinet and he extracted what seemed to be a venerable bottle of schnapps and two glasses. Otto felt reasonably safe. Richter could no more reveal his true identity than he could identify the former SS officer.

~

He tore himself away from his musings. It would not do to miss his plane. He showered and dressed quickly, packed his carry-on, and paid his bill. To find a taxi was rather easy in New York, and he arrived at the airport in plenty of time.

Trust Richter to do things well. Streicher had a first class seat, and he was soon installed with a glass of whiskey in his hand. He closed his eyes and instantaneously picked up his reminiscences where he had left off in the hotel room.

He remembered that day, in his first office, almost thirty years ago, a year and a half after the war, holding two glasses and a bottle of schnapps.

Streicher had felt the need to talk to someone who knew him, and the two men had sat together for a long time sharing memories. Streicher was smart enough not to share everything with Richter. There were things that would be locked forever in his memory, and he remembered them well indeed.

Otto Streicher had been arrested by Yugoslav partisans in 1945 and it was not an experience he was about to forget. For many years, he had intimidated, frightened, and killed, and now the roles were reversed. He was not really afraid; he had seen death so often and in so many shapes and forms that it did not frighten him, not even his own. He could put up with hardship of any kind. What disturbed him and for the first time in his life made him feel insecure and off balance was his complete sense of powerlessness and the fact that no one, not even anyone among the female partisans, was afraid of him. It was as if when he lost his power over others, he had also lost his *raison d'etre*. He realized that it was only power that gave meaning to his life.

While climbing a rugged hill to the partisans' camp, he had stepped on a rock, twisted his ankle and stumbled. Streicher would never forget his blind rage when one of the partisan guards hit him in his kidneys with a rifle butt. He had turned in a flash, his fist raised, ready to strike, and found himself facing the rifle aimed at his stomach. What made him sick, however, what nauseated him even many years later, was that the guard, a mere adolescent in his late teens not only stood his ground but stared him down with a grin on his face as if taunting him to strike. It was at that very moment that Otto Streicher, former police detective, former Gestapo agent, understood that life without power over others was not worth living. Oddly enough, he felt almost as if he were emerging from a shell, saw himself in a new, different, but truer light. He realized that all his life he had deluded himself; he had always believed that power over others was important because it enabled him to satisfy his sexual and sensual needs. He understood it was much deeper than that. It was the core of his being; without power, he was dead. For anyone else, that insight might have been a reason for pause, for introspection, perhaps for trying to put something else, something less transient, less destructive in what was left of one's life. Otto Streicher, however, was not capable of such introspection. When the realization hit him that power made life, he simply set about to reacquire the power that he had lost.

His first goal was to escape. The hardships of captivity did not frighten him. What really scared him was the realization that others had power over him. He did not know how long he could keep his temper in check, and if he were to lose control he would surely be killed. Besides, if the war ended while he was in captivity, his identity as a Gestapo agent--an identity which he had managed to conceal from his captors--would be revealed, and that would be the end of Otto Streicher.

Richter refilled his glass of schnapps, and looked outside. The rain was still falling, and outside it was cold and foreboding. It was warm in the dingy office, and it felt good to drink schnapps and listen to an old comrade. Funny, he had never thought of Streicher as an old comrade before.

"How did you manage to escape, Otto?"

"Well," replied Streicher with fake modesty, "it wasn't hard. I met another prisoner, a Wehrmacht sergeant, who was really good with horses. These Yugoslav bastards liked him, and he enjoyed a comparative amount of freedom. So, one good night, we put the partisan guard to sleep, hopped on two horses, and that was the last we saw of them and they of us."

Richter nodded enthusiastically. "They must have learned that a good German cannot be kept down."

It was getting late, and the two men parted company. This was the first of a series of meetings which would be profitable to both in the years to come.

☙

"Would you like a pillow, sir, or perhaps another drink?" The stewardess's voice startled him, and Streicher stared at her with vacant eyes.

"Another drink," he stammered.

He had not told Richter the whole story of the escape. That story was known to nobody and would never be known by anybody. He wanted to forget it himself, but sometimes it intruded in his mind, and it was there now, stirred by the reminiscences of his first post-war encounter with Richter in 1946.

The Werhmacht sergeant's name was Hans Knoppel, a fact which Streicher had been careful not to reveal to Richter. Hans was a large man, every bit as big as Streicher, and looked almost as tough. Unlike Streicher, however, he was a gentle soul with a perpetual grin and a dazed expression. Hans was a Bavarian farmer, and all his dreams and hopes revolved around going back to his farm, his animals, and his wife, in that order.

The two big men gravitated toward each other and often talked in the evening. That is, Hans talked and Otto listened.

Hans was not a member of the Nazi party, partly because he did not understand Nazi propaganda and partly because there was so much to do around the farm that he had no time to attend meetings where he couldn't even understand what was going on. He was not in the army because he wanted to be but because he had been told to join. He witnessed atrocities with distress and incomprehension; he even participated in some because he was told to. Once, in Russia, his platoon had occupied a small village and bivouacked at

85

that village for several weeks. Hans had befriended a young Russian child named Stepan, whose mother had died and whose father, a soldier with the Russian army, had not been heard from for over a year. Stepan and Hans would spend time talking together in the evening, and he would teach the child German words and learn some Russian from him. Hans often thought that he would take Stepan with him to the farm after the war. Then, the order came for the platoon to retreat, and on that same day, several German soldiers had been killed by Russian partisans in a well-planned ambush. Hostages, including male children, were rounded up and executed.

Hans shot Stepan because he was told to.

"I didn't want to do it, Otto, honestly, I didn't, but what else could I do? Orders are orders. I remember how he looked at me as he died. It really bothered me for a while, but not anymore."

The Yugoslav partisans liked Hans; he was enormously strong and did the work of at least two men. He had disarmed them with his gentleness and good humor, and he enjoyed more freedom than the other prisoners. It was what attracted Streicher's attention. He managed to ingratiate himself with Hans, a simple task indeed. Hans was flattered by Otto's attention, yet he did not feel comfortable in his company. He couldn't quite put it into words but there was something about Otto that frightened him. He felt dominated by him, and almost against his wish, they became inseparable. The partisans soon became accustomed to seeing the two big men together, and Otto benefited from the semi-freedom which Hans enjoyed.

It did not take him long to work out an escape plan. Up in the mountains, the partisans allowed themselves to relax their vigilance since an attack by German troops was most unlikely. When darkness came and the prisoners were locked in their compound, there were only two guards watching them. One guard watched the horses picketed downwind from the bivouac area. Much to his surprise, convincing Hans to escape with him turned out to be the most arduous part of the plan. Hans enjoyed life in the mountains and liked the partisans. As far as he was concerned, the war was over, and maybe not in the too distant future, he would go back to his wife and the farm. Eventually, Otto concocted a story according to which he was a high-ranking SS officer hiding his identity and threatened Hans with a court-martial after the war unless he fulfilled his duty as a true German soldier, which was to escape from the enemy. As usual then, Hans accepted because he was told to.

"But, Otto, the war is almost over. Why risk our lives?"

"Hans, that is strange talk coming from a German soldier. It borders on treason. How about your oath to the Führer?"

Hans would sigh, not quite understanding. He did not remember giving an oath to the Führer, an imposing and frightening figure in faraway Berlin. Yet, he dared not say so. He could not look at Otto straight in the eye. He was frightened but remained stubborn for the first time in his life.

"Otto, I like it here. These men are my friends. They treat me well."

Otto sighed. This wasn't quite going as expected.

"All right, Hans! But before making up your mind definitely, there is something that I must tell you, and when I do, I'll put my life in your hands. I want your solemn word of honor that you will never, ever share this information with anyone."

Hans looked around him like a cornered animal and eventually said, "You have my word."

"Well," said Otto with a crooked smile, "my name is Otto Streicher, but I am not an enlisted man. My rank is Obersturbamführer in the SS. If the Yugoslavs knew my real identity, they would have killed me right away."

"That is true, but they will never learn it from me."

"I know, but I have my duty to perform. As an SS officer, I must try to escape. I cannot do it alone. That is why, even though I understand your reluctance, it is, as I said, my duty to order you to do so."

Hans felt as if he were drowning. All his instincts told him to refuse to obey this order. But the man was an officer, and Hans always did what he was told. Yet, he had a bad feeling about it. Something in the pit of his stomach was biting him like an animal. If Hans knew how to label his feelings, he would have said, "I am deathly afraid." But he didn't know. It was just a bad feeling.

The actual escape proved easier than what Otto hoped for. At night, when the few prisoners doing chores around the campground were herded into their compounds, Otto and Hans simply hid behind a hut, and in the darkness, their absence was not noticed. A little after midnight, they carefully made their way toward the horses. It was child's play for Otto to sneak behind the sentinel and break his neck in two quick snapping movements. The horses were becoming restless, and Otto was glad for Hans' presence. The big farmer knew horses, and these particular horses knew him, since it was part of his daily chores to care for them. The horses were bridled but not saddled--*A minor inconvenience*, thought Otto. As stealthily as they were able, they led two horses away and walked them for approximately one mile, then they vaulted on top of them and took off at a gallop.

Streicher would not soon forget that eerie ride through the mountains, in mortal fear that a horse would tumble and break a leg.

He was not a very good rider, and without a saddle, he hung on to the mane and felt that, at any moment, he would be thrown against the rocks which passed on each side of him at a dizzying speed.

It was dawn when the horses finally slowed down and stopped. The sky was very blue and the air so pure that it was like drinking cold water. He was free; at long last he was free.

Not quite, he thought as he glanced at Hans. He was free of the partisans but not free of "Otto Streicher." His true identity had to die, and he would be reborn with a new name. He was under no illusion that the war could be won, and he could see the inevitable end coming. At the end of the war, Otto Streicher and his past would be quite a heavy burden to bear. What Otto did then was not impulsive. He had thought about it, rehearsed the scene several times in his mind. When Hans had his back to him, he picked up a rock and hit Hans on the back of the neck. Like a tree befallen by an ax, the big German fell to his knees, then on his face. The first blow was deliberate and calculated.

Then something happened to Otto Streicher, something terribly frightening, something that would haunt him for many years to come: he lost control of himself and was unable to stop. His arm lifted and came down with increasing but silent fury. He only stopped when, in sheer exhaustion, he couldn't lift his arm again. After a while his ragged breathing slowed down. As usual, he did not try to understand the meaning of his loss of control. He only knew that if he wanted to remain alive, he could never allow this to happen again. Hans' features as well as the back of his head were unrecognizable. Otto shrugged. That was what he wanted anyway.

With a thin razor blade that he kept in his pocket, he slit the sole of his boot, extracted his Gestapo identification, and carefully inserted it in Hans' inner tunic pocket. He took Hans' papers, which the Yugoslavs had allowed him to keep, and put them in his own pocket. Exit Otto Streicher; from now on, he was Hans Knoppel.

The ensuing years had been hard but comparatively safe. He never returned to Hamburg, where someone might have recognized him. He settled in Munich, where he opened the Hans Knoppel Detective Agency. His business had prospered, but God, how he missed the old days, how he missed them.

Eventually, the plane landed in Detroit. In about an hour he would see Richter again.

☙

Destinies take strange turns. It matters little where we are born. It matters little how well we had planned our futures. The path taken is often beyond our control. Lives started at different times and different places intersect with such intensity that they are changed forever.

Thus it was that while Otto Streicher, alias Hans Knoppel, born in Hamburg, former Gestapo strongman, was landing in Detroit, David Castro, born in Salonica, Holocaust survivor and former CIA agent, was planning his return to the place of his birth. Simultaneously, a Palestinian youth was sitting on a pier in Beruit, overlooking the sea, while a middle-aged State Department functionary in Fairfax, Virginia, was wondering at which point his life had taken a wrong turn.

And all these different people, born in different places, meant for other destinies, unknown to each other, would soon clash, and their lives would take unexpected paths.

Chapter 9

Alysha and Ibrahim

It was a small white house on the outskirts of Beirut, looking more like a shoebox than a real house with a very small patch of grass in the back. There were two chairs on the sidewalk. The house was decrepit, the paint peeling, but somehow the Lebanese sunlight managed to give it a cheerful appearance. It was cool and peaceful inside with fine scents of freshly baked bread and a perpetually simmering soup.

It was cool, and the atmosphere was warm and inviting. Yet, Ibrahim did not like to go inside the house because of his father. Not that he did not like his father. In fact, he adored him, but the sight of his father helpless in a wheelchair filled him with rage and pain. His father, Yassir, had always been a big, strapping man. His bushy, black mustache and a scar on his forehead gave him a fierce and foreboding appearance which hid a most gentle and kind man. Ibrahim was twenty-one but he still remembered the breathless, wonderful feeling of being thrown up in the air by his father and the rides on Yassir's shoulders. He remembered being so high on the tall man's shoulders that he could almost touch the sky. Ibrahim and his father had done many things together: went to the market, worked in the field, played soccer.

Ibrahim and his younger sister, Alysha, would listen to his father's stories. The one he liked the most was about their little village in what was now Israel, with its field of gnarled olive trees and the village square. There was a deep sadness in the big man's voice, and he would say:

"Someday, there will be peace with the Israelis, Ibrahim, and then we'll be back. We should have never left. They told us we could stay, and I wish we had believed them. But we didn't. Instead, we listened to the Syrians, who promised that the Israelis would be driven into the sea and we would come back to a bigger and better village. We should have never listened to them."

90

Ibrahim would, indeed, listen, at least when he was a child. As he became a teenager, however, he was less and less patient with Yassir's tales. The word "peace" especially always struck a negative chord in him.

"Papa, if we wait for peace, you will die of old age and so will I, and so will my children. Why not go in there and fight for what belongs to us?"

His father would sigh. "It is hard, Ibrahim, my son, to move to another place, to a different home, but we can do it. It is not possible to bring back the dead. I have seen so many people die. I don't want to see you die. Besides, who can say what is ours and what is theirs? We could have stayed, but we left because we wanted to return as conquerors and take what was theirs. In the process, we lost what was ours. Yes, I want to go back to our old home, but with a branch of olive tree and not with a sword in my hand."

"But when, Papa, when? How long must we wait?"

And then the accident happened. Ibrahim was sixteen years old when Yassir stepped on a land mine and lost both of his legs.

That day was the worst day of Ibrahim's life and etched in fire in his memory. The boy was returning from a soccer game. His team had won the game, and Ibrahim was happy, doing tricks with the soccer ball. That was when he saw the crowd in front of his home and felt like a hand was squeezing his stomach. He forgot the ball and raced toward home like a madman. There were women and men blocking his path and looking at something on the ground. Ibrahim was very strong. He shouldered them aside and there on the ground was his father. His father, unconscious, appearing to be dead, covered with blood--and he had no legs, he had no legs, he had no legs! Ibrahim felt a scream swelling from inside him and bit his lips so cruelly that blood flowed. Nobody heard him scream, and years later, he still felt as if that scream, that wail, was still trapped within him, wanting but not being able to come out.

They took Yassir to an Israeli hospital. The doctors there saved his life, but his legs had been shattered beyond repair. If the day had been the worst of Ibrahim's life, the night was no less horrible. His mother and sister had stayed at the hospital, and the small shoe box of a house seemed immense. He wandered from room to room, unable to lie down, unable to sit, repeating over and over, a single word, "Papa, Papa, Papa." He was terrified that if he said more than just that single word, something would break, something would happen that would never, never stop.

When at last they brought Yassir back from the hospital, Ibrahim ran away. He spent two days and two nights wandering through the war torn streets of Beirut. It was a miracle that he did not get himself killed. When finally exhausted, famished, and desperate, he returned home. He felt rigid as a board as he approached the invalid's bed. He tried to shake his father's hand, but Yassir pulled him against him, embraced and kissed him. It was not the same; it would never be the same. Ibrahim loved to hug his father and smell his scent of Arak, perspiration, and tobacco. Now he smelled of hospital, of medicine, and all his strength was gone.

Ibrahim sometimes thought that it would have been easier to see his father dead than helpless in a wheelchair. There was something in him that violently rebelled at the sight of his father so helpless and so dependent. He knew that he should have stood by him, helped him, listened to his stories, and nurtured his father as his father had nurtured him when he was a child. But he couldn't; he just couldn't.

"Ibrahim, help me put Father's chair outside, so that he can get some fresh air."

"Yes, Mama." He would obediently help his mother wheel the invalid's chair by the side of the front door; then, his hands in his pockets, somewhat hunched, he would walk away, feeling his father's gaze like a hot poker through his shoulders. He would not glance back, and Yassir would never ask him to stay.

Ibrahim never liked the Israelis, but after the accident, he started hating them with an obsessive, single-minded hatred. The fact that the land mine on which Yassir had stepped was a land mine left behind by a retreating Arab unit did not matter at all. The fact that his life was saved by Israeli doctors was, in a perverse way, an additional injury. If it were not for the Israelis, there would have been no land mines.

It was around that time that he began frequenting the hangouts of other young Arab radicals. He found that his hatred of the Jews, his intolerance of the status quo, and his need for violent action was shared by many. He became intoxicated by the rhetoric of armed resistance, the romanticized, conspiratorial atmosphere of the back rooms of small cafés where young Arabs met. Somehow, he was not affected by the religious fervor which seemed to permeate all their activities. Even though he was a Muslim, he had grown up among Christian Arabs and absorbed much from their attitudes, strongly influenced by the French liberal thinking which had prevailed in Lebanon for many years. He kept his opinions to himself, however, in as much as he felt quite confused about them. On one hand, he felt uneasy, somewhat amused at, and somewhat repelled by the fundamentalist views of his friends, and then he felt sometimes guilty at not being able to share them, although he desperately wanted to be able to do so.

It was not as if he didn't belong. He truly felt part of his comrades and fully accepted, even admired by them. One evening while Beirut was burning, he and some of his friends had discussed Existentialism. None of them, of course, understood the meaning of the word. They vaguely knew that Existentialism advocated personal choice. That was laughable, indeed. Didn't everyone know that Allah dictated one's choices and that Islamic law prescribed one's daily life? Ibrahim did not laugh. There was something seductive in the idea that people made their own choices. Ibrahim was convinced that his way of life, his hatred of the Jews, and his need for violence were choices that he had made and that nothing and no one had influenced him.

One day, he had crossed into Israel and crawled as close as he dared to a kibbutz, and for quite a while, several hours in fact, he had observed the kibbutzniks' activities. He couldn't get over how clean and new the place looked. The people were young men and women in shorts. Ibrahim was enough of a Muslim that the sight made him feel uncomfortable. They did not cease to work, and Ibrahim couldn't help compare their activity to the idleness of Arab men in Arab villages. It was only toward dusk that things slowed down, probably for the evening meal. That experience had left an indelible impression on Ibrahim. Thinking of what he had seen, even after many months, stirred some very strange longings in the young man. Very deep inside of him, flickering like a light, was the unspoken, unacceptable feeling that he almost wanted to be like the Israelis. He knew that such longings, such feelings were evil, and they further inflamed his great rage at the Israelis.

Ibrahim had many friends, but he confided in only one. Yussuf was his age, a Lebanese Christian who, although not harboring much love for the Jews, thought that sooner or later the Arabs had to come to terms with Israel, and the sooner the better. The two friends had interminable, sometimes heated arguments on the topic, heated, that is, on the side of Ibrahim. Yussuf was calm, logical, and with an amused shrug would say, "Ibrahim, smile," and he seemed not to really care if he could convince Ibrahim.

Ibrahim, however, desperately wanted to convert Yussuf to his way. It was as if Ibrahim's hated doubts would disappear if Yussuf would agree with him. Ibrahim had shared with many of his friends his clandestine visit to the Israeli kibbutz, but he had confided his evil longings only to Yussuf. Much to his surprise, Yussuf lost his usual amused grin. Instead, he had become very serious and said, "I know what you mean." The two friends let it go at that.

He never discussed his activities with his father, and Yassir never asked him. He knew that his father would neither condemn him nor ask him to abandon what Ibrahim called "The Struggle." He also knew, however, that Yassir would not approve, and Ibrahim dreaded to see disapproval--more than just disapproval, sadness would be the right word--in his father's eyes.

Sometimes, after Ibrahim had helped with his father's chair and before he had time to leave, his father would gently ask, "How are you, my son? Is everything well with you?"

Ibrahim would answer, "Yes, Papa, everything is well." Oh, how he longed to sit by his father in the dusk of a warm Beirut night. How he longed to empty his heart to the old man and share with him all his troubles as he used to do when he was a child. But he could not; he was afraid that he would burst into tears and never stop crying. So, he would only say, "Everything is well, Papa," and he would rush off. He never heard his father's sigh.

He loved his father so much, and the thought that he would cause him pain was unbearable. He knew that he could not convince his father of the rightness of his cause, and perhaps, deep down, he feared that his deep love for his father could make him stray away from the struggle.

He had shared that fear with Yussuf, and Yussuf said, "No, my friend, you are not afraid of that. You are afraid that you may use your love for your father as an excuse to stray away from your so-called struggle." Ibrahim had hit him and immediately regretted it. With tears in his eyes, he stooped to pick Yussuf up while he mumbled, "I am sorry, I am sorry."

Yussuf looked at him and replied, "I know, Ibrahim. I know and I understand."

Ibrahim felt that Yussuf understood, but he did not know what it was that he understood and was afraid to ask.

So, a gap had developed between father and son, a gap that grew wider from day to day even though the bond of love remained intact, and that had to be sufficient.

Very rarely at night, when it was too dark to see, Ibrahim would sit on the stone floor by his father's wheelchair, and Yussuf would put his hand on his son's shoulder. Ibrahim would then reach and hold his father's hand. During these rare encounters, Ibrahim would feel such a fierce, overwhelming love for his father that, after a while, it would become unbearable, and he would move away.

As a child, Ibrahim had always been protective of his younger sister, but the two were never close. This began to change after Yassir's accident. The two teens, equally afflicted, learned to lean on each other. For the first time in their young lives, they began to talk to each other and discovered that they had much in common, especially that Alysha shared Ibrahim's belief in a violent struggle, although her hatred for the Jews was much less virulent and less conflicted than Ibrahim's.

Rhetoric was soon followed by action, and Ibrahim and Alysha were quickly inducted into an underground cell.

The induction was somewhat melodramatic and impressed the two youths. Their views were well-known among the crowd they frequented, and after Ibrahim and Alysha made discreet inquiries about how to join the movement, they received an anonymous note instructing them to be at a downtown café the next night at 11:00 pm. They were ecstatic, although they had to lie to their parents in explaining why they had to be out so late.

Before they had time to enter the café, they were accosted by two men whose features they could not distinguish in spite of the café's subdued neon light.

"We have to blindfold you," said one of the men.

Alysha and Ibrahim acquiesced, and after being blindfolded, they were helped into a car. While in the car, they held hands, sensing each other's anxiety. It was a long ride, and when the blindfolds were removed, they found themselves in a pleasantly cool but windowless room, probably underground. There were few chairs against the bare walls, a table in the middle of the room, and three masked men were sitting behind the table. Two chairs in front of the table were meant for Ibrahim and Alysha, and they were invited to sit.

"We know of you and of your family. We welcome you, but you cannot both join our cell, and you will not ever be allowed to work as a team," said the man in the center.

Alysha and Ibrahim stood up together. "But why?" stammered Alysha.

"The first thing you must learn," said the masked man, "is never to question the orders and decisions of your superiors, but since you are not yet one of us, I will answer your question. In the course of a mission, you may be called upon to make decisions which endanger the life of your partner but which, nevertheless, have to be made. This is much more difficult to do when your partner is a close relative and the mission may be placed in jeopardy."

"Sir," said Ibrahim in a subdued voice, "what you say is true. On the other hand, a brother and a sister who have grown up together can be tuned to each other and anticipate each other's moves better than any two partners. This could be a plus for any mission."

The interview lasted for one hour, and at the end of it Ibrahim and Alysha were told that they would be notified of a decision.

Back at their parents' home, Alysha and Ibrahim felt somewhat dejected. The thought of not being together and having to worry constantly about each other was intolerable, although they agreed to abide by the cell's decision. Three days later, again via an anonymous note, they were notified that they were accepted and would be allowed to train and operate as a team. Their joy was boundless. Shortly thereafter, they were sworn in.

The training area to which they had been assigned was a makeshift camp in a deserted area among the hills of Beirut. It was dusty, baked by the sun, and two decrepit barracks offered no relief from the stifling heat. The training was hard, exhausting, and the instructors were capable but hard and rigid. Alysha and Ibrahim became proficient in hand-to-hand combat, learned to handle different kinds of weapons, learned to manipulate explosives, and to arm and disarm mines.

Ibrahim, even more than Alysha, threw himself whole-heatedly into the training. Initially, he felt very alone. Yussuf had categorically refused to join, and Ibrahim felt little in common with his fellow "freedom fighters" except for their common goal.

And then he met Abdullah. Abdullah was a big, simple man, older than Ibrahim, but not as old as Ibrahim's father.

"Why did you join the struggle, Abdullah?"

"Why not? The Israelis took my home. They took my father's home. I want them back."

"Do you hate the Jews?"

"Hate? Ibrahim, my friend, I don't know what the word means, really. I just want our homes back."

Ibrahim thought for a moment, remembering his father's words. "Is it true that the Jews had asked you to stay?"

"It is true, but we were in the middle of two fighting armies. We were afraid for our lives.

"Is it true..." Ibrahim swallowed audibly. "Is it true that you expected to come back and take over the Jews' possessions?"

"Yes, that is true for some, but not for all of us. I could not care less about the Jews' possessions. All I want is my home and my father's home, and I will fight until I get them back."

Ibrahim's conversations with Abdullah always made him feel better. The big man's uncomplicated convictions always reinforced his own beliefs. It bothered him a little that Abdullah did not hate the Jews, but then, it did not matter. He was a dedicated fighter. Learning to handle guns and his increased proficiency at hand-to-hand combat gave him a sense of empowerment. He felt that he was regaining a sense of identity which wavered whenever he talked with his friend Yussuf. He saw Yussuf less and less. In fact, he avoided him. After each of their meetings, his sense of balance, acquired during his training and his talks with Abdullah, was affected.

One late evening, they had taken a long walk along the quay of Beirut, an area bustling with activity but much more peaceful after dark. Scents of tar, of grilling shish kebab, a flavor of salt were wafting, pushed along by a slight breeze. The two young men had studiously avoided discussing "the struggle." They had stopped for a while, staring at the sea.

Yussuf turned to his friend and abruptly said the words that Ibrahim had said to himself more than once, but with fear and self-loathing.

"Ibrahim, my brother, we must not see each other again."

"Why?" stammered the youth.

"It is not anyone's fault. I have my destiny, and you have yours. We must follow it without influencing each other. Do you remember our discussion on Existentialism a long, long time ago? I will always love you like a brother, more than a brother."

Ibrahim said nothing. He was afraid that if he said a single word, he would cry. He simply opened his arms. The two young men hugged and held each other tightly for a long time, unwilling to let go. Eventually, they held each other at arm's length, turned around, and walked away without a backward glance.

The memory of Yussuf never left Ibrahim and remained tucked into a corner of his heart. He made an effort not to think of Yussuf and immersed himself in the training. He and Alysha saw their parents less and less.

It was toward the end of the training that Ibrahim and Alysha were summoned to a meeting with a leader of the underground.

The meeting took place in the dimly lit basement of a nondescript building in one of the least destroyed areas of Beirut. There was a touch of surrealism to the whole scene, which made Ibrahim feel somewhat uneasy.

"Comrades Ibrahim and Alysha, the leadership has closely followed your progress and has been impressed by it. You are two of our best recruits and in about a week, your training will be completed. You will then be ready for your first mission." The shadow remained silent.

Ibrahim and Alysha felt their hearts beat precipitously but said nothing. Indeed, no answer was expected. The man continued.

"When your training is completed, someone will bring you written instructions. You will memorize them and destroy them immediately. That is all." And the shadow disappeared.

Ibrahim and Alysha talked very little about the meeting. They were uneasy, perhaps afraid, and avoided sharing the fear with each other.

What am I afraid of? mused Ibrahim. *Certainly not death. To live in Beirut these days is like living under a death sentence that could be carried out at any time. I am not afraid to fail. I am well-trained, and so is Alysha.*

He silently repeated the instructions which he had memorized:

You will travel to Jerusalem using the entrance permits attached herewith. To any inquiry you will respond that you live in the Gaza strip and visited relatives in Lebanon. You will proceed to the address indicated below. You will be expected, given valid passports, enough money, and two plane tickets to Athens. The password to be recognized is: 'Have you visited Salonica?' Your liaison's response will be, 'What a beautiful city.' You have reservations at the Hotel Grand-Bretagne. The hotel will host an international convention of jurists. You will locate an Italian lawyer by the name of Francesco Venchiarutti and will not lose sight of him. Venchiarutti will be contacted by an American agent named David Castro. At some point, documents will pass from Venchiarutti to Castro. You are to seize these documents by whatever means possible and bring them to the P.L.O. representative in Athens.

The instructions were clear, unambiguous. There seemed to be nothing especially difficult or unusual about the mission. The only tricky part was not to miss the document transfer from Venchiarutti to Castro. Ibrahim did not worry about that. Both he and Alysha were masters at shadowing unsuspecting prey. Yet he had a sense of foreboding which he could not shake off.

He was sitting on a pier, looking out at the magnificent blue sea. The training had been over for two days, and they were leaving in the morning. Even for a short time, it would be good to leave Beirut, once a jewel of the Mediterranean and now a disintegrating city, blood-bathed and bent on self-destruction. It was painful to deceive their parents, and they had concocted a story to explain their hopefully short absence. He wasn't sure that his father had believed him, but the old man had said nothing. Anyway, they had no choice. The mission would be brief and successful. *Inshá Allah!* (If God wills it.)

Chapter 10

On the Way to Salonica

The train rushed through the night. Huge shadows, woods, and mountains appeared and disappeared through the picture window, and occasionally one could discern a meadow with pinpoints of lights, homes where people lived and faced their daily problems and small satisfactions, oblivious to the train gliding through the darkness.

There was something lonely about a train in the night. There was something ominous about these foreboding mountains, where more than thirty years ago, people fought and died for their land, people with few weapons, little food, little support, bitter and alone but fiercely independent with a common love for their country and a hatred for the invaders. They had managed to defeat the greatest and most malignant war machine humankind had ever known. How many acts of heroism, of cruelty, how many tears, sufferings, how many sacrifices had been witnessed by these dark mountains and would never be written in history books?

David felt a poignant sadness at the thought that the world would never know and that whatever was known would someday be forgotten. He remembered few lines from a poem by Victor Hugo about sailors lost at sea and whose names were forgotten except by their widows.

> *When time, at last, has closed their eyes*
> *No one remembers your names*
> *Not even a humble stone in a graveyard at dusk*
> *Not even the tree losing its leaves in the fall*
> *Not even the ballad of one old beggar*
> *At the corner of an old bridge*

David shook his head. His thoughts were carrying him away and becoming morbid. It was no longer 1944 but 1976, and he was in the first class compartment of a comfortable train going from Athens to Salonica. The ride was a lot smoother than he expected, and he thought that it would take him a while to realize and accept the fact that Greece had joined the ranks of industrialized nations. He was not sure that the change was to his liking. His week in Athens, except for his meeting with Venchiarutti and the unforgettably dramatic encounter between the Italian lawyer and Mihali, the mountaineer, had been disappointing in many respects. He remembered Athens as a peaceful, beautiful, and romantic city. He remembered his lonely walks along the beautiful coastline of Phaliron. He remembered the Acropolis in the moonlight and the people talking in hushed voices. The Athens that he knew was gone forever, replaced by a bustling metropolis, with lethal traffic and a polluted air reminiscent of Los Angeles.

After returning from Mavropotamos with Mihali and Venchiarutti, he had ventured to the Acropolis one evening and had been sickened by the experience. The sight of loud tourists with their red and orange shirts, with their cameras bouncing on their stomachs and rear ends, walking in droves through the Parthenon where Socrates had lectured, and the quaint homes of the Plaka transformed into bars spewing forth rock music had made him beat a hasty retreat. He would probably never go back again.

Thoughts of the Acropolis always brought Xenia to his mind. Beautiful, gentle, kind Xenia was, perhaps, the only relationship in his life tinged with guilt. They had met in school while working on their undergraduate degrees. He had liked her immediately, attracted by her chiseled, strong, yet gentle face; her slender, elegant appearance; her quietness; and her intelligence. Xenia had fallen in love with him, and her love had been unconditional, undemanding, and, to her, so natural. She just loved him as she breathed and lived. That was all there was to it. There was something exquisitely distinguished about Xenia, and her nickname as a child, a nickname which she had shared only with him, seemed so appropriate. The child of well-to-do parents, she was born and raised in the Pinde mountains and liked to ride on horseback. She was known and liked through all the villages, and the mountaineers had named her "The Princess of the Pinde." David knew how Xenia felt, and he tried, desperately but in vain, to reciprocate her love.

David often wondered. Xenia was everything he had wanted in a woman. She could listen, always conveying to him the feeling that what he was saying was important to her. She could talk, and her description of her beloved mountains enthralled him. They would sometimes remain silent, just enjoying each other's presence. With her fine figure, her long silky brown hair, and dark Mediterranean eyes, she was truly beautiful, and David enjoyed being seen with her. But he sensed that when they were together he could not let himself go. He could not say the words of love that part of him wanted to say and that she wanted to hear. It was only many, many years later, during his conversations with Dr. Rosen, that he realized he was just protecting himself, that at some unconscious level he was terribly afraid of getting close to anyone for fear he could lose that person again. Had he met Xenia two decades later, he would certainly have fallen deeply in love with her. But at the age of 17 or 18--he couldn't quite remember--he didn't know what he knew now twenty years later, and he became convinced that he did not love her. Xenia sensed the barrier, but it did not matter.

In those days, the Bay of Varkiza was still wild and practically uninhabited. He and Xenia would board a rickety old bus at Omoneia Square. The bus, which had seen better days, carried mostly young couples, lovers in search of a lonely beach. Lonely beaches were in abundance, then. After a ride which would sometimes last forty-five minutes, sometimes an hour and a half, according to the driver's whims, they would get off at a small restaurant, café, or taverna in the middle of nowhere. He and Xenia would walk along the unending beaches, which would eventually become rocky, until a huge rock, almost a mountain, prevented them from going any farther.

For a while, leaning against the rock, facing the sea, became their favorite spot, until on a warm Sunday in the summer time, they became adventurous and climbed the rock. The climb was arduous but worthwhile. On top of the rock, they discovered a sort of vertical tunnel which led them to a cave at sea level. The cave was large, a huge chamber made of two flat rocks. One of the rocks was lapped by the sea; the other was higher and completely dry. The cave was invisible to passing canoes, and David thought that very few people, if anyone, knew of its existence. They would sit on the flat rock, half-covered by sea water.

"Sometimes I miss the mountain, David."

He would not reply, just hold her hand very tightly.

"Sometimes, David, you frighten me. You never let go. At times, you look so sad that my heart breaks. At other times, there is such anger in you. Yet, you never scream."

"Why do you stay with me?"

"I love you. It's as simple as that. I know that our ways will part, and I want to keep as many memories of you as I can."

"But..."

She interrupted with a smile.

"I know that you like me very, very much. I know that you would never hurt me. I also know that you don't love me, at least not as I love you. Yes, you want to love me, I know. But you see, love and hate are not feelings that we can control at will. So, it happened to me, and I want to drink as much of it as I can. Then, when my love interferes with your life, I will go back to the mountains, and I will be a very rich woman because of the treasure I gather every minute we spend together and which I will carry with me."

They shared their lives for almost two years, then Xenia returned to her mountains. They never saw each other again, and when thinking of her, he always felt in awe of having received such love and so regretful that he had been unable to love in return. Still, the memory of her was like a precious jewel that he would never want to lose. Shortly after Xenia's departure, he emigrated to the United States.

The train's soft, rocking motion was having its effect on David. He stood up and stretched. He thought of joining Venchiarutti and Mihali in the dining car and then thought better of it. He would feel like an intruder. The two men were like long lost friends, although they had never met face-to-face before. Each was thirsty for knowledge of the other, and it seemed as if they had been made suddenly aware of a bond forged through self-sacrifice, through twenty-five years of bitterness and hate, and an explosion of gratitude and love. David admired the two older men and envied their relationship.

He longed for a friend, for someone he could sit with and open his heart to. He missed Master Kwang and he missed Bill. The truth be told, he also missed Bill's family.

"Why don't you visit more often, David?" Bill would ask.

"Well, you know, my work is unpredictable, and it's hard for me to make commitments, and..."

Bill would laugh and interrupt. "That is a lot of bull. You must have more interesting things to do. But seriously, David, whenever you are with us, you close up or something. It is so hard for me to explain. Do you remember our talks in Korea? We had shared so much. What has happened since? You know how much we love you, and I know that you love us just as much."

Bill was right. But how could he tell him that he avoided them because he needed them too much? He had briefly talked about that with Dr. Rosen.

"I have no friends, Dr. Rosen. I want no friends. Some of the other drivers have invited me to visit with their families, and I always say no."

"You are so self-sufficient, David. You need no one, and yet..."

"And yet, when I am alone, I sometimes feel such a horrible, terrible emptiness."

Dr. Rosen said nothing, and the two men remained silent with their thoughts. Eventually, the old psychologist said, "I am sure that you would enjoy being with their families, but they are not *your* family."

David nodded. "It would have been okay if I had my own family, my wife, my children."

"Then it would not feel as if you are taking all the time and not giving."

As usual, the old man was right. Whenever he was with Bill and his family, he felt as if he was living their life, that he was taking so much that did not belong to him. No, that wasn't true. He did not mind, in that instance, taking what did not belong to him. The problem was that he had nothing to give in return.

So he would say, "Yes, Bill, I know you love me, and you know that I love you and your family more than I have ever loved anyone in this world, except my sister and my parents, and they are dead. I will try to come more often." But, of course, he would not.

And as he watched Mihali and Venchiarutti, he felt that same old emptiness, but this time without bitterness, perhaps because the warmth and love shared by the two older men in some inexplicable way reached out to him.

Soon they would reach Salonica, the city where he was born and had spent his childhood, at the same time synonymous with love, warmth, fear, and death.

☙

"David, tell me about Salonica, tell me about your home."

"It was a big, rambling home, Dr. Rosen, and I had a room all to myself. It is somewhat vague in my memory, but I remember sunshine slanting through the window in the morning, and it always made me want to laugh with joy. There was a big veranda in the back, and early on summer days, mother would sit there and clean string beans or peas, and she would sing old Spanish songs, sometimes even operatic arias. Her favorite was *Madame Butterfly*, 'Un bel di Vedremo.'"

"These are good memories, David."

"Yes, they were, and then it all ended. It did not come crashing down at once. It was so insidious, like a cancer gnawing at our daily lives. We had to move from our big home into a very small apartment with another family in a section of town which had been cordoned off. I remember the day Dad came home all bloodied up after the Germans had beat him. I was so scared, Dr. Rosen, I was so scared."

"Even your parents were powerless, David. Who could you trust?"

"No one, nobody. I was so alone. My world was coming apart. I hated the yellow star that we were obliged to wear. I thought that everyone was looking at me. For a while, I thought that there was something wrong with me, and I would look at myself in the mirror, wondering if something had changed in me. One day, I was standing with Nico at a street corner. Nico was my friend and much smaller than I, and that big Greek boy approached us and sneered. For some reason, he ignored me but concentrated on Nico, called him a name and then slapped him. I became enraged, like, you know, a premonition of these terrible rages which I told you about and made me come to see you. I picked up a stone lying by the curb and, God help me, I was going to split his head open. Then two German soldiers walked by. My rage instantaneously turned to fear. I took Nico by the hand and we walked away. I was a little boy, Dr. Rosen, but I swear to you, if I ever see that fellow again, ever, I'll kill him."

"I understand, David. When he slapped your friend, he killed part of you, and you feel that you cannot reclaim that part until you have hit back."

"That is exactly right."

That is what he liked about Dr. Rosen. He never moralized. He never approved or disapproved. He listened, and David always believed that the old gentleman understood.

Chapter 11

The Old House

The railroad station was new and no different than the many stations he had seen in his thirty-some years. They hailed a taxi that took them to a brand new hotel very much like any Hilton in the United States. Their rooms were large and airy, with a fine view of the White Tower, the remnant of a castle built by Venetian invaders many centuries ago. David felt uncomfortable and out of place; this was not the Salonica of his youth, it was not at all what he remembered.

He was allowed to use one of the empty ballrooms and went through his daily karate ritual. Meditation was difficult today; too many memories were stirred up, too many thoughts and feelings. It was as if he lived in two worlds at the same time, going through two separate existences: his childhood, a sharp break which was like death, and a second existence as an adult in the United States, totally separate from the first. As usual, he became totally immersed in the Karate moves. One form followed another with lightning speed, and his movements were graceful yet denoted power reminiscent of a jungle cat stalking, then attacking its prey. There was something lethal and frightening about his kicks, and a bell boy who opened the door by mistake quickly retreated, closing the door behind him. When he finished, he was bathed in sweat but totally relaxed, peaceful, even contented. In his mind, he bowed to Master Kwang. Following a long, hot shower and a change of clothes, he met Mihali and Venchiarutti in the hotel bar.

From the bar, they adjourned to the hotel restaurant. David liked the blue tablecloths and the white, immaculate napkins. He liked blue and white combinations always reminiscent of Greece. There were some beautiful paintings on the wall and a huge bay window which led onto a terrace. The place was empty. It was, indeed, far too early for Greek diners.

"It is too late now to do anything," said Venchiarutti. "You see, the Italian consulate was located on property which we had leased from the Catholic diocese of Salonica. After the war, the building reverted back to the church and, according to my information, currently houses a number of sisters. They retire early, and before retiring, they must have supper and pray. I suggest that we wait until tomorrow. I am not as young as you, my friends, and after our trip, I would not mind a peaceful evening and a long night's rest." Mihali and David had no objection to the old gentleman's plan and, after an early dinner, each went his separate way.

The Greek waiter followed them with his eyes in utter puzzlement. Dinner at 5:15 p.m. Only foreigners could do something as bizarre as that.

It was a little past six o'clock in the afternoon, and the sun was just beginning to set. David wandered through the streets in utter confusion. He could recognize neither streets nor buildings. It was as if, phoenix-like, a new city had been reborn from its ashes. In desperation, he caught a cab and gave the driver the address of the place where he had grown up. The old house was still standing and seemed so much smaller than he remembered it. It was surrounded by new and bigger houses. It was, in fact, slated for demolition. A steel fence surrounded it and barred its entrance. David wondered whether he should vault over the fence or go around it to try to find an opening. It was at that moment that a policeman approached him.

"That is a very old house, and nobody has lived here for many years. Is there something I can do for you?"

"Yes," said David. "I was born and spent my early years in this house. I have been away for a very long time, and I would like to see it one more time before it comes down."

The policeman gave him a curious glance. "Jew?" he asked, and David nodded. "Come, I guess you have a right. Follow me."

They walked around the side of the house to an opening in the fence. "Take all the time you want. I'll see that you are not disturbed."

David nodded his thanks and walked through the garden. Entering the house was difficult. It was as if a part of him refused to move. What was he afraid of? Was he afraid to re-enter a previous life? No, not a previous life but a previous incarnation. Was he afraid that he would be swallowed by it, lose his identity, confuse the past and present? What the hell was happening to him? He thought that he had exorcized the demons during his sessions with Dr. Rosen.

He entered the indoor stairway, the granite steps that neither time nor neglect had been able to touch. He knocked at the door, then realized how silly that gesture was. The door was, of course, open, and he forced himself to enter. The rooms--large, airy, sunny rooms filled with magnificent furniture, his mother's pride and joy--were empty and littered, with the windows closed and a musty smell and the paint peeling from the ceiling and the doors. Something once vibrant, young, clean, and beautiful was now old and broken. There are people and places that grow old in a gracious way, fulfilled by life, surrounded by loved ones. His home, his lovely home was dying a lonely death, alone and abandoned. It was dying the same death as his parents at Auschwitz. For some unknown reason, he thought of his father, his poor, poor father. He had died alone and in the dark, and he had seen his wife and daughter die with him, choke to death, cry in pain, cling to him, and he could not protect them. He could not save his wife and daughter. He could only die with them. *Oh, my poor, poor Dad!*

҂

He had talked about his father with Dr. Rosen three months into his therapy. He had talked about him many more times, but the first time stood vivid in his memory.

"I loved him so much, Dr. Rosen, I loved him so much. When he would come back from a trip, I would try to stay awake so that I could catch him coming through the door. You know how some children feel on Christmas Eve waiting for Santa Claus? Except that *he* was Santa Claus, and every day was Christmas. You know, in those days, there were no buses in Salonica, just street cars. I knew exactly which car he would ride to come home after work, and I would wait for him, walk back home with him holding my hand. I can still feel his hand around mine, Dr. Rosen, after all these years, do you believe it? I could tell him anything. He would always understand. I would tell him about the windows I broke playing ball, all the berets I would lose coming back from school, all the different kinds of mischief I would get into. He would always bail me out, always plead my cause with Mom, who was more on the strict side. He never let me down."

"He must have been a remarkable man, David, and I love him just from hearing you talk about him."

"Everybody loved him, Dr. Rosen, and people referred to him as 'the last gentleman.' For a long time, I did not understand what that meant until an older cousin explained to me that they called him that because he had never cheated or lied to anyone and because everybody trusted him. I was so proud that day that I remember wanting to shout out loud, 'My father is the last gentleman.'"

"You wanted the whole world to know the kind of person your father was."

"Absolutely! He frightened me once, only once. It was during the winter of '41. This was a horrible winter. Not only was it very, very cold, but a real famine was sweeping the city. Little children would die of starvation, be dumped on door steps, and be picked up by municipal trucks for mass burial. It was then that our fine furniture began disappearing piece by piece. It was much later that I learned how it was bartered for food. It was early morning and freezing cold outside. Dad was shaving at the kitchen sink, and a man came to the door asking for food. The way things were, any food that could be spared was religiously reserved for children. After a while, the man started cursing and kicking the door. Under the kitchen sink, there was a cabinet where we kept an axe which we used to split wood for the stove. Suddenly, without saying a word, Dad bent, opened the cabinet, took the axe, opened the kitchen door, and swung the axe at the man. Had he connected, he would have split his head wide open. Fortunately, he missed, and the man jumped backward, turned around, and ran. Still without saying a word, he closed the door, put the axe back under the sink, and continued to shave as if nothing had happened. His hands weren't even shaking. I was petrified. I had seen a side of my father that I did not know existed. Yet, somehow, in spite of my fear, I felt even closer to him, safer. I don't know how to explain it."

"I think I understand, David. This potential for violence you saw in your father, this unexpected ability to act, protected the family against harm and intruders."

"You are right. Later, when I became an adult, I was glad that I had witnessed this incident. It gave Dad an additional dimension, one that, for some reason I never could understand, made me love him and admire him even more."

"You realized that he--who is capable of such extremes, to be able to kill in order to protect his family and yet able to be so kind and gentle and loving--is a complete human being, indeed."

"That is it, Dr. Rosen. That is it. That is perhaps why I enjoy full contact karate so much and, on the other hand, why I feel so bad when I hurt someone."

"Perhaps, David, perhaps."

"My father is dead, Dr. Rosen. He is dead, and I'll never see him again, and I miss him so much. Even after all these years, I think of him at night before I fall asleep, and I imagine that I still tell him all my sorrows, all my troubles, but now he cannot fix them. At the end, he could not even save his wife and daughter. Dr. Rosen, what must have gone through his mind, at the last moment, when he was choking, when he knew that his wife and daughter were dying and there was nothing he could do? Oh, my poor, poor, beloved father, what a lonely, cruel death. Dr. Rosen, when I think of those who did this to him, I feel like I want to vomit blood. I don't want to kill them with a gun. I want to hit them, hit them with my hands, grind them into the ground, stomp on them, see fear, see horror in their eyes. I don't know what I am saying! But, you know, when I hit that man with the two-by-four on Fisherman's Wharf? I wanted to kill him. I wanted to destroy him."

"But he didn't die, David."

"No, he didn't die."

"Why not, David?"

"I don't know."

"Why not, David?"

"I don't know, I don't know! Yes, I know, I know. I held back, I held back. At the last moment, I held back. Oh God! Thank you, God!"

"David, what happened when your Dad hit the man with the axe?"

"I remember. He waited for a split second, gave the man time to jump backward. He didn't want to kill him."

"David, if your father were here now, what do you think he would say to you?"

"He would say, he would say... He would say nothing. He would just hug me."

"Thank you, David. I think this is enough for today. We'll meet again in three days."

ɛʃ

He went through all the rooms of the house again, feeling as if he was visiting a cemetery. The veranda in the back where his mother would sing was much smaller than he remembered it. The backyard, his "jungle" as he called it, was now an impenetrable bush. There sat his parents' bedroom. Here was the family room; there was a ceramic stove, and, on winter evenings, when everyone would be in bed, he would get up, wrap himself around the still warm stove, and read some of his favorite adventure books. He always suspected that his parents knew what he was doing, but they never said anything. Here was Liza's room with a chest of drawers in that corner and toys all over the floor. That was it, then. Generation upon generation of good people, a peaceful, caring family... and all that remained was littered, empty rooms and a house slated for demolition. There was no looking back. He walked slowly through the hole in the fence without glancing back. The cop, still standing at the corner, looked at him. David went to him and put a one hundred dollar bill in his hand.

The man touched the brim of his cap and said, "I am so sorry."

109

David walked away and hailed a cab.

That same night, after dark, the Greek policeman sat on his back porch sipping a glass of *ouzo*. In his hands he held the one hundred dollar bill, a tidy sum for a Greek policeman whose salary was nothing to speak of.

"What is the matter, Costa? You look so pensive."

He stood up and held his wife very long and very tight. "I love you, Heleny. I love you. Don't ever leave me."

"Costa, are you all right? What happened?"

"I saw something today, something so sad, so very sad! You see this? It's one hundred American dollars. God knows we can use this money, but I want you to give one fourth of it to the church. We must thank God! We must thank God!"

Chapter 12

Salonica

Ibrahim and Alysha reached Athens without difficulty, and their room at the Grande Bretagne Hotel, where they registered as Mr. and Mrs. Ibrahim and Alysha Khalid, awaited them. It was a large, luxurious room which provided them with a new experience.

"Typical Western decadence," said Ibrahim, and then he added with a sigh, "I wish we could stay here for a few extra days. I could get used to this kind of decadence."

The first two days were uneventful, although they were intrigued by an unexplained happening at the end of the second day. Two men, one younger and the other much older, had left the American's room, and a few seconds later, the American followed them. It was obvious, however, that they were not together and that the American did not want to be seen. It was Alysha who shadowed him as she and Ibrahim thought that a woman would be less conspicuous. They were walking through the streets of Athens past deserted residential avenues, animated boulevards with sidewalk cafés, and laughing customers. Alysha reluctantly gave credit to the American for his ability in following the two Greeks; in fact, once or twice he almost became aware that someone was following him. The first time, she had to quickly turn around and pretend that she was walking in the opposite direction, and the second time, she hid in a doorway. When the two Greeks reached their destination, the American turned around and went back to the hotel.

Alysha was thoughtful as she returned to the hotel, and Ibrahim was quick to detect her mood. He looked at her questioningly, and she shrugged.

"This man is more than just a messenger, Ibrahim. He is good, very good. He came within a hairbreadth of finding out that he was being followed, and believe me, it was a short distance.

Ibrahim bit his lower lip. "We were told he was an agent, but then, there are agents and *agents*. What else?"

"Well," added Alysha, "there is also the matter of the two men who left his room and whom he followed. Who are they? How do they fit into this? Obviously, they are not his friends, otherwise, he would not have followed them. Are they working for the Italian lawyer whose name I can't pronounce? Mark my word, brother. There is more to this than just a transfer of documents."

Ibrahim listened carefully and nodded.

"You are absolutely right, but what else can we do? We must retrieve the papers, Alysha, and that is what we shall do. In the meantime, it won't hurt to keep our eyes open and be alert. Right now, let's go and have dinner."

The dining room was like nothing they had seen before, especially in war-ravaged Beirut. Of course, the pre-war hotels in Beirut could easily compete with the Grande Bretagne. Ibrahim and Alysha had been too poor to even enter the lobby of these hallowed places, let alone eat in one of their dining rooms. Still, they managed to hide their awe quite well. In fact, they made quite an impression upon the staff and the guests. Tall, dark-haired with chiseled features, dressed soberly but with taste, they cut quite an elegant picture and looked more like brother and sister (which they were) than husband and wife. They ate well, and the food reminded them of their native Lebanon, only more refined and much better prepared. They enjoyed their appetizers, especially the kalamata olives and the grape leaves in lemon and olive oil served cold. They passed on the meat dishes and selected two magnificent trout cooked on a charcoal grill and smothered in lemon and oil again. They hesitated before ordering wine, yet went ahead with it, not wanting to be singled out and later remembered. The pastries were delicious, much more Parisian than Middle Eastern, but then again, Ibrahim and Alysha had never been to Paris and could not have a considerate opinion. They could enjoy and eat the pastries and did not deprive themselves of that experience.

They went through an awkward moment as they entered their quarters. When they had taken possession of the room earlier in the afternoon, it was daytime and all seemed very simple. Ibrahim and Alysha had grown up together, had few unhealthy inhibitions. They made an elaborate show of protecting each other's privacy, and Ibrahim chose the sofa while Alysha slept on the bed.

The next day went by without incident, but the third day, Ibrahim and Alysha knew several hours of panic. "The Target," as they had nicknamed the American, had disappeared and so had the Italian lawyer. All their efforts to get a line on their whereabouts were in vain. The reception desk did not know where they were, and all they could learn was that they had not checked out of the hotel. They did not inquire into possible telephone communications. Indeed, they were certain that the information would not be forthcoming, and besides, they were afraid to arouse suspicions.

They felt as if they had become a permanent fixture at the bar. From the bar, they could watch the entrance to the lobby, and soft drink followed soft drink, with an occasional *ouzo* in between. They were truly worried but had to make a decision. This could not go on forever.

"Ibrahim, what do you think we should do?"

"I don't know," he replied. "I hate the idea of calling Beirut. This is our first mission and a fairly simple mission. To admit that we have flubbed, it makes me sick to my stomach. They will never trust us again."

Alysha remained pensive. "What do you say about searching their rooms? Maybe we can find a clue as to their whereabouts."

"Yes, but it is risky. I am not worried about what may happen to us, but if we are arrested, there goes our mission. Let us wait at least one more day before we call Beirut or search their room. What do you think?"

"Yes," started Alysha, then she almost shouted with relief, "Ibrahim, Ibrahim, there they are!"

Indeed, the target and the Italian lawyer were entering the lobby of the Grande Bretagne accompanied by a third man, a huge Greek wearing boots and riding breeches somewhat reminiscent of mountaineers in their own Lebanon. The presence of the Greek worried them; their instructions, which they had both carefully memorized, did not mention a third party, and they were afraid that his presence might somehow interfere with the successful accomplishment of their mission. The intrusion of the other two unknown Greeks the preceding night added to their confusion, although they did not recognize the Greek accompanying their target as one of them. Again, they toyed with the temptation of contacting Beirut, and again, they decided against it. It was their first mission, and they were going to carry it out to its completion by themselves as they were expected to.

The tall Greek accompanied the target and the Italian lawyer and, to Ibrahim's and Alysha's surprise, boarded the train with them. The two Palestinians barely managed to buy their tickets and climb into a different car. During the trip to Salonica, Ibrahim and Alysha did not make use of the dining car but bought sandwiches and a bottle of retsina wine, which they consumed in their compartment. It would not do to be seen and perhaps later recognized by the target or the two other men.

They did not turn the light on in their compartment. There was something ghostly about the trees and the mountains furiously passing by the bay window in the darkness. They exchanged few words. Both of them felt like something was squeezing their chests. Was it fear?

113

"I don't think so, Ibrahim. I'm not afraid. I mean, not afraid for myself, perhaps afraid to let our comrades down, but it's really not that. I don't know what it is. We are so far away from home and all this is so new, so foreign to me. Sometimes, I feel like I am floating and can't hold on to anything."

"I think of father," said Ibrahim. "I love him so much, and if I were to die without telling him so, that would be the worst fate in the whole world."

Alysha gave him a furtive look. Ibrahim did not often display his feelings. She reached for his hand. They held on to each other's hands and dozed fitfully through the night.

Upon arrival at Salonica, they experienced few moments of anxiety. It was an easy task to follow their target to their hotel. No reservations, however, had been made for Ibrahim and Alysha by their handlers.

They waited for a while to make sure that their quarry was duly registered and were fortunate to find a room in a more modest hotel, the Thessalonica. There was a small café across from the Glyfada, the hotel where the American and his party had registered, and from the terrace of the café they could see the hotel entrance. It would serve as their headquarters.

Alysha and Ibrahim registered together, and Ibrahim went immediately to the café. Indeed, they did not want to let the American out of their sight for longer than was absolutely necessary. His short disappearance while in Athens was still fresh in their minds, and they were not about to let this happen again.

Alysha unpacked, took a quick shower, and rushed to relieve Ibrahim. She ordered an *ouzo* and swirled the ice cubes in the licorice liquid, which quickly became opaque. She liked the scent of *ouzo*, which reminded her so much of their Arak in her native Lebanon. In fact, much about Salonica reminded Alysha of Beirut, not the present Beirut, but the Beirut of old, before the shootings, the killings, and the fires started. It was such a beautiful city, a city of light and pleasures, of elegant buildings and beautiful white, pink, and yellow houses. She was too young to remember when her parents had made the decision to leave the refugee camp and try their luck in Beirut; she knew that they had been criticized by some for "falling into the hands of the Israelis."

Alysha was not yet born when the first Arab-Israeli war broke out in 1948. She had no memory of, no sentimental attachment to what was then Palestine. She would have been quite content to spend her life in beautiful Beirut. In fact, if her father had decided to leave the camp, he was, no doubt, right. She would never say it to anyone, but secretly, she held in contempt those who lived in squalor and did nothing to ameliorate their fate except complain and curse the Israelis. Her father was not one of them; he liked to take his fate into his own hands, and he never complained. Their beginnings in their very modest home in Beirut were a struggle from morning to night, but it did not matter. They were all together, and they had a future. She and Ibrahim were going to a good school; they had many friends, enjoyed the beaches, and liked roaming the streets of Beirut, so long as their homework was done and they returned home at a decent hour. Sometimes, she would look at the beautiful bungalows ensconced in flowers, but she was never jealous. She had the unshakeable conviction that one day they would move into one of those fine houses.

Then, the bad things started happening. The civil war and her father's accident occurred almost at the same time. She was no longer allowed to go to the beaches or to downtown Beirut, which had become a city of thunder and blood. She did not mind. She and Ibrahim had to work to supplement the family's income after the accident. She was not trained for anything and, therefore, could do everything. She worked as a maid, a nurse's assistant, a companion for older people. The rest of the time she stayed home to help her mother take care of her father. The accident had brought the three of them closer, and oftentimes in the evenings, she would sit next to the wheelchair and her father would put his hand on her shoulder. They would be silent, listening to soft, melancholic Arab music from the radio in the kitchen. She felt safe and contented at those times, and the war and its ravages seemed so far away.

She was angry at Ibrahim, however, for his changed attitude toward their father, and she knew that the old man felt hurt. One evening, as Ibrahim was about to walk away, she said angrily, "Where are you going?" He turned for a second, said nothing and left. She had time, however, to see his face streaked with tears. They never talked about it, but somehow, her anger left her. She could fathom, for the first time, Ibrahim's gut wrenching pain at their father's condition. Their father must have sensed it too. Even though she could see the sadness in his eyes, he never once asked his son to stay longer by his side. From that day on, she and Ibrahim became closer than they had ever been, and when his involvement with the Palestinian movement began, she followed in his footsteps.

She was happy to have been chosen for this mission together with her brother. She was happy and proud, proud because she and Ibrahim must have been well thought of, and happy because, at least for some time, they would be away from the grisly scenes of daily carnage in their once beautiful Beirut.

The American was coming out of the hotel lobby; she had already paid the check and located the taxi stand. When he got into a cab, she followed in the next one. "Suivez ce taxi." Like drivers all over the world, the man understood a smattering of English and French and asked no questions. Soon, they left the downtown area and were driving through suburbs. The American was obviously not sightseeing. Indeed, he seemed to know where he was going. This puzzled Alysha, and what she did not understand irritated her. Was the American familiar with Salonica? If so, how would this affect their mission? She made a mental note to discuss this with her brother.

The taxi stopped by a run-down, old, but large house in a neighborhood which must have seen better days. She asked her driver to stop at a safe distance from the American's taxi, paid, and asked him to wait. She hid, out of sight, behind a wall, saw the American talk to a policeman, and then both entered the house. After a very short while, the policeman reappeared by himself. The house was obviously empty, and she wondered what the American was doing in this dilapidated ghost-like place all by himself. She could not go through the main entrance, which was within sight of the policeman. She gave some thought to scaling the walls and abandoned the idea as too risky; besides, the American could come out the front entrance while she was busy trying to climb the walls or entering the house through a side door.

The wait was not very long, and when the American came out, he looked somewhat different. He was more stooped and his gait was slower. It was as if he had aged in barely twenty minutes. Her taxi followed the other and returned to the hotel. Alysha waited at the café until midnight. Then, satisfied that the American would not come out again, she returned to her room. Ibrahim still had his doubts and took up the vigil until 3:00 a.m.

⌀

Back at the hotel, David sat at his window, nursing his glass of *ouzo* on the rocks and reviewing the events of the day. When they got off the train upon arrival in Salonica, early in the morning, he had an uneasy feeling which he had not shared with his friends, a feeling of being exposed and vulnerable with which he was but too familiar, a feeling that occurred whenever he was followed and was not able to locate his shadow. Whoever was following them was pretty good. Today it did not matter, but tomorrow, especially after he entered into possession of the documents, he would have to be more careful. He wondered who was following him. Whoever it was must be aware of his mission, and therefore, there must have been a leak somewhere--CIA, FBI, or State.

He glanced at his watch. It was 8:00 p.m., therefore noon in D.C., a decent time to call. With a sigh of regret, he put down his *ouzo*, moved over to the head of the bed, and picked up the telephone. Telecommunications in Salonica left something to be desired, and it was a good fifteen minutes before the operator called him back. Bill was not at his desk, and David was reluctant to leave the information as a message. He would call again in the morning.

The visit to the old house had drained him. He knew that he would never go back, but he was glad that he had made the pilgrimage. He was glad also that he had been able to cry. There had been a time when he would have gone through the old place dry-eyed and feeling nothing.

℘

It was a huge breakthrough in his sessions with Dr. Rosen when he talked about crying for the first time.

"It started when the German knocked me unconscious that first night in Auschwitz. When I regained consciousness, Mom and Dad and my little sister were gone. That first night, Dr. Rosen, was the worst night of my life. I couldn't stop crying. I wanted to scream 'Mom, Dad,' and I knew that I couldn't. I was so frightened, so terribly frightened, shaking all night. The other prisoners, all men, were kind and protective, but it didn't matter. I wanted my mother and father, and without them I was lost and would die. And then, something strange happened the next morning, and I stopped crying. To this day, more than twenty years later, I haven't shed a tear. I wasn't afraid either. It was as if something had died in me. All that mattered was to have enough food and stay out of the way of the German guards. I guess in that one night I had become a different person."

"No, David, you had not become a different person. You had entered a different world and you had to change in order to live in that alien world."

"I guess you are right. Perhaps. Anyway, thank you for saying that. I feel less ashamed."

"Ashamed?"

"Yes, you know, for having no feelings, no compassion, for not caring. Someday, I will tell you about Mazel. But not yet. Anyway, there was a night in the camp when an inmate was told that his wife had died. His wife was in the women's compound. He sat on the edge of his bunk, which he shared with two other men, and was sobbing, not just crying, but sobbing. His whole body shook. Some of his friends were trying to comfort him, and many were crying. I couldn't feel a thing. I was sitting in a corner, just staring at him and wishing he would stop."

"Why?"

"Why what?"

"Why did you want him to stop?" Dr. Rosen asked.

"I don't know."

"That is not good enough, David! Think, why did you want him to stop?"

"I was afraid that the German guards might hear."

"Would they, and would they care?"

"I guess not."

"Then why, David, why?"

"You are pushing me, Dr. Rosen, and I don't like it."

"David, what were you afraid of?"

"Nothing, I was afraid of nothing. I just was feeling sorry for him."

"But you just said that you could not feel anything."

"That is true. I said that. Maybe I was wrong, maybe I could feel."

"No, David, you could not feel. You were afraid..."

"Damn you, yes, I was afraid," shouted David, barely sitting on the edge of the yellow chair. "I was afraid that if he cried much longer I would have cried too, but not for him. I would have cried for myself and been destroyed. I was afraid to cry for me."

The old man leaned over and put his hand gently on David's arm.

"I understand, David. I understand so well."

"Oh! Dr. Rosen, Dr. Rosen, will I ever be able to cry again? You know, Dr. Rosen, I think that meeting Bill and my karate teacher was a monumental happening in my life. It is hard to explain."

"I believe that I understand. The stone heart of David had begun to melt a little, but only the outer shell was affected. The core remained hard and cold."

"That is exactly right. Somehow I didn't want it to be so, but I couldn't help it. Why was that?"

"Perhaps, because inside the core was something very fragile, very precious, very tender, and the cold, hard core wouldn't let it become exposed and vulnerable," Dr. Rosen explained.

"I really think that had I spent more time with Bill and Master Kwang, this would have happened. I could feel some tenderness, something soft stirring in me. I was peaceful with them. When I left Korea and said good-bye to Master Kwang, he hugged me, and it was the closest I felt to tears, but I did not cry... I couldn't."

"Yes, something had happened, David, and it wasn't just the softening of the outer core. Isn't that true?"

"Yes, it is. The real softness, the tenderness, the ability to cry for myself as well as for others, the ability to be afraid, were still sealed inside, but something had leaked out, and it was brutal and corrosive."

"What was that, David?"

"Anger, rage. Even as a child, I had violent temper tantrums. You remember the story I told you of the Greek boy who had slapped my friend and how I would have hit him with a rock were it not for the two German soldiers who happened to walk by. Well, in the camp, and for a long time afterward, I felt no anger. I could defend myself, hit someone if necessary, but coldly, without feeling anything."

The old man stood up and walked around the office. "Pay no mind, David. At my age, I need to stretch once in a while. And by the way, when did you become aware of it, your anger, I mean?"

"When I reached San Francisco. I was working, in fact I still am, as a delivery truck driver. Now, I can go out in the evening, have a drink at a bar, take in a movie, but until I started seeing you, I would go home after work and sit, and I had violent thoughts. I wanted to hit, not kill but hit. I could feel it in my arms. I would go nowhere, just stay in my small apartment, hold my head in my hands, and just try to stop the thinking. Memories from the camp swirled in my mind, out of nowhere. Things that I thought I had forgotten. The more I remembered, the angrier I became. When I think that it was only six months ago, I hardly believe it. When I closed the door to my apartment it was, at the same time, a feeling of doom and relief."

"Being in jail was safer than being free."

"That is exactly true. You know, the only place I would go was the gym, and as I think of it, it is a miracle that I killed no one. I refused to spar because I did not trust myself. I remember that after my very rare sparring sessions, my arms and legs ached from the tremendous effort at control. It was only after our session when I became aware that I could have killed the man on the wharf but didn't, and that my father could have killed that man during the war but didn't, that I began to trust myself again. I still have fits of anger, but they are becoming less and less intense."

Two sessions later, David told Dr. Rosen about Mazel.

"He was an old man in the concentration camp--no, not really old, perhaps 45 or 50, but he looked terribly old, if you see what I mean. He was emaciated, ugly, blind in one eye, limping with wooden shoes that made an uneven sound when he walked. We did not know his name, but when things were really bad, he would smile, shrug, and say, 'Mazel, next year in Jerusalem.' So we called him 'Mazel,' and his smile was very gentle. When he smiled, his whole face was transformed. Do you remember some weeks ago I told you that I felt nothing, not even anger? That was true, but what I did not tell you was that, occasionally, I would react instinctively, like a flash when something was in my way. I don't remember feeling anger. It was as if my body reacted, not my feelings.

"Anyway, there was that very cold, freezing morning in the camp, and it was dark outside. I walked through the snow to the shack which served as latrine and wash room. I was washing my face at one of the sinks, and I remember distinctly that my teeth were chattering. Mazel was behind me, waiting for his turn, and his feet apparently got all tangled up in his wooden shoes, and he fell against me. My face almost hit the faucet. Without thinking, without even knowing who it was, I turned around and hit him. I was only thirteen, but tall and very strong for my age, and poor Mazel was not a heavyweight. He flew across the width of the washroom, fell on his back, and hit his head against a pipe. I never forgot the look on his face. I feel cold every time I think of it. Anyway, it's one of the few things I feel guilty about. I wanted to tell you for a long time, but I couldn't. Perhaps I just couldn't hear myself talk about it. Now you know."

"What happened to Mazel, David?"

"He died a few weeks later. We found him one morning on his straw mat. Few people paid attention. But I still remember him."

"David, I would like you to write a spoken letter to Mazel, and in that letter simply say what is in your heart this very minute."

"Okay." David paused a while to collect his thoughts, then began. "It has been so many years, I hardly know what to say. I remember the sound of your shoes. I remember your smile when you said 'Mazel' and how it made your ugly face look so radiant and serene. I remember the day I hit you and the expression in your eyes. To say, 'I am sorry?' No, I did not mean to harm you. Perhaps I am sad, so deeply, deeply sad for the pain I saw in your eyes. Mazel, I wish you were alive. I wish I could put my arm around your bony shoulders and tell you, 'Smile, smile again. Someday we'll be in Jerusalem together.'"

"David, close your eyes and concentrate. Imagine that in your mind's eye. You see Mazel. He cannot talk to you, but look at his face, look at his eyes. What do you see?"

"I see his smile, and his eyes are very gentle."

"And what do the smile and the gentle eyes say to you?"

"I think they say... I think they say, 'Thank you.' It's crazy, but I think they say, 'I love you.'"

ↄ

A poet once said that the future belongs to no one but God. Yet we plan for it, dream of it, and, sometimes, we help our dreams come true. David had but one immediate goal. He would get Dr. Assael's papers with the help of Venchiarutti and deliver them safely to his friend Bill. He fervently hoped that a result of his effort would be the arrest and conviction of one Dieter Von Eckardt, in a previous incarnation SS Colonel Johann Richter, a vulture feeding off the remains of dead people. David had never seen Von Eckardt but, as an adolescent, had nightmares about him. To punish him would be to put some additional closure to the cycle of misery, despair, fear, hate, and, more recently, hope and light, within which he had been swirling for the past several years.

The goal of Alysha and Ibrahim was just as simple; they would take possession of whatever documents the Italian would give to the American and give them to their superior. There had been a slight change in their instructions. Instead of delivering the papers to the P.L.O. representative in Athens, they were to take them to a deserted house on the outskirts of Salonica and wait for their contact. The password would be "Athens didn't work," and the contact would reply, "Salonica is so much easier." Neither Ibrahim nor Alysha knew the nature of the dossier, and had they known, they would not have cared. They simply wanted to carry out their orders.

Otto Streicher was after money. Successful retrieval of the documents would net him a vast sum of money, and if he had to knock a few heads together to do it, he would rather enjoy the exercise. He never killed for the sake of killing, but he was not averse to it.

The stakes were highest for Johann Richter. His future, his fortune and that of his family, perhaps even his freedom and his life could be in jeopardy if the documents fell in any hands but his. The planning had to be faultless, and nothing could be left to chance.

Chapter 13

Detroit, Michigan

Otto Streicher's plane landed safely in Detroit. He was one of the first passengers to deplane. Having no baggage to claim, he quickly exited the airport, hailed a cab and gave the driver Richter's address. It took a good half-hour before the cab stopped in front of a big, beautiful house, almost a mansion. A maid opened the front door and, after he identified himself, asked him to follow her. Richter's study was just like Streicher remembered it: comfortable, luxurious, and somewhat pretentious. Richter, sitting behind his desk, stood up to welcome him, and they shook hands effusively.

"Hello, Otto, it has been a long time, my friend. How are you?"

"Hello, Johann, it's good to see you. What a beautiful study!" Streicher cared about power but was not impressed by its trappings. He knew, however, that his statement would please Richter.

"Sit down, sit down," said Richter. "You really didn't change much over the years. Cigar? Maybe a dash of cognac? I haven't had any schnapps for a long time."

That figures, thought Streicher, *the son of a bitch is as vain and snobbish as he ever was. Yet his cognac isn't bad at all.* "Yes please, thanks."

After a few perfunctory pleasantries and attempts at keeping each other superficially appraised of what they had done over the past few years, Richter finally explained the reason for his having requested Streicher's services.

"Here are plane tickets to Salonica."

"To where?" said Streicher, startled.

Richter himself could not stem the flood of memories. It was so many years ago and yet so vivid in his mind; the glory days, the days of the master race when all of Europe was at their feet, when Aryan power and efficiency ruled supreme, and when he, Richter, was not just a well-to-do industrialist but the master of life and death over multitudes.

"You heard me, Otto, Salonica. You knew me in Belgrade, but Salonica was not much different, perhaps even better. Anyway, your mission is fairly simple. As I said, here are the tickets and enough money to cover expenses. Here are the address, the keys, and the lease of a house in an out-of-the-way suburb of Salonica. You will stay there until someone comes to visit you. That person will simply give you a full briefcase. The password which will help you identify yourself is 'Athens did not work.' The answer will be, 'Salonica is so much easier.' You will take the briefcase and bring it back to me. Incidentally, I do not wish the messenger to be hurt--unless it is absolutely essential. Any questions?"

Streicher remained silent for a long moment, and Richter sighed. He knew what was going through the mind of the former policeman, and after all, why not tell him? They were bound to secrecy by the knowledge of each other's past. Neither one could threaten or blackmail the other without betraying himself. Richter firmly believed that the indications to the treasure which he had looted from Jewish homes and which Athanassopoulos had so well hidden were among the documents. He did not worry much about Streicher's curiosity. Everything would be written in Greek or French, a language common to Jews in Salonica, God knows why. At any rate, Streicher, Richter knew, could only speak German and a smattering of English.

"Okay, Otto, the briefcase contains documents which can reveal my true identity. In the wrong hands, they can spell the ruin of everything I have built and achieved during the past twenty-five years. I cannot risk that and will not allow it to happen."

Streicher smiled. This was more like it and a motivation he could well understand. His question was direct and blunt. "How much?"

"Twenty thousand American dollars."

"Thirty thousand."

"You drive a hard bargain, my friend. Thirty thousand it is. It is worth that much to me," Richter said.

They shook hands, and without another word, Otto Streicher left the room. Richter was annoyed, yet not surprised, that Streicher had not asked for a down payment. He realized that the omission was not a sign of trust. Streicher knew that Richter would not dare double cross him, and that belief was true. Richter was afraid of Streicher, and that knowledge rankled.

After Streicher left, Richter poured himself a second cognac, sat in his big comfortable chair, stared out the window, and one more time carefully and painstakingly reviewed in his mind every facet of the operation. He had done that several times already, but it didn't matter. Richter was a careful and methodical man, and in this instance, mistakes were not allowed.

Let us see, Streicher... He still had a hard time thinking of the ex-Gestapo agent as Knoppel. Yet, he must make an effort to identify him, even in his thoughts, as Knoppel. Johann Richter and Otto Streicher were dead and should remain dead. *Well, Streicher/Knoppel knows nothing of the American former CIA agent and the Italian lawyer, and that is the way it should be.* Richter was a great believer in the "need to know only" system. *All he knows is that a package will be delivered to him by an unidentified person and that he will bring the package to me.*

The P.L.O. knew about David Castro and Venchiarutti, the Italian lawyer, and they had no knowledge of the package contents. They had asked no questions and had readily stated their willingness to carry out this mission. Richter had contributed heavily to their cause and was entitled to a shady favor or two. Yet, his trust in them was limited. His original plan to have the package delivered to the P.L.O. representative in Athens had left him somewhat uneasy. Indeed, this could give them ample time to check the contents of the package, and unlike Streicher, the P.L.O. representatives were master linguists.

He had come up with the idea of renting a small isolated house in the outskirts of Salonica. This proved to be rather easy through the good offices of a Greek businessman for whom he had done a favor or two. Setting the meeting between Streicher and the P.L.O. agent in Salonica rather than in Athens would drastically cut the time that the package would remain in the P.L.O.'s hands. Besides, while he knew that the P.L.O. representatives in Athens would easily recognize the value of the documents, he seriously doubted that their field operative would have that kind of sophistication. As for taking the documents from the American, that should prove an easy task for two trained field agents.

He sighed contentedly; he would give himself credit. His planning had been imaginative and thorough. In very few days, he would be on his way to becoming an extraordinarily wealthy man and the last vestiges of threat from his past would be eliminated forever. He deserved a third cognac. The presence of Otto Streicher had not allowed him to enjoy the first drink.

Chapter 14

Salonica - The Second Day

In the hotel's empty ballroom, in the early dawn, David went through his daily ritual. Sometimes, these two hours were the best part of the day. It was unlike the beginning, when karate was literally his reason for being, his haven, his refuge from the memories which tormented him. Karate had become a more appropriate but perhaps even more meaningful part of his life.

For a short while, especially while working for the CIA, it had become an activity in which he engaged in order to ensure his survival, but this was no longer the case, and he deeply enjoyed it for its own sake.

He adopted a fighting stance, and his two fists--quick as lightning--struck an imaginary opponent in the stomach and the forehead. He pivoted to the left, and his left hand, rigid as a board, deflected a knife blow. He pivoted to the right, and a side kick knifed the air as potentially lethal as a bullet. He kept on pivoting, and flying through the air, he delivered a flying side kick. His movements were fairly simple but extraordinarily fast and precise. Old Master Kwang would have been proud of him.

He liked the feeling of his strong muscles, the quickness of his reflexes. He enjoyed the intricate pattern of movements into which he glided effortlessly. Karate was not only a fighting art but a communion with himself and nature. It was like walking in the rain, swimming in quiet waters. When the moves accelerated, it was like listening to the wind howling through the winter night. He liked the meditation before and after the practice session. It left him renewed, refreshed, and in harmony with himself. After finishing his session, he returned to his room and took a hot shower. He smiled ruefully. In spy novels, the secret agent always took a cold, invigorating shower. If there was anything he disliked more than cold weather, it was a cold shower. He dried himself and changed into clean clothes.

It was still early, and Venchiarutti and Mihali would probably not be down for breakfast for another hour. The air was clean, not yet violated by the pollution typical of Western cities. It had that peculiar luminosity which he remembered so well from his childhood, a luminosity which gave buildings, people, and trees a softer yet brighter appearance. The avenues were wide and modern, and he remembered with a bit of nostalgia the dusty streets of his childhood and the city water trucks which would sprinkle them to settle the dust and the clean, fresh smell which would linger after their passage.

There was a café across the street, and on an impulse, David crossed the avenue and walked toward it. There was a lone customer sitting at an outside table who seemed to leave in a hurry when he saw David coming. David followed him with his glance, and there was something peculiar about the man's gait. Indeed, it was not a "he" but a "she"--and a young woman at that, judging from her straight stance and firm steps. Now, why would a young woman be at the terrace of a café at a time when most people either went to work or were already at work? He remembered the uneasy feeling of being followed which he had experienced upon arrival at the train station. Again, the possibility of an information leak crossed his mind. He had forgotten to call Bill again last night, and now it was too late. There wasn't anything his friend could do. He would just have to cope with events as they unfolded. He felt annoyed and irritated and couldn't quite put his finger on the reason for his annoyance. His sessions with Dr. Rosen had taught him to try to find honest reasons for emotions which puzzled him. He ordered a Turkish coffee and allowed his mind to wander and reminisce while he slowly sipped the hot and sugary beverage.

℃

"Something strange happened yesterday, Dr. Rosen. For no reason, at least no apparent reason, my boss changed the route of my delivery truck. It was no big deal. In fact, it really made no difference whatsoever to me. Yet, I really felt pissed. I didn't say anything because I realize that it would be childish to complain about such a small matter. In fact, later during the day, I learned that he was simply trying to combine two shorter routes. Yet, I couldn't help the way I felt."

Dr. Rosen leaned back on his chair, his two hands on his stomach.

It's amazing, thought David, *he never takes notes but remembers almost everything.*

"What can you associate to the feeling? Do you remember feeling that way before, ever?" Dr. Rosen asked.

"Come to think of it, it wasn't just irritation. It was more than that, like a feeling of having lost my bearings, not knowing where I was. Yet, I am quite familiar with the new route. I mean, I have been over it several times."

"Lost your bearings, like being out of your element, in a strange world, in a different time, perhaps?"

"No, not so much in a different time, but certainly in a different world."

David remembered a long silence during which disconnected images flashed through his mind, the army, basic training at Ft. Knox, Seoul. Nothing rang a bell. Bill's departure for the States. That had the same flavor but not quite. It went further back, but he couldn't pinpoint it.

"It's no use, Dr. Rosen, I can't put my finger on it."

"You said it wasn't a different time, but it was a different world. When did your world begin to change?"

"Oh my God! It changed so many times and in so many different ways. I think that the very first time I knew something was wrong was when the Germans beat up my father and he came home and there was blood all over his suit. We talked about that, and I remember that I was so frightened because if my parents couldn't protect me, then who could? You remember. But as I think about it now, it was more than fear."

"What was it like?"

"It was like... It's hard to explain. It's like everything is stable, and then, suddenly, it's stable no longer. It's like, like...."

"An earthquake."

"Exactly, exactly. That is exactly what it was like. When Dad came back from the Gestapo headquarters, it was as if the earth started shaking and things which had been in the same place started falling off. Funny I should say that because, as you know, as the famine was getting worse and worse, Dad starting selling our furniture off, one piece at a time. All the beautiful things that my mother loved so much began disappearing, and the rooms seemed emptier and larger. She must have felt so sad. Then, it was no longer furniture but people. As the Germans were emptying sections of the ghetto, friends and relatives began to vanish, and then it was our turn. And then I was alone."

"So, when the boss asked you to change routes?"

"It was as if he had started another earthquake, and in some strange way, I felt threatened all over again."

❦

David sighed and continued to sip his coffee. Maybe this was happening again. Maybe the possibility of someone following him was disturbing the web of memories which he had begun to build with his pilgrimage to the old house. No matter; this was not a time for too much introspection. Today was an important day and required all his concentration. If all went well, they would retrieve the package today, and tomorrow morning they would fly back to Athens. The documents would be delivered to the CIA station chief, who would send them to Langley via diplomatic pouch. His role would then be over and he had made no further plans. He would probably return to the States or maybe choose to remain in Athens for a few more days; too early to tell.

He glanced at his watch. It was 9:00 a.m., time to meet his friends. Indeed, he found them seated at a restaurant table, and they waved at him.

"Am I late?"

"No, not at all," said Venchiarutti. "Mihali and I have just arrived."

Mihali and Venchiarutti had ordered fruits and croissants. He knew that croissants made in Salonica compared quite favorably to French croissants, but he needed a more robust fare.

"Eggs and bacon," he said and smiled at the waiter's contemptuous glance.

Mihali harrumphed and in his most severe tone said, "David, having been raised in Greece, you should know better. Eggs and bacon, indeed. That is close to being insulting to a Greek waiter. I guess we'll have to forgive you because of the nefarious influence of all your years in America."

Venchiarutti glanced at them over the rim of his glasses.

"If you two youngsters are through with your adolescent pleasantries, may we get down to business?"

Mihali and David looked duly contrite, and Venchiarutti proceeded.

"Early this morning, I called and talked with Mother Veronica, the mother superior of the convent where Assael's papers were and hopefully are still hidden. During the war, it was part of the Italian consulate. After the war, the Italian government donated it to... I believe it was the Carmelite order, of nuns or maybe it always belonged to the church and we were leasing it. I can't remember. I told the good woman who I was and asked to see her today with two of my friends. She was most gracious and agreed to see us at twelve o'clock. David, I did not tell her that you worked for your government. It was my understanding that your government did not wish to appear involved in this matter and that is why they requested your service. Am I right in this assumption?"

"Yes, sir, and I thank you," David replied.

"Well, then," continued Venchiarutti, "when we get there let me do the talking. The lady speaks French, as we three do. This way you will not be left out of the conversation. I wondered if you should have hired a private security guard, David, but Mihali assured me that you could probably take care of any eventuality that may come our way…"

"With all due respect, Francesco," interrupted Mihali. "I did not say 'probably,' I said 'certainly.' I remember a hotel room in Athens, not too long ago, my poor nephew with his bruised ribs and me with my hand still hurting. And that was in the dark, mind you, and… he did not expect us. He half-killed us."

"It wasn't so bad," David demurred. "I am sure that if something happens, Uncle Mihali will be a worthy ally."

"That is settled then. Let us enjoy our breakfast and take our time."

෬

Alysha had seen the American cross the street toward the café and made a hasty retreat. Maybe she shouldn't have. She probably had drawn attention to herself. On the other hand, had she stayed, he would certainly have seen her features and been able to recognize her should their paths cross again. That was totally unacceptable.

She left the café, walked around the block, came back, hid in a doorway, and, after a long wait, saw her target get up and walk toward his hotel. She quickly took her light jacket off and put it back on, this time inside out, messed up her hair, stooped, and changed her gait. The transformation was instantaneous, and she was unrecognizable as a slightly disheveled old woman.

She followed the American into the lobby, and through the glass panes of the restaurant, she saw him and his two friends having breakfast. They had not yet ordered, therefore there was still time. She walked out of the hotel walking slowly, dragging her left leg as befitting an old woman who didn't want to attract attention. Half-a-block away, she broke out into a run, and it did not take her long to reach her hotel.

Ibrahim was waiting, and she dressed up quickly. Both wore black leather trousers and black sweaters. In a black carry-on, they put two Berettas and two black ski masks. They had rented a car, which they had not yet used, not wanting to risk being seen driving it. They were certain that today would be the day when the document transfer would occur.

"Alysha, I guess that is what we have been trained for. Are you okay? Do you feel ready?"

The young woman smiled and extended her arm in front of her. Her hand was steady as a rock.

"Good," continued Ibrahim. "Let us go over the plan again. While at breakfast, I overheard something about a Carmelite convent. We shall, of course, follow them, and if indeed they go to a convent, we both agree that will be the best place to strike. Still, how can we be certain that the documents are there? What if they are not? They will be on their guard more than ever."

Alysha shrugged and said, "Why would three men--I assume only one of them is Catholic--why would these three men visit a convent? Certainly not for the salvation of their souls, Ibrahim. Besides, I am sure that they know they are being followed. If we are wrong, then we'll just have to try again."

"Okay!" said Ibrahim. "Let's go for it. As you said, we probably won't find much opposition. The Italian is an old man. The Greek is pretty big, but he is not young either. We'll have to watch out for the American. Besides, they are not armed. Let us go."

It was not hard to find a parking space in front of their target's hotel, and when the three men got into a cab, the Arabs were right behind then. Ibrahim was happy at the way events were developing. If things went well, as he expected, they would have possession of the package and turn it over to their contact before the end of the day. Tomorrow they would fly back to Athens and, perhaps, enjoy the sinful pleasures of this decadent civilization for a day or two, buy a few things for their parents, then return to Beirut. He felt proud and content that they would strike a blow for the cause. In his imagination, he could see Alysha and himself standing in front of their superior and proudly announcing that their first mission had been a success.

ⷭ

It was close to noon, and the cab containing David and his two friends was making its way to the convent when David said suddenly, "Driver, make a left turn at the next intersection."

Venchiarutti, who until then had given the driver instructions, looked surprised but said nothing.

"Now, turn right and make an immediate left." After the driver complied, David turned to his two companions. "We are being followed. Look behind, that blue Mercedes. I am sorry, Mr. Venchiarutti, for having so rudely interrupted your directions."

Venchiarutti dismissed his apology with a wave of the hand, and David continued. "There is nothing we can do or should do. To lose them we would have to speed, and I don't want to attract the attention of the Greek police. Let us just be on our guard."

The convent was a stark building of medieval architecture, gray and foreboding. The front door was massive, oak with iron bands. The inside, however, belied the exterior. The person who answered the door was a young nun in a starched white habit with a pleasant and engaging smile. The hallway was peaceful and cool with small end tables along the walls, each carrying a vase of flowers.

"Please wait here," said the nun. "Mother Veronica will be with you shortly." Indeed, thirty seconds had barely elapsed when the mother superior made her entrance. She was, or at least looked like, a most remarkable person. She was tall, regal, and even her austere habit could not completely hide the voluptuous curves of her body. Her eyes were inquisitive and searching, although her traits were serene. Her smile was dazzling yet with a tinge of sadness. David fleetingly wondered as to what set of circumstances had made such a woman withdraw from the world.

He remembered then, as a little boy of six, how he had severely cut his knee while playing soccer and his mother had taken him to an infirmary manned by Catholic sisters. He distinctly recalled the same feeling of coolness and peace and the beautiful, smiling face of a young sister who ministered to him and looked like an angel. He kept his thought to himself but he couldn't help but wonder if this was the same place and the mother superior the same young sister. But no, she was far too young.

"Please, come with me, gentlemen," she said, and they followed her into a large wood-paneled room with a ceramic floor. The room seemed to be at the same time austere and warm. The walls were adorned with a single beautiful ivory and gold crucifix. There was a wooden desk, two wooden chairs in front of the desk, and three more against the wall. There was a large bookcase full of books. But there was also a mischievous ray of sunshine intruding through the window and touching the bookcase and the wall with a magic touch of gold. There was a good smell of furniture wax polish, which reminded David of his childhood home, and a most incongruous row of dolls on the top shelf of the book case, each wearing different attire. David recognized an Epirotiko costume, a doll dressed in the manner of women in Crete, a doll from Brittany, and a doll which surely must have come from an Israeli kibbutz. Mother Veronica followed his glance and smiled.

"We all have our weaknesses, young man. Mine is dolls, and when our parishioners go abroad, they always remember to bring me a doll from the country they visit. You see, there is much more kindness and generosity in the world than we give it credit for."

131

David could have disagreed with Mother Veronica, especially when the memories of the camps revisited him, but he simply nodded. Venchiarutti began the conversation as soon as they were seated.

"This is such a beautiful and peaceful place, Mother, that I do not feel comfortable bringing into it discordant notes from the outside world, but please believe me, I have no choice, and I hope that you will forgive me."

"Of course," replied Mother Veronica. "Not only have I received a letter from our bishop instructing me to collaborate with you in every way I can, but he also spoke of you in glowing terms. Tell me how I can help you, and I shall do my very best."

"Thank you, Mother Veronica. But first, let me introduce myself and my two companions. As you know from the bishop's kind letter, I am Francesco Venchiarutti, an attorney practicing in Rome. To my right is Mr. Diamandopoulos, a retired colonel in the Greek army, and to my left is my American friend, David Castro. Both are interested in my mission here. Mihali's relatives were shot by the Germans in a small village called Mavropotamos in 1942. David was born and spent his early years here in Salonica. His parents and little sister died in Auschwitz. And now, I will tell you why we are here.

"The story I am about to tell you unfolded many years ago, in fact, about thirty years ago. In those days, this very building was part of the Italian consulate. In fact, my own office was at the end of this hallway. But please believe me when I say that it was far from being as gracious and peaceful as it is now. At any rate, those were dark, terrible times. Perhaps you know that Salonica, for hundreds of years, boasted a large, flourishing, vibrant Jewish community. A year after having occupied the city, the German authorities applied the Nuremberg Laws to the Jewish community in all their ferocity. In less than two years, a remarkably intellectual, hard-working, avant-garde community became disintegrated, annihilated, and eventually all its members were massacred. Out of 75,000, only 2,500 survived. Those years were the most shameful chapter in the history of humankind. The most despicable atrocities were committed in this very city. They were of such magnitude that decent people cannot fathom them and have a difficult time believing that they happened. Only the few surviving victims and those of us who saw all this happening can bear witness. No one else can really understand."

"I believe that I can, Signore Venchiarutti," Mother Veronica said.

"You, Mother?" His tone was incredulous and clearly implied his doubt that anyone living behind the protection of the thick walls of a convent could understand the monstrous events of those days.

Mother Veronica was listening intently. Her face had become pale, and her fingers held a book of prayers with such force that her knuckles were white.

"Yes, I know, Mr. Venchiarutti. Few people know what I am about to tell you, although it is not a secret. I am a German. My father was an officer of the Whermacht, and I was engaged to a young Jewish boy whom my father liked very much. We had helped my fiancé hide in the country. Then, my father came back on leave from the Russian front. Somehow, at about that time, the Gestapo found out about my fiancé. My mother and I managed to escape, but my father refused. He was a solider and could not desert when the enemy was at the gates of the Fatherland. But he also refused to tell the Gestapo where my fiancé was hiding, and they tortured and shot him, an Oberst, Mr. Venchiarutti, a twice-wounded full colonel in the German army, holder of the Iron Cross with God knows how many clusters. They tortured and shot him. Later, they found my fiancé anyway, and he died at Auschwitz. Then, I only had two choices: I could become a murderess, or I could become a nun. I chose to become a nun."

Mother Veronica stopped abruptly. Her breathing had become ragged, and her eyes were flashing. She gave herself a moment to regain her composure and continued.

"I haven't talked about this for many, many years, but, somehow, it seems that the three of you--at least Mr. Castro, Colonel Diamauloupoulos and I--have shared the same kind of pain, and it feels good to talk even at long, long intervals."

David knew exactly what the woman meant. She had chosen to become a nun. He had almost chosen to become a murderer and, in fact, would have become one were it not for Dr. Rosen. He felt a surge of gratitude for the old man in the rumpled suit and military bearing, and snatches of one of their sessions flashed through his mind.

ငာ

"Usually, Dr. Rosen, I remember happenings that are so painful that I blot them out of my memory. There was something that happened and that I never forgot but that I wanted to forget. It was not as traumatic as the other things, just irritating and annoying."

"Would it help to talk about it?"

"I guess so. When the German army occupied Salonica, a column of trucks camped in our street, and all the children quickly made friends with the German soldiers. My little sister, Liza, was smitten with a driver. I still remember his name, Otto Reck. The other children, probably jealous of Liza's popularity, pointed at her screaming, 'Juden, Juden!' The German was nonplussed, and when he asked Liza, she said that of course she was Jewish and would show him our house. So, she took him by the hand and dragged him into our home. Mom and Dad were out for some reason, and I was alone. The German looked around, looked at me, and shook his head repeatedly. He knew a smattering of French, and we had learned few words of German. Basically, what I think he said was that he didn't believe that we were Jewish because our home was clean, we were clean, and we didn't have crooked noses, long hair, and long, dirty fingernails."

"Is that all?"

"No, there is more to it. Three days after that episode, the column of German trucks left. Then, a year and a half later, it was winter and very, very cold. It was past midnight, and there was a knock at the front door. Now, you must understand, Dr. Rosen, that there was a curfew, and a knock at the door after curfew hours never bade good tidings. We were hesitant to open the door when a voice said, 'Kleine Liza. Kleine Liza.' Liza's face lit up, and she said--I think she screamed--'It's my friend, Otto!' She rushed to the door and opened it. Sure enough, there he was, big as Dallas and with another German, whom he introduced as his co-pilot. Both men were carrying heavy canvas bags, which they deposited on the floor and proceeded to open. The bags were filled with food stuffs, condensed soups, breads, cheeses, chocolate bars, and what have you. In those days of famine, the contents of these bags were worth a fortune. The two Germans explained that they were in Salonica for one night, on their way to join Rommel's Africa corps, and they had heard that there was a severe famine in Salonica. They also apologized for coming in the middle of the night and, somewhat embarrassed, explained that they did not want to be seen entering a Jewish home."

"Is that all?"

"That is all, Dr. Rosen, except that instead of being grateful for this manna, which literally came from the sky when we needed it so much, I resented the Germans, and I was mad at Liza for being so friendly with them."

"Do you know why?"

"Not at the time, and not for many years."

"And now?"

"Now I understand, or I think that I understand. How can I hate all Germans if even one of them is good? Otto Reck challenged my hate and I didn't like him for that."

∾

David did not resent Mother Veronica; in fact, he liked her very much, and his heart ached at her story.

Venchiarutti remained silent for a long moment and so did Mihali and David. Finally, he sighed, and his words sounded so sad, reflecting perhaps the agony which Mother Veronica had gone through so many years ago.

"Thank you. We feel honored, and knowing what you shared with us renders my mission easier."

"And now," said Mother Veronica in a matter-of-fact tone, "please tell me about your mission."

"As I was saying, this convent was part of the Italian consulate, and we Italians, I am proud to say, did all we could to help members of the Jewish community. Giuseppe Castruccio, Commandatore Castruccio, had followed Count Zambone as consul general and even more so than his predecessor had encouraged us to do all we could to thwart the Nazis' efforts. At one time, the basement of the consulate was filled with Salonica Jews, whom we eventually provided with fake Italian passports so that they could escape to the Italian zone of occupation. One of these unfortunates was a noted scholar, Dr. Assael, who later became a very dear friend. Dr. Assael refused to escape and stayed because he wanted to 'bear witness,' as he said. He interviewed as many people as he could, collected all the evidence he could lay his hands on, and thus built a voluminous file, an indictment against those who destroyed the Jewish community. Unfortunately, his task was interrupted when my country signed an armistice with the Allied countries and Marshall Badoglio took over the Italian government. The Germans took over the consulate. Professor Assael and I both managed to escape. I was able to return to Rome, and he remained in hiding until the war ended. We hid his documents in a secret place in this convent before we left. I never saw Professor Assael again and learned that he had died on a trip to Israel. I was always under the impression that he had managed to rescue his files before his death. It is only recently that I found out that the files are still where we left them. These files contain information which may lead to the arrest and conviction of some of the Nazis perpetrators of very heinous crimes. That is about all, Mother Veronica, and I hope that you will permit us to retrieve these documents."

Mother Veronica tapped her fingers lightly on her desk and asked, "What is your friends' interest in this matter, Consigliere?"

"Mihali is a very old and dear friend. Since I do not speak Greek, he volunteered to come with me and pave my way, so to speak. As for David..." Venchiarutti's voice trailed. He did not want to lie to this fine woman but did not feel at liberty to explain David's role. David sensed his hesitation and stepped forward.

"Mother Veronica, like you, I did not want to become a murderer, but unlike you, I did not seek refuge from my anger in religious life. I cannot forgive, and I do not want to forget. I do not seek revenge, but I do seek justice. I am here to make absolutely certain that these documents reach the proper authorities which have a legal right to prosecute and, if appropriate, punish those whose names appear in Professor Assael's documents."

Mother Veronica remained impassive and silent while the three men waited. After a while, she nodded, and her words were soft but determined.

"I would like to forgive. I have not achieved full forgiveness, but every day that passes, I am closer to my goal. I wish everyone could forgive, but I realize that I cannot. In fact, I do not have the right to impose my beliefs on others. I truly believe that you are not after revenge but after justice. You shall have your documents."

Before Venchiarutti had time to reply and thank her, Mother Veronica pushed an intercom button on her desk and said a few words in Greek. Almost immediately, the door opened, and the young nun who had welcomed them when they arrived walked in carrying, with some difficulty, a huge briefcase of discolored, stained, and frayed leather. It was bound in leather straps and had two old-fashioned, formidable looking locks. Partly because he wanted to give Venchiarutti the pleasure of receiving the briefcase to which so many memories were no doubt attached and partly because he remembered the car that was following them, David moved away from the tight little group formed by his two friends and the two sisters and stood by the side of the door.

༂

Alysha and Ibrahim saw the three men enter the convent and were not sure of their next step. They had two options available to them. They could enter the convent and take the documents, or they could wait until they left the convent, follow them, and wait for another opportunity. The idea of storming the convent appealed to them. It was highly unlikely that the sisters of charity would put up any kind of resistance. If they waited for another chance, they might never encounter another opportunity where their quarry would be as effectively cut off from outside help. It never entered their minds that the three men would fight back. Two of them were pretty old; as for the third, the American, their target, he was young and looked in good shape but he probably was a Washington bureaucrat who would faint at the sight of their Beretta. None of them was armed, they were pretty sure of that. Except for the old, white-haired man, the other two wore slacks and short-sleeved shirts.

Pistols are not easy to dissimulate. The only problem was that the documents which they were seeking might be elsewhere, and by entering the convent they might give themselves away, and from then on, the three men would be on their guard. But, no, this would not happen. This was it. Every fiber of their beings said so. This was the moment. They each tucked a Beretta in their belt, to the left side for easy accessibility, held a ski mask in their left hand, checked the deserted street, stepped out of the car, and walked toward the convent.

ᏋᎧ

Mother Veronica saw the puzzled expression on Venchiarutti's face, smiled, and explained, "We found this three years ago while making some renovations in the convent. It wasn't ours, so we decided not to open it, although opening it would have been the only way to identify its owners. We trusted that, sooner or later, God would see that this be returned into its rightful hands. Please, take them, Consigliere."

As Venchiarutti was about to thank her, he was interrupted by a loud noise. The door to the office burst open, and an older nun was pushed violently forward, falling on her knees. Behind them were two black clad figures, each holding a gun. Their attention centered on the small group surrounding the briefcase, and they were not yet aware of David's presence, half-hidden by the opened door.

"No one will get hurt," said one of the intruders in heavily accented English. "All we want is the briefcase. We'll take it and be on our way. Now!"

Oblivious to the threat of the pistols, Mother Veronica rushed to the aid of the old nun who had fallen on the floor. Venchiarutti defiantly put the briefcase behind him.

The black clad man raised his pistol at arm's length and said in a slow, cold tone, "I shall count to three. If you have not given me the briefcase at the count of three, I shall put a bullet between your eyes."

Until then, David had been loath to intervene. The guns, 9mm Berettas, were pointed at his friends, and the risk was too great. A diversion might help. He let go a blood-curdling "kia" so terrifying that Master Kwang would have been proud of him. Indeed, the man pointing his pistol at Venchiarutti whirled in a beautifully controlled, smooth movement and, without hesitation, fired at David. David, however, was too fast for him. His left foot--in an incredibly fast, fluid motion--went from right to left and hit the wrist of the gunman just as the shot was being fired. The gun was deflected, and the bullet harmlessly buried itself in the ceiling plaster. After anchoring himself again on his right foot, David pivoted slightly to his right, and his left foot again hit the man in the center of his chest. At the last second, however, David held his kick. He did not want to kill or severely injure the man. Besides, he needed information. Still, the kick was hard enough that the man held his chest and fell, while the gun clattered on the floor.

The second intruder barely turned to see what was happening, but that was enough for Mihali. The former Greek colonel tackled the intruder like a professional football player. It was too late, however, and a shot rang out. Enraged, Mihali picked the assailant up in his powerful arms, lifted up, and was about to crush the intruder against the wall when David's scream stopped him.

"No, Mihali, no! We need to know who they are."

Mihali dropped the assailant on the floor. It was then that they became aware that Mother Veronica was slumped on the floor. The two intruders had recovered a measure and, holding each other, were backing off toward the door. Mihali started after them, but David stopped him.

"Let them go. They will come back. They still want the briefcase. Right now, the sister needs our help."

To their incredible relief, however, Mother Veronica was getting off the floor unaided.

"What happened?" inquired David.

"When I heard the first shot," said Mother Veronica, "I became afraid for Sister Athanasia, so I laid on her to protect her. This probably saved my life. Otherwise, I would have been hit by the second bullet. As for you, my friends, you are like a three-man army."

"More like a two-man army," grunted Venchiarutti. "In the first place, I am an unreconstructed civilian, and in the second place, I am too old for these kinds of games."

Once they ascertained that the old nun, Sister Athanasia, and the young one who had brought the briefcase were unharmed, they collected the two Berettas and took their leave of the Mother Superior. David was sorry to go. He wanted to stay and talk with the older German woman who had chosen to become a nun rather than a murderess. He thought that talking with her would help in the healing process which had begun with Bill and Master Kwang and had continued under the tutelage of Dr. Rosen.

It was as if Mother Veronica had read his thoughts. She shook his hand and said with her half-dazzling, half-sad smile, "If you ever come back to Salonica, come back to this convent. There is much that we can share."

"Thank you, sister. I believe I will," and he meant it.

Chapter 15

The Eye of the Storm

It was only two p.m. when David and his friends returned to the hotel. It was hard to believe that so many things had happened in only two hours and that the coveted documents were, at last, in their possession. Venchiarutti and, to a lesser extent, Mihali were not used to this pace of events, particularly violent events. David was unperturbed. If it were not for the personal meaning of the documents to him, it would have been all in a day's work.

They were sitting around a table, and Venchiarutti ordered half a bottle of white wine while Mihali and David nursed their *ouzo*. After a while, they ordered, and for a time they ate in silence, each absorbed in his own thoughts.

"They will come back," warned David. "They want the documents, and they are not about to give up. What I want to know is how they found out about us, how they knew the precise moment at which the documents would be in our hands. Either we get the answers from them or in Washington when I get back. And by the way, Signore Venchiarutti, speaking of things that we don't know, what was that about a bishop's letter to Mother Veronica? I did not know that I had friends in such lofty circles."

"Oh, that!" replied Venchiarutti in his most innocent tone. "I have a younger brother, you see, who plays chess with the Pope, and when he won the game, he asked the Pope to ask the bishop to send a letter of introduction to Mother Veronica. Nothing to speak of, really."

"Nothing indeed," mumbled David in mock disgust. "You ask your brother, who asks the Pope, who asks the bishop, who sends a letter. It sounds like a variation of 'Old McDonald had a farm.'"

"Mac, who?"

"Never mind. I just want to say that it is good to have you on my side. Now, what do we do about our friends, who surely will make another attempt?" David asked

"I know what I should do," said Mihali in his booming voice. "I still have few friends and some influence left with the police department here. They can canvass the hotels, find them, bring them to a police station, and I will spend an hour or so in *tête-à-tête* with them. By that time, I guarantee you that you will know all they know and more."

Venchiarutti shook his head and smiled. "Mihali, my old friend, you are still the same impetuous youth that you were in 1942 in Mavropotamos so many years ago. Those days, my friend, are gone. I don't know who those two rogues are, but I am willing to bet that they are not Greeks. Their accent had a very distinct Middle Eastern flavor. If the German--how did you call him David? Von something or another--has learned of your mission, he may well have hired someone to take the documents away from you. It is not the first time and it won't be the last that Nazi thugs and the P.L.O. have worked hand in hand. If my guess is correct, Mihali, your friends may have a hard time explaining their actions to their superiors. The Greek government is rather partial to the P.L.O. these days. Let's see if perhaps David might come up with a more subtle plan."

"Lawyers," grunted Mihali. "Lawyers, they are the same the world over. If we listened to them, we wouldn't get anything done. Okay, let's hear what the boy has to say."

"Okay," said David. "What are their options? They can steal the papers from our hotel room, and if so, they will have to try this tonight. They will expect us to leave as soon as possible, and as a matter of fact, we are returning to Athens by plane tomorrow morning. Their second alternative is to attempt the steal on our way to the airport. That would be much more difficult for them. They know that we are on our guard. They know we can defend ourselves, and what they don't know but may guess at is that Mihali's friends can provide us with unobtrusive but efficient protection to the airport. The third possibility is for them to wait until we pass on Dr. Assael's documents to someone else. Now, if there has been a leak somewhere in Washington, they will know that the package will be delivered to the U.S. embassy in Athens. Once they are inside the embassy compound, no power on earth can steal them. I believe they will choose the first alternative. It is true they do not know whether the papers will be in one of our rooms or in the hotel safe. They may well believe that we will decide not to let the papers out of our sight, and besides, if they fail, they will still have the other two more dangerous options."

"It sounds good to me," replied Mihali. "But let us hear the details."

"Simple. You may have noticed that there are many vacant rooms in our hotel. I will rent the room across the hall from mine. If it is occupied, we shall ask the occupants to move to another room, paying their hotel bill if need be. I will concoct a suitable story to explain why I need that particular room. I'll make sure that I have enough coffee to keep me awake, and I'll wait. If and when they come, I'll have to make an on-the-spot decision either to apprehend or to follow them. I would prefer to follow them and get as much information as possible. As for the documents, I will, as soon as we leave here, buy a brand new leather briefcase into which I'll transfer the contents of the old one and put it in the hotel safe. I will fill the old one with newspapers and put it by my bed. One more thing--" David turned to face Mihali. "In the unlikely event that they may try to force the hotel safe before or even after they enter our room, if they become aware of the substitution, could you have the lobby covered by a couple or three of your tough guys?"

By then, Mihali was quite interested and had a gleam in his eye. He continued where David left off. "No problem, you Machiavellian young character. If you ever want to join the Greek police, I'll give you a first class recommendation. But one more thing. If you follow them, I'll go with you. My room is adjacent to yours, and you can bet your life that I'll be awake. Someone has to keep an eye on you and protect you from the bad guys."

"That's fine," added David. "Mihali, you will make sure we have a good car parked outside the hotel. Taxis in the middle of the night may be iffy."

"What about me?" said Venchiarutti in a plaintive tone. "Where do I fit in?"

"Mr. Venchiarutti," said David seriously. "Someone has to hold down the fort. I don't know what may happen tonight. Should we be in need of help, there must be someone we can call. Mihali will leave with you the names of two of his contacts in the Greek police."

"Why do I have the feeling that you are trying to protect me?" complained the old Italian gentleman. "But you make sense. Okay, let's go."

The three men finished their coffee, paid their bill, and went out. Venchiarutti went to the front desk to rent the room across from David's room. Mihali went in search of a suitable automobile. David went to buy a new leather case. He was carrying the old one with him, fairly certain that it was too early for their adversaries to mount a new operation.

⁊⊃

It was late afternoon of the same day, almost dusk. David was sitting cross-legged on his bed, hundreds of pages from Dr. Assael's manuscript--a few typewritten, most of them handwritten--strewn on the bed cover and the floor. One of the Berettas taken from their unknown assailants was also on his bed, under a pillow.

David stood up, walked over to the bathroom, and threw up, then he drank deeply from a carafe of water in which ice cubes were melting. He felt dirty inside and out. He had just descended into depths of human cruelty and depravity next to which Dante's *Inferno* was a vacation resort. He wondered how such horrible things could have happened around him without his being aware of them. After all, he was eleven or twelve, not a baby. He realized with a start the lengths to which his parents must have gone to protect him and Liza from the hellish waves swirling all around them.

Tears welled in his eyes as he picked up some of the handwritten sheets and started reading again.

11 April 1941.	*All Jewish papers are ordered to cease their operations.*
June 1941.	*The Rosenberg Commando descends on Salonica and steals every rare book or manuscript, every precious artifact, Torahs, silver goblets, and candle holders it could find in the many Jewish synagogues in Salonica.*
Winter of 41-42.	*An indescribable famine afflicts the city.*

At least David was aware of that part. That was when his mother's fine furniture had begun disappearing. The mortality rate among Jewish children was extremely high.

13 July 1942.	*Nine thousand Jewish professionals are arrested and conscripted to do heavy work for the German army. Most of them perish of malnutrition.*
6 December 1942.	*The centuries-old Jewish cemetery is destroyed.*
6 February 1943.	*All Greek Jews must wear a distinctive yellow star.*
25 March 1943.	*The Jewish population of Salonica is crowded into a ghetto.*
14 March 1943.	*The deportations to Auschwitz began.*
8 December 1944.	*There were eight Jews left in Salonica in the Pavlos Melas prison. They were shot. Thus*

> *ended the Jewish community in Salonica,*
> *which was flourishing when the Apostle Paul*
> *visited the city and which, according to some*
> *sources, began 400 years before the birth of*
> *Jesus Christ.*

Professor Assael's memoirs were not only mere descriptions of events. They also contained facsimiles of German orders and decrees. There was a copy of the decree ordering the wearing of the yellow star, a copy ordering the confiscation of Jewish properties, and many others. The name of Johann Richter figured prominently on many of the documents. There was enough there to hang the bastard many times over. David wondered at the dogged determination of the old professor, the heartache it must have been for him to describe these horrors so meticulously, and the ingenuity he must have demonstrated to obtain this mountain of evidence. He really did not deserve to die without having seen justice prevail.

David bent to retrieve a sheet that had slid under the bed. It looked somehow different from the rest, it was written on different stationary. Curiously, David read the first line, and soon his attention was riveted to the document.

> *On Thursday, April 12, 1945, I was informed*
> *that a Greek collaborator by the name of Antonio*
> *Athanassopoulos, awaiting execution at the Pavlo Mela*
> *jail, had requested to see me. His request, for which no*
> *reason was given, was granted, and I met with Mr.*
> *Athanassopoulos on the afternoon of that same day. He*
> *said that he knew that I was a man of honor and that*
> *he had a story to tell before his death. I did not ask him*
> *how he knew of me and of my whereabouts, nor did*
> *he volunteer the information. He had, indeed, a very*
> *strange story to tell.*
>
> *Athanassopoulos had become the associate of*
> *SS Colonel Johann Richter. I, as almost everyone*
> *in Salonica, knew of Richter. He was the Gestapo*
> *official responsible for the cataloguing and disposal of*
> *Jewish properties. While the Rosenberg Commando*
> *concentrated on Jewish assets of historical or*
> *archeological value, everything else fell within the*
> *purview of Richter, such as gold, jewelry, diamonds,*
> *paintings, tapestries, rare furniture, etc. What was*

not common knowledge was that Richter sent only part of the loot to his superiors in Germany and, with the help of Athanassopoulos, had managed to divert a large part for his own usage. The stolen property was stored in a warehouse, and it was Richter's intention to retrieve it a few years after the war and Germany's inevitable victory.

Things, however, did not turn out as expected. Richter had to leave Salonica in a hurry, a step ahead of the partisans. Athanassopoulos had eventually been arrested, convicted of treason, and sentenced to death. Before his arrest, however, he had managed to buy a small house in a village approximately 80 kilometers from Salonica and had transferred the stolen goods into that home. He had paid a caretaker to keep an eye on the property, had paid him well, and had informed him that it would be many years before he returned. His instructions were to allow no one on the premises without a written authorization from Athanassopoulos. After he finished his story, he wrote the authorization, and it is attached to this narrative.

I asked him why he was doing this. Very concisely he said that, had he known of Richter's whereabouts, he would have given him the instructions to the treasure because "after all, a deal is a deal," but since he had no idea of how to get in touch with him, he would be just as happy returning the stolen property. What he said exactly was: "I have no family, nobody. After I die, my name will soon be forgotten. Perhaps some of the people we wronged will have a kind thought for me." I believe that he meant what he said. I asked him why he had not tried to bargain for his life with his captors. He laughed and said that he knew the partisans too well. They would probably take the treasure and shoot him as well. Maybe he was right, who knows? After all, it was his choice.

My own sincere belief is that the remnants of the Jewish community of Salonica are the rightful owners of whatever Richter and Athanassopoulos stole. I shall wait for a while until the present chaos subsides and law and order are restored again. I plan to leave for

> *Palestine for four to five weeks to visit relatives. Upon my return, I shall give these two documents to the representative of whatever Jewish population is left. In the meantime, and since I am still allowed access to the former Italian consulate, I shall keep them together with the rest of my papers, which Francesco Venchiarutti and I hid so carefully.*

David dropped the sheet of paper, took another long drink of water, and remained pensive for several minutes. He had witnessed and experienced most of the events described by Dr. Assael; he had experienced the fear, the sorrow, and the despair, but it was much later that he understood the meaning. It was after the war that he understood the greed, the cold-blooded, well-organized measures, and the conspiracy of silence. Yet, there was something he could not understand.

℘

"You are a Jew, Dr. Rosen, aren't you?"

"Yes, David."

"You are such a wonderful person, Dr. Rosen."

"Thank you, David."

"So was my father, so was my mom. My relatives, my friends, they were all good people. If they weren't Jews, they would still be alive. I don't understand. Is it so important to pray in a synagogue rather than a church or a mosque? Is it worth the lives of so many millions? If there is a God, isn't that God everywhere?"

"I don't know, David."

"The Inquisition, the pogroms, the Holocaust. It is a vicious cycle. You know, Dr. Rosen, if I ever marry and have children, I don't give a damn if they become Buddhists, Muslims or Christians so long as they don't bear the curse of being Jewish, and they will know that their children and their children and their children's children will never be persecuted or killed."

"To die is too high a price for one's religious beliefs? I don't believe that is what you are saying."

"What am I saying then? I believe what I am saying is that death is too high a price to pay for the rituals of religion. It becomes a monstrous price to pay when one does not believe in religion to begin with."

"I think you are right, you are absolutely right, and yet..."

"And yet, I would never deny my Jewishness, not even if my life depended on it," David said.

"You are not making sense, David!"

"Yes, I am. I would change my religion to save my life, but I would never deny my ancestry. I am proud of my people. Over thousands of years, we have overcome so much, and from Moses to Jonas Salk, we have made more contributions to humankind than any other race."

"Would you die for the right to proclaim your ancestry, David?"

David remained silent for a long, long moment.

"No, Dr. Rosen, I would kill for it."

෬

That session, unlike most of the others, had left David with a sense of dissatisfaction. So much more talking needed to be done, but they never discussed the matter again. He seemed to have drifted far away in time and place.

He picked up and re-read Dr. Assael's letter.

No wonder Richter was so eager to get his hands on the papers. Not only would he eliminate every vestige of evidence against him, but the son of a bitch would enter into possession of incalculable wealth, which, like the carrion that he was, he had stolen from the dead. David was not about to let that happen.

David very painstakingly made two copies of Dr. Assael's handwritten note. Then he carefully tucked the original and Athanassopoulos' authorization in his money belt. These he would give to the president of the small Jewish community before they left or, if that proved to be impossible, he would return to Salonica immediately after having delivered the papers to the embassy in Athens. One copy he kept for himself, and he would decide later whether to destroy it or give it to the head of the Jewish Agency or the president of the American Zionist Organization. The second copy would go to Bill, who would decide whether or not he would give it to his CIA superiors. Since David was a free agent and not part of the CIA, he had no compunctions about having examined the contents of the briefcase and would assume full responsibility for having withdrawn the material pertaining to Athanassopoulos. Knowing Bill, he would probably destroy the copy sent to him, realizing that this matter did not concern the CIA.

By the time he'd finished reading, it was 10:00 p.m. and completely dark outside. It was time to get ready for the night. David transferred all of Dr. Assael's papers into the new briefcase, stuffed the old one with folded newspapers, placed it by his bedside, and took the new one down to the lobby. As he approached the counter, which bore a sign saying "SAFE DEPOSITS," he noticed that three burly men, strategically located and apparently lazing in deep leather chairs, automatically turned their heads toward him. *Well*, he thought, *this is reassuring. The safe deposit box is well guarded.* He came back to his room, called room service, and ordered a large pot of American coffee.

When the coffee arrived, he first checked that his wallet and passport were securely zipped in a back pocket, checked his money belt, which contained Dr. Assael's note plus what was left of the five thousand dollars Bill had given him before leaving Washington, checked the loads in the Beretta, which he stuck in his belt, took the coffee pot with him, and moved into the empty room across the hall. He placed a comfortable chair in such a manner that he could easily and swiftly go out, opened the door a tiny crack, turned the lights off, and settled in for a long wait.

❦

At approximately the same time, Alysha and Ibrahim were sprawled on the large queen size bed of their hotel room with a large pan full of ice water between them. A bottle of whiskey and two glasses sat on the bed stand. They had been resting there after their foiled heist.

"My God," groaned Ibrahim, "I never saw him move. I never saw the kick coming, and I thought my reflexes were pretty fast. Who the hell is that guy, anyway? They told us nothing about professionals, and you know what, these guys are better than professionals."

Alysha could only moan. "I hurt all over. If the American hadn't told him to put me down, he would have crushed my head on the wall. For a moment there, I was sure that I was going to die."

Ibrahim looked at his sister with great tenderness. The very thought that she could be hurt filled him with dread. What the hell were they doing here, anyway? And why didn't their superiors in Beirut warn them that they were going against truly dangerous people?

"Ibrahim," uttered Alysha in a small voice, "what are we going to do? Do you think that we should give up and go back to Beirut?"

"No." Something in Ibrahim rebelled against the prospect of returning empty handed. They would give it one more try. "Look," he said, "we must rest first, then think. Still, we must act tonight. They may well leave tomorrow, and then it will be pretty much impossible to do anything about it. They will be surrounded by people and we cannot risk a daytime assault on them.

Besides, to be really honest, we were not very successful even with the element of surprise."

"Then maybe there is nothing we can do?" Alysha murmured hopefully.

"Alysha, I said no. We must try one more time. They will probably keep the package with them, not let it out of their sight. Tonight, after midnight, I'll try to enter their room and take the briefcase. I know it is risky, but you know how good I am at this sort of thing. Even before we were trained, I could move like a shadow. Do you remember when we were younger, when I would come home late and didn't want Dad to find out? Remember? He never did."

Alysha smiled at the memory. "Tell me your plan."

"Okay, right now, I'll be going into the lobby to have an *ouzo* and a cup of coffee. This whiskey is for foreigners and does nothing for me. In the meantime, you'll take a long hot bath and go to bed. We'll ring room service for dinner. I'll take a shower. You'll use the bed, and I'll sleep on the sofa. I will pay the hotel in advance and sleep for about four hours. Then we'll pack, leave our things here, and I'll drive you to the house where we have been ordered to deliver the goods. I looked at the map, and the house is not hard to find. Besides, there won't be any traffic past midnight. I don't want to stay here any longer than absolutely necessary. As soon as I come back with the briefcase, we'll drive back to Athens. No planes, no trains."

Ibrahim slowly, gingerly rose from the bed. "All right, little sister, you have forty-five minutes for your bath, then I am back."

Chapter 16

The Depth of Evil

David, all his senses alert, was sipping his coffee in the dark in his room. Something was bothering him, and he knew exactly what it was. One of the two men who had attacked them, the one Mihali had almost crushed against a wall, was not a man at all but a woman. He remembered the woman who had left the café in a hurry when she saw him coming that same morning. It seemed ages ago. That did not surprise him, as the P.L.O. had several female agents. It did, however, make him feel quite uncomfortable. It would be trite to say that he disliked hurting women. That was true, but it only partially explained his discomfort at the thought of the P.L.O. female agent. He remembered having discussed his feelings about women with Dr. Rosen a long, long time ago...

"I like women, Dr. Rosen. I feel comfortable with them. It is easy for me to talk with them, and the truth be told, I enjoy them sexually very much. But I have never really loved a woman. I have had many short and enjoyable liaisons, and the women and I always parted on amicable terms. So long as it was clearly understood that we could enjoy each other's body and company on a temporary basis, without any emotional entanglement, there was no problem. There was one exception, and that was Xenia. I remember telling you about her once, when we first started our meetings. Haven't I?"

"Very briefly. Tell me again."

"She was one of the most extraordinary persons I have ever seen. She was so bright and knowledgeable that just talking with her was an experience. She was one of those rare people with a brain and a heart, if you see what I mean. She was sensitive, compassionate, kind, and she loved me very much, a totally unconditional love, expecting nothing in return. She was also very beautiful. Truly, she looked like a princess. Not regal like a queen, but delicate, distinguished, and... and... beautiful. I can't think of a better word. In fact, the villagers in her native mountains, when she rode on horseback, used to call her the Princess of the Pindes.

No one had ever impressed me like she did. For a while, I really thought that I could spend the rest of my life with her. She was the only woman to whom I did not make it crystal clear from the beginning that our liaison would be temporary and without any kind of emotional commitment. I didn't because I really wanted our relationship to last. I wanted desperately to fall in love with her, but I couldn't. I would have never left her because I knew how much it would hurt her. But, true to form, she left me. One day, she just wasn't there anymore. She left a note which said, 'I love you, live your life.' She didn't want me to stay with her out of a sense of duty. I never heard from Xenia again. I missed her terribly, yet I must confess that I also felt a sense of freedom and relief. Sometimes I wonder if I am defective in some way. Do I really lack the ability to love?"

"What other women have you been close to, David?"

"My mother, of course, and my little sister, Liza, and I loved them very much, but, of course, a different kind of love."

"And they both died."

"You know, when I think of what happened to them and of what happened to my father, I have different feelings, well not altogether different, but... let me try to explain. When I think of Mom and Liza, I feel a deep sense of despair and sadness, of pity for what they went through and rage at those who killed them. When I think of Dad, it is all this and something else too. The horrible, horrible knowledge that his wife and daughter were dying and that he could not save them because he was dying too. Just thinking about it makes me want to scream."

"You would rather be alone forever than experience what your father went through."

"You are right. Wait a minute, are you saying that the reason I cannot fall in love is that I am afraid that someday my loved ones may be in danger and I won't be able to rescue them?"

"Perhaps, David, perhaps."

"What you just said reminds me of something that happened only a few years ago. I was staying with Bill's family for a while, and I took his youngest sister for a walk in the woods. I remember it so clearly. It was morning in the springtime, one of those rare very beautiful spring mornings in Pittsburgh. The air was so crisp and dry that breathing felt like drinking cool water. Trees wove a green and white tapestry all around us, and it felt so good to hold Annie's warm little hand in mine. I remember feeling suddenly overcome by a terrible sense of fear, and I remember also saying over and over 'Please,

God, don't let her suffer like Liza.' Annie must have sensed that something was happening, because she said, 'What is it, Uncle Dave?' Her voice broke the spell, the fear evaporated, and we had a wonderful time. Strange, I had completely forgotten that incident until it popped into my mind just now."

"Just one thing, David. No one is emotionally defective who can care as much as you do."

℘

At about the same time, Ibrahim left his sister off at the house where they expected to meet their contact. The place had been hard to find, and he was in a hurry to get back to the hotel and try for the briefcase.

Alysha waited in the dark until Ibrahim's car turned around the corner. When she could no longer see the red taillight, she sighed, turned around, and briefly hesitated before ringing the bell. There was something sinister about the house which made her shiver. It was isolated, dark, nondescript, and, in the moonlight, appeared unpainted. She shrugged. *I am being childish,* she thought. *This is the perfect house for a meeting of this nature.* Resolutely, she rang the bell, but nothing happened. She waited for a long while, then pushed the button again.

"What do you want?" The voice coming from behind startled her. She turned around and saw the man silhouetted against the moonlight. He was big, enormous, probably an illusion created by the shadows of the moonbeams shining through tree branches.

"Who are you, and what do you want?" he repeated in heavily German-accented English. Alysha could not remember whether there was a password agreed upon for the meeting with this man. She did remember, however, the password used with their contact in the Gaza strip and said "Have you visited Salonica?"

The man's grip was like steel pincers as his fingers dug into her shoulders and turned her around. His voice was deep, like the roar of the sea.

"Don't play games with me, girl!"

He opened the door, propelled Alysha forward, followed her, closed the door, and turned the lights on. The room was large, sparsely furnished, and surprisingly clean. The furniture was rustic but solid. Against one wall was a massive, finely chiseled fireplace, and Alysha had a fleeting, incongruous thought that fireplaces were rare in Salonica and wondered where this one had come from.

"Where are the papers, woman?"

151

She tried very hard to speak in a calm, deliberate manner, but her voice was still trembling and her knees were weak.

"My brother is in the process of getting them and will be here within the hour."

"You lie," said the man. "Who sent you? Who are you spying for?"

"Nobody, I told you..." Before she had time to finish her sentence, he cuffed her on the side of the head so hard that everything spun around her, and for a brief moment, she thought that her jaw was broken.

"I said, 'no lies.' You didn't know the password, and that was pretty stupid to put yourself in my hands. What happened to the P.L.O. agent? Did you arrest him, or was he killed? Not that I give a damn. All I want are the documents that he was carrying, and all you have to do is tell me where they are and you can walk out of here free and unharmed. Otherwise, you and I are going to have a great time together. Now, woman, what is it going to be?"

Alysha looked around her like a trapped animal. It didn't matter what she would tell him, he wouldn't believe her. And he probably would kill her anyway.

He sensed the panic in her and became afraid that she would do something desperate before giving him the information he needed. He tried what could pass for a smile and somewhat lowered his voice.

"I'll tell you what, I'll make us a nice cup of coffee. This will settle us both down and we'll talk. Okay?"

Alysha nodded, not trusting herself to speak.

"But, in the meantime," continued the man, "I will tie your hands, because I don't trust that you wouldn't try to run away. Not that I would blame you."

He bound her hands together before her then tied them to the door handle of a heavy china chest. He disappeared into the kitchen, and Alysha heard the clattering of dishes and the sound of running water. A few minutes later, he reappeared holding two steaming mugs of coffee and handed one of them to her. Alysha forced a smile and glanced at her hands.

"Oh! Yes, how inconsiderate of me." He bent, freed her hands, and handed her the coffee. Quick as a flash, Alysha flung the hot coffee into the man's face and ran for the door. Her legs betrayed her, however, and she stumbled. With a mighty roar, half-blinded by the scalding coffee, the man rushed after her and grabbed the collar of her leather jacket. Alysha slid out of the jacket and tried to run again, but she was too late. The man caught her blouse and ripped it off her. Naked to the waist, she faced him like a cornered deer facing a hungry wolf in a deserted forest. She picked up a poker standing by the fireplace and, even in her panic, remembered the words of her instructions: *When you use a stick, thrust, do not hit.* She came close, but the man almost contemptuously deflected the poker with his right arm. At that moment, the documents were forgotten and, half-crazed with lust and the pain of his burned face, all the man could see were two beautiful breasts with erect red nipples. He grabbed Alysha by the shoulders and drew her to him. Game to the end, Alysha clung to him and with her right leg kneed him in the groin with all her strength. With a roar of pain, he flung her against the wall; she fell hard, smashing her neck and the lower part of her cranium against the edge of the fireplace. With furious, raging movements, the man tore the rest of Alysha's clothes off. Her neck had snapped in her backwards fall. Otto Streicher never found out that he had raped a dead woman.

ھ

David barely heard the footsteps in the dark. Whoever he was, the man was good. But David was even better. Even absorbed in his daydream, he sensed the alien presence and was instantly alert. The intruder had no trouble unlocking the door to David's room and entered using a hooded pencil flashlight. David couldn't tell whether or not the man was surprised to see the bed untouched and the room empty. He had toyed with the idea of rumpling the bedding and putting two pillows under the blankets, but he had decided against it, however, for two reasons: First, unlike what most people would think, it is not easy to fool a trained eye. Second, if the man had realized that the bed had deliberately been rumpled, he would immediately smell a trap. He had preferred to leave the bed intact and watched through the barely opened door of the room across the hall from his own, which they had rented as planned. At any rate, the man came out of David's room within twenty seconds and walked through the hallways without rushing. Evidently, he preferred the stairway to the elevator. Indeed, there was less danger of meeting someone who would recognize him later. This excess of caution served David fine and made it easier to follow the man. Without turning around, he knew that Mihali was behind him. They emerged from the lobby just as the man was getting into his car approximately 50 yards down the street.

"You drive, Mihali, you know the place better than I do," said David. "But remember that I am too young to die. All you Greeks drive like maniacs."

"Teach your grandmother to suck eggs," was Mihali's jovial response. "I was driving trucks in the mountains when you were still in diapers."

To follow the man was a fairly easy task. The man was not speeding, and at 1:00 a.m., the traffic was practically nonexistent. It took them approximately twenty minutes to come out of the city limits, and now they were driving on a one-lane narrow paved road. It was tricky to drive without headlights, but Mihali was a truly remarkable driver. The trees, like sentinels along the road, and the moonlight through the occasional clouds incongruously reminded him of Ichabod Crane and Sleepy Hollow when he would read the story to Bill's sister Annie and she would squeal in frightened delight. This, however, was no laughing matter; David felt a knot in the pit of his stomach- -a precursor to unpleasant things to come.

The man finally stopped his car in front of an old house, a house standing alone far from neighbors. The man got out of his car, knocked, and entered the house. It took David and Mihali ten to fifteen seconds to reach the house. They were about to reconnoiter and try to find an open window or a side entrance when they heard the scream.

It was unlike anything they had heard before in their life. It was not fear, nor rage, but all these together and more, like the scream of an animal being slaughtered, like the scream of a primeval man in a prehistorical jungle. Without a word between them, without a moment of hesitation, David and Mihali put their shoulders against the door and tore it from its hinges.

Chapter 17

The Wrath of God

In one corner of the room lay a beautiful, half-naked woman, and under her neck was an ever-widening pool of bright red blood. A man was standing in front of the fireplace, not a man, but a red-headed giant with massive shoulders and huge, powerful legs. He was holding another man above his head, as if he were a toy. He turned around as the door crashed, and surprise registered on his face. He put the man back on the floor; no, he did not put him back on the floor, he dropped him negligently as one would drop a sack of flour, and the man remained motionless.

"Who are you?" he asked David.

David looked at him, then looked at the naked girl. The man on the floor dragged himself to the dead girl, held her head against his chest, and moaned, rocking back and forth.

"Who are you?" he repeated. He followed David's glance and became aware of the other man, holding the woman.

"The Arab brat," snarled the giant in heavily accented English. The accent was unmistakably German. "You just saved his life when you battered the door down. Now, tell me who you are, or I'll beat it out of you. Now!"

David couldn't talk. He wanted to move but couldn't. He couldn't see the man because of something that felt like a red mist obscuring his vision. Yet, there were images in his mind, horrible, atrocious, but familiar images--his father dying in a gas chamber while his mother and Liza were killed not far away, perhaps in the next gas chamber. The bloody face of the little girl on Fisherman's Wharf in San Francisco. He almost touched the part of his head where the German had hit him the first night of his arrival at the camp. The huge man facing him was a German, he was all Germans, all Nazis, all concentration camp guards, and David was going to kill him.

155

"My name is David," he said in a surprisingly soft voice which betrayed nothing of the insane fury which had paralyzed him for a few seconds. "I am a Jew," he added as an afterthought. "And who are you?"

The giant threw his head back and laughed, an uproarious laughter, with surrealistic undertones in this room where death had struck and, no doubt, would strike again in a few minutes.

"A Jew! That is beautiful. It has been a long time since I killed a Jew, but I haven't lost the habit. So, you want to know my name, Jew? I am Hans Knoppel. Not my real name, of course, but my real name does not matter. And now I am going to kill you, then finish off this Arab louse, and maybe there is still something left in his sister."

David realized that the German was not aware of Mihali's presence. The Greek colonel had wisely chosen to remain unseen in the shadows.

"Well, Mr. Knoppel, would you mind satisfying the curiosity of a man who is about to die?"

"No, not at all," replied the German with a fake joviality. "What is it that you want to know?"

David slightly cocked his head to the right. "Well, not much. Just what are you doing here, who sent you, and what are you after?"

"Okay, no harm in telling you. Dead men tell no tales. Old friend of mine named Von Eckardt--and I am sure you have heard his name, except that it's not his real name either. This here Arab monkey was bringing me some documents. He is P.L.O., I believe, and they owe Von Eckardt. I was to take the documents and bring them back to him, kill the P.L.O. people if necessary, and this, my friend, is just what I am going to do, kill you, kill them, and bring this here briefcase back to Von Eckardt. Now, I have satisfied your curiosity, and it's your turn. Your name is David, you are a Jew and probably American, but where the hell do you fit in all this?"

"One more thing," said David. "What is your real name?"

"Real names don't matter," snarled the giant. "Why not? Dead men are entitled to a last wish. My name is Otto Streicher, and Von Eckardt was, once upon a time, known as Johann Richter. Now answer me, what the hell are you doing here?"

"What about the girl?" asked David again ignoring Streicher's question.

"None of your goddamn business, Jew, but if you must know, she just happened along, and she wasn't cooperative. Didn't do her much good. Now talk," he added roughly.

"Mr. Streicher, can you pray?" The question was so incongruous that it threw the German momentarily off balance.

"What, what did you say? Can I pray? What the hell kind of question is that?"

"Mr. Streicher, if you believe in a God, make your peace with him for in a short while you will rejoin him."

David had hardly finished his sentence when the German rushed him. David had anticipated the move. In fact, his last statement had been designed to provoke it. He nimbly jumped to the left, and as the giant went past him, he pivoted to the right and with his left fist hit him in the lower back. It was a short and wicked blow with all the power of David's left shoulder behind it. The German stopped in his tracks, turned around, and with his right hand massaged his lower back. Otherwise, he seemed unaffected by a blow which would have felled most men. He sneered, but this time there was caution in his eyes.

"Is that the best you can do, Jew or American or whoever the hell you are?"

David said nothing. The time for words had passed. This was the deadly game in which he had engaged only very few times in his life. This time, he would not have to hold his blows, and the thought gave him a feeling of deliverance. David had waited for this moment for a long, long time. He feigned a side kick to the body. The German smiled contemptuously and did not even try to block it. He stood in the middle of the large room, his arms akimbo, like an immovable statue of granite. David adopted a classic Tang-Soo-Do karate stance and circled around him. Streicher did not move; he only pivoted slightly so that he would always face the younger man. He was, David thought, like an impregnable fortress. Yet, there was no such thing as an impregnable fortress.

David, imperceptibly and tantalizingly, came closer to the bigger man. As he hoped, Streicher jumped forward to grab him, but David was no longer there. He crouched suddenly, and his left foot hooked behind the German's right ankle and pulled. Streicher lost his balance and fell on his back with such a tremendous impact that the furniture shook and books fell from a shelf. David stood up and aimed a front kick at the man's face. He was too late, however, and with a remarkable agility in a man his size, Streicher was up and out of harm's way.

It was David's turn to be off balance and vulnerable. The German got behind him and tried to put one hand around his neck and the other around his face so that he would break his neck in a swift gesture. He did not have the time. David felt the man's arm trying to get around his neck; he knew that if the other hand were in place, the fight would end in a matter of seconds. He backpedaled desperately, and Streicher's back hit the china closet. Streicher loosened his grip, and that was all the break David needed. He bent suddenly, grabbed the cuffs of Knoppel's pants and pulled with all his might. The move was so unexpected that, instead of holding on to David's neck, as he should have, the German let go to break his fall.

David took a step forward to give himself space and unleashed a back kick, the same back kick which would have broken all the ribs and probably punctured the lungs of Mihali's nephew that night at the Hotel Grande Bretagne had David not chosen to hold back his kick. This time, he did not hold back, and his foot was a missile aimed at the man's chest. He felt the impact and heard a groan. As he turned around, the German was already beginning to get up. David's kick had made contact as he was falling, and instead of connecting with his chest it had hit him flush in his face. The German's nose was broken, his face was covered with blood, and there was a hideous gap where several teeth had once been. David looked at the horrible sight and felt no pity; in fact, even his anger was gone. He was going to kill that man and felt nothing. Once, as a child, he had walked around an ant to avoid stepping on it, but this man deserved no mercy.

David's mind was empty, and he kept on fighting, totally unaware of the terrible, clinical, methodical way in which he was taking the man's life. The German kept coming at him, waving his arms like some kind of huge prehistoric monster. There was no room for David to retreat, and he met the German on his terms in the center of the room, trading blow for blow. The German tried desperately to grab David, counting on his vastly superior strength. He put a bear hug around David, and David felt an excruciating pain in the small of his back. He could have broken the hold in several ways, by slapping the German's ears or gouging his eyes, but something inside him didn't let him. Instead, he obeyed some strange, crazy impulse and inserted his arms inside the German's arms, matching strength for strength, and slowly, imperceptibly the vise of the giant's arms loosened. The German gritted his teeth and spat blood and mightily tried to hold onto the bear hug, but to no avail, and suddenly he let go. He looked at his hands, stupidly, in sheer disbelief, and with a roar, he threw himself at David. He no longer attempted to grab David but only to hit him, hit him with all his strength, and his blows were punctuated by groans as if he was a wood cutter trying to fell a tree with an axe.

The two men stood toe to toe, and the epic battle was like that of two jungle animals. It was there that Master Kwang's teachings paid off. Streicher's blows were powerful, but David's hands were like a blur. Few of Streicher's blows connected, blocked by two hands which moved so fast that they were like a protective blanket. At times, it seemed as if there were not two hands but twenty. Eventually, Streicher's huge strength waned, and he slowed down and that was when David hit him repeatedly. His blows were sharp, cutting like a surgeon's scalpel. Soon Streicher was covered with blood, but he would not go down, and in some perverse way, David was glad that he didn't. Now the German was backing up, and David had more room. A flying side kick sent Streicher reeling, but he did not fall. As he kept coming, David let go with three flying, spinning kicks, one after the other, and each made a horrible thud as they connected with the German's skull. At the third kick, the German's legs buckled, he fell flat on his face, and he remained motionless.

David stopped. His arms were like lead. His clothing was covered with blood, but it was not his blood. In fact, while he ached all over, he was not marked. He was tired, however, so terribly tired. He no longer wanted to kill the German. In fact, he hoped he was still alive. He would certainly stand trial for the murder of the young woman, or the P.L.O. would get him. David had done his part. Let someone else finish the job.

"Watch out!"

The warning came from the shadows, where Mihali was standing. David raised his head and witnessed the incredible happening. Otto Streicher was up. With one hand, he was holding himself to a chair, and with the other he held a gleaming kitchen knife. He lunged at David and thrust. The man was an experienced knife fighter. David easily deflected the knife with the flat of his hand, but because of weariness he did not follow through at Streicher's unexpected resurgence of speed and strength. The German came at him again, his blade held low, and at the last minute transferred his knife from the right to the left hand and cut a wide swath. David saw the switch too late and only a backward jump saved him. Even so, a thin red line appeared on David's shirt. Sensing victory, the German rushed in for the kill. This was his last mistake. David had seen him coming in plenty of time. A well-aimed crescent kick hit the German's wrist and the knife clattered on the floor, almost at David's feet. He picked it up just as the German rushed him again. David later speculated that the German, blinded by the blood, had not seen the knife. Surprised by the mad rush, David did not quite manage to back off, and Otto Streicher impaled himself on his own knife.

"This time, he is really dead." It was Mihali coming from the corner where he was standing.

"I know," said David. "Thank you for the warning and thank you for not interfering. That was my fight."

"It was a good fight, and it's over now. I think he is dead."

Otto Streicher was dying but was not quite dead yet. His body was broken, and he knew not where he was. He was drifting somewhere in a misty sea of forgotten experiences, but the voices were so clear.

"Otto, listen to your father. He does not like it when you hang around with those hooligans. Nothing good will come out of it."

"Mama, why don't you move into the new house that I bought for you? You like flowers, and there are so many flowers. Away from all the filth and the cabbage smell."

"You and your friends are shaming Germany. Your mother and I will stay where we are."

"Fuck you, Father. I love you but you never loved me."

The face of Katya--gentle, loving Katya, with the dark hair and the deep blue eyes. Katya, the only person who ever loved him. There was blood on the grass when he took her, then walked away from her and never saw her again. There was blood on the grass, and that blood haunted his nights for a long time.

Blood, so much blood. In every Gestapo wall, on every torture rack. There was blood on Hans Knoppel's face disfigured by blows. *I am Hans Knoppel. No, you are Otto Streicher, and there is blood all over you, Katya's blood, Hans' blood...* The blood of all those he had interrogated in the cellars of the Gestapo, Jewish blood, so much Jewish blood, children, women, old people, so many of them. Jewish blood does not count, he used to say. He was drifting, people, places, long forgotten. He raised his hand to his face, and it was crimson with his own blood. He was dying, and a Jew had killed him. Life for life. It was just, it was fair.

"I should have listened to you. You always loved me, but I turned away from you and Mama. Oh, God! I let you both die, but you are just and terrible. Oh, God!"

Otto Streicher died with the name of God on his lips. David was trying to make a bandage of his shirt, but Mihali restrained him.

"Too late, he is dead."

Mihali and David stared at the huge body on the floor. Until now, neither one of them knew of Otto Streicher, former policeman, former Gestapo strongman, former private investigator and murderer and rapist many times over. Something evil seemed to emanate from the dead man.

David shivered. "For a while there, it was touch and go."

Mihali remained silent and pensive, then said in a hushed tone, "If I hadn't seen it with my own eyes, I wouldn't have believed it."

It was only then that they turned to Ibrahim and the dead girl. Ibrahim was still holding her, but his moaning had stopped. He was crying, great, silent tears. David sat on the floor next to him and very gently put his arm around him. Then, suddenly, without warning the silent tears became loud, convulsive sobs, the sobs of a child, a child hurting alone and in the dark. David put both arms around him and held him tight.

❧

It was a long time ago, it seemed, one of the very rare times that Dr. Rosen had initiated their session.

"You were eleven or twelve, David, when you entered the camp on that terrible night. Weren't you?"

"Yeah, about that... whenever I think of that night, I feel the same fear and the same loneliness. No, loneliness is not the right word... I feel the same *aloneness*. My parents were gone, and I was so desperately alone."

"David, I would like you to have a fantasy. I would like you to close your eyes and go back in time, as far back as you can go. Way, way back until in your mind's eye you see yourself as an eleven-year old little boy. Take your time, go back, way, way back. Can you see yourself?"

"Yes."

"What do you look like?"

"I am skinny. I wear a tennis shirt and short pants, short blue pants. My hair is all messed up."

"Get acquainted with yourself at eleven, touch your face, touch your hair. You are now only an eleven-year-old child. And I want you to imagine yourself in a big empty room, empty except for a tall, life-size mirror against one of the walls. And since it is only a fantasy and we can make anything happen in fantasy, let us make this a magic mirror. As you look at it, you don't see the little boy. Instead, you see a silhouette, rather vague, and as you keep looking at it, it becomes more and more distinct, and it becomes you, the you that you are today, an adult, a big, strong man. And since this is all magic, I want the adult you to step into the room next to the child you. And now, there are two of you, the child you and the grown-up you. And I want you, in your fantasy, to be the adult first and talk to the child."

"Hi there, little boy," David said.

"Now, be the child," asked Dr. Rosen. "Can you answer?"

David shook his head.

"Now, be the adult," said Dr. Rosen. "Look at that little boy. Look at his face. Look at his eyes. You know how expressive a child's eyes can be."

"He looks scared," David said, "so terribly frightened."

"Would you want to help him?"

"Oh, yes!"

"How can you do that?"

"I could tell him..."

Dr. Rosen interrupted. "Tell him."

"David," said David, talking to his child self. "Don't be afraid. Everything is going to be all right."

"Now, look at his eyes again," Dr. Rosen asked. "What do you see?"

"A little better, but still frightened."

"What else can you do?"

"I could hug him."

"But you are so big, and he is so small."

"I could kneel, but I don't want him to be frightened."

"Stoop down to his size and very gently take one of his little hands and hold it. How does it feel?"

"It feels good," said David. "Warm, so small."

"Ever so gently, take his other hand," Dr. Rosen said. "Now, look at him, what do you see?"

"He looks so peaceful now, and he is crying."

"How do you feel about this little boy?"

"Oh, I love him, I love him."

"Then put your arms around him and tell him."

David put his arms around himself, sobbed and rocked back and forth.

"Now," said Dr. Rosen, "be the little boy and say something to the grown-up. Anything you want."

"Please, don't leave me," David said, as the child. "Please don't go away."

"Will you do that?" Dr. Rosen asked of the adult David.

"Oh, yes," David said to the child. "I'll do that. I'll never leave you. I'll protect you. You will never, never, be afraid with me. I'll never, never let anyone hurt you ever!"

"I want you to be the adult, now," said Dr. Rosen, "and experience what it feels like to hold the little boy. Then, I want you to be the little boy and experience what it feels like to be held by a strong adult. Go back and forth, become the adult, then the child, then the adult again, and when you feel ready, let the two blend into one and open your eyes."

David cried for a long time. It was then that the core of the stone heart of David melted and he learned again to cry. It was then that Dr. Rosen, in his infinite wisdom, taught David not only to cry but to become a man.

☙

David looked at the dead German on the floor. He had kept his word to the little boy and had protected him. He held the young Arab man close to him. He was a child, and David would protect him also.

Ibrahim's sobs subsided, but he looked dazed, his eyes staring fixedly into space as if he didn't know where he was or what was happening to him. David looked at Mihali and shook his head. The Greek shrugged, but David could see deep compassion in his eyes.

"The boy needs help," said David.

"I know, but what can we do? We don't even know who the hell they are."

David nodded in understanding, "We'll have to find out, of course. In the meantime, we'll have to clear this mess. Mihali, my friend, how solid are you with the police?"

"Somewhat. I have never done any police work, but I do know a couple of higher-ups with whom I served many years ago. They were in intelligence, and when they returned from the army, they joined the police force in Salonica. Greek colonels, or even generals for that matter, can't really survive on their pension alone. This is how I got us the three guards for the hotel lobby."

Former generals in army intelligence, now serving with police forces, thought David. *Not my favorite kind of people, but then beggars can't be choosers.*

"Okay, can your influence get us a disposal team with no questions asked?"

"I can try," said Mihali, a man of few words. On the china chest, to which Streicher had tied Alysha's hands, stood a telephone, a rarity in a rural area. Mihali picked the telephone up, and David couldn't understand everything that he was saying; the Greek of his childhood was very rusty indeed. He sighed with relief when he saw the frown on Mihali's face disappear.

"Well?" asked David.

"It was touch-and-go for a while. He wanted to know what was going on, what the hell could I tell him? I couldn't even make up a story that would sound halfway plausible. But he believes that he owes me, and by God, maybe he does. We were two young officers, he was a first lieutenant, and I was a captain, and we were leading a platoon on a fairly perilous mission. We never made contact with the enemy, but he lost his footing and fell off the edge of a cliff, and I tell you, it was some cliff. We could see him from up above, and he looked all broken up. I believe that my men would have tried to go down and bring him up, but I did not want more than one man's death on my conscience. I was their commanding officer and responsible for their lives, so I asked them to lower me down to where he was. We tied together all the ropes we had, and by God, David, if he were two meters further down, he would have been a dead man. As it was, the rope was fifteen centimeters short. I managed to tie him securely, and they lifted him up. When my turn came to climb up the rope, a gust of wind swung me against a protruding rock, which damn near ripped my arm off. Both of us had the devil's own luck. Some lacerations for me and a few broken bones for him, nothing that time couldn't cure. So this is the story. I had to swear to him on my honor that this matter had nothing to do with the internal security of the country. Now, the team will be here in about fifteen to twenty minutes and we better be on our way before they get here."

"Mihali," said David, somewhat hesitantly, "is it possible that they keep the two bodies separately? I don't care what they do with this bastard, but the boy, well, he may want to take the girl's body back to their country, wherever that may be."

Mihali shook his head in mock disgust. "I am a step ahead of you, youngster. And by the way, what do you think back in America, that we Greeks are all barbarians? Yes, they will take care of that. Now we better go."

It was easier said than done. Ibrahim would not say a word but clung to Alysha's dead body, and it took the combined strength of David and Mihali to pry his fingers loose. As soon as his fingers lost their grip on the dead woman, his taut body seemed to relax, and he docilely followed Mihali while David brought up the rear. In the car, nobody spoke, and when they reached the hotel, they crossed the lobby rapidly and went directly to Venchiarutti's room. His relief was evident when they entered his room.

"My God!" he exclaimed. "Whatever happened to you? Five more minutes and I would have gone after you." For the first time, he noticed Ibrahim, who had been hidden by Mihali's huge body. "And who have we here?"

"Too long to explain just now," replied David. "What this young man needs is sleep. Mihali, do they sell over-the-counter sedatives in Greece?"

"Of course we do, what do you think we are? I'll go get some. With your Greek, they'll probably give you a laxative."

Ibrahim was slowly coming out of his daze by the time Mihali returned with the sedatives, and he seemed puzzled by the presence of the three men.

"You killed the German," Ibrahim said with a hoarse voice. "You also saved my life. For that, I thank you. I would have liked to kill him myself, but I couldn't. Why did you do it? To get the documents back?"

"You never had the documents, my friend," said Mihali, brusquely, as he handed the young Arab two sedatives along with a glass of water.

The young man slowly swallowed the two pills, chasing them down with water, and stared off into space, recollecting the events that had occurred that night. "But," he stammered, "the briefcase?"

"The briefcase was filled with old newspapers. The woman died, and you risked your life for nothing. We followed you to find out who you were. We don't like being robbed at gunpoint," Mihali gruffly explained.

Ibrahim closed his eyes for a long moment, then said, "All for nothing. Still, you could have let the German kill me. Why didn't you? Why didn't he?" He pointed at David.

"It is late," interrupted David. "Tomorrow, we'll talk about it."

Ibrahim tried to say something, but the sedatives were having their effect. The sedatives, Alysha's death, the day's events, suddenly caught up with the young man. He tried to stand up but instead fell back on the bed, breathing heavily, and before long, he was totally asleep.

"He'll be all right," said David. "Mr. Venchiarutti, if you don't mind, please use my room tonight. I'll grab a blanket and sleep on the sofa."

In the silence and the darkness, he reviewed the events of the day.

He had killed a man yet felt no regret, no remorse. The man he had killed was one of those who had murdered Liza and his parents, who had destroyed his childhood, the childhoods and lives of millions like him. He deserved to die, and that was now behind him. He gave more thought to the quirk of fate which had made him save the life of this Arab man, who, on that same morning, had tried to kill him. That poor bastard! David would not soon forget the sight of him holding the dead woman's body and rocking back and forth in grief and despair. It was that more than anything else that had enraged him. The repetitive cycle of death and murder of the weak by the strong. Well, he was one of the strong now and would and did use his strength to protect the weak. This did sound somewhat melodramatic, didn't it? The fact was, however, he was strong, and he hated the arrogant, strutting, domineering, cruel people who littered the world with corpses and despair. Maybe he didn't care so much about protecting the weak; maybe all he wanted was to cut the bastards down. It really didn't matter.

He also thought of the convent and the mother superior. It was hard to believe she and the man he had just killed were both Germans. He tried to remember the words she had said, "I tried not to become a murderess," or words to that effect. He marveled at her courage and her strength--a greater strength than his. Her way, however, was not his. Sleep was long in coming; there was something lurking in the back of his mind, and suddenly he remembered. The leak! How did the young Arabs know about the documents and about him? That part was easy. The information came from Richter and the planning was also probably his handicraft. Before dying, the German had practically said so. But how did Richter know about it? Where did he get the information? Where did the leak originate?

It was past three in the morning when David finally fell asleep.

Chapter 18

May

In the morning of the next day, they were all four in Venchiarutti's hotel room in a small sitting room adjacent to the bedroom. David had slept for four hours, devoted one hour to his karate exercises, and had shaved and taken a long, hot shower. Except for some bruises and aches where the German had managed to hit him, he felt like his old self again. Venchiarutti still looked tired, and the indestructible Mihali looked as fresh and rested as a baby after his nap. In fact, he had already managed to retrieve the young Arabs' luggage from their hotel and had stored them in the extra room which they had rented for the man.

"We have much to talk about," said David. "I suggest that rather than going downstairs for breakfast we ask room service to bring us something up here."

Mihali took everybody's orders, and the four men remained silent for a few moments, awkward, not knowing how to begin. The young woman's death and her brother's grief gave an altogether different tone to what could have been a straightforward interrogation. However, it had to be done. David cleared his throat and began.

"We must tell you, first, that we are so terribly sorry about your sister's death. That she was avenged means nothing. Hers is still a life cut at its beginning, and I have no words to assuage your pain except to tell you that I really know how you must feel. I had a sister killed many years ago by the likes of Streicher. Only she was just a child."

Ibrahim shot a surprised glance at him and nodded in acknowledgment.

"Much as we dislike doing this, we must know who you are, who sent you, and what you are after. After all, you attacked us, and we have not only the right but also the duty to protect ourselves."

166

Ibrahim shrugged and in a slow monotone said, "You already know what I can tell you. My name is Ibrahim, and my sister's name is Alysha. You know that my sister and I are P.L.O. operatives. Our mission was a simple one, yet we failed. It was to wait until your friend gave you some documents and take them. After taking them, we were to deliver them to someone at the address of that house. That is all."

"Can you tell me the name of your P.L.O. contacts in Athens and Beirut?"

"I can, but I won't."

"Do you know what these documents are all about?"

"I have no idea."

"Have you ever heard of Otto Streicher?" David asked.

"I have never seen him until last night and never heard his name before."

"Do you know who Von Eckardt or Richter is?"

"I have no idea."

Ibrahim's answers were straightforward and rang true. Ibrahim's contact with the P.L.O. was of no interest to David. He was going to continue his interrogation when Venchiarutti restrained him gently.

"I believe him, and I think I know what happened. I did not spend all my professional life advising prime ministers and high government officials. For many years, I interacted with people like Streicher and Richter. Believe me, it is not a pleasant experience, but at least I acquired some familiarity with how their minds work. I remember that, when we first met, David... My God! It was only about a week or so ago, yet I feel as if I have known you forever... Anyway, when we first met, you told me that, according to the FBI, Richter had several contacts with the P.L.O. and probably gave them money."

"Richter? He and Von Eckardt--are they the same man?" interrupted Ibrahim. The boy seemed slightly more animated and more interested in what was going on.

David answered. "Von Eckardt is a very wealthy American industrialist in Detroit who was persecuted by the Nazis before emigrating to the States from his native Germany. Only his real name is not Von Eckardt. It is Johann Richter, and instead of being persecuted, he was one of the worst persecutors, a former colonel in the SS. The documents which you and your sister were after contain irrefutable evidence of his true identity and his activities during the war. How they came to be in our possession would be too long to explain. And now I want to hear the end of what Mr. Venchiarutti was saying."

"I am sorry, Ibrahim," continued the old gentleman. "I should have explained to you about Richter and the documents. At any rate, what I think happened is this. Richter, probably... no, certainly, enlisted the help of the

P.L.O. in retrieving the documents, of course without telling them the nature of their content. Since he was a financial contributor to their cause, the P.L.O. was probably glad to comply. After all, it was a fairly simple request. Richter, however, was afraid that if higher-ups within the P.L.O. found out about how the documents implicated him, they might have tried to blackmail him. So, he made the necessary arrangements so that the briefcase would be delivered to his henchman who probably had a free hand to do what he wanted with the P.L.O. people. Streicher practically admitted this before he died."

"Whoever he is, Richter double-crossed my people, and as a result, Alysha is dead," Ibrahim said. "What will I tell my father?" For a moment his eyes filled with tears, and he tried to regain his composure.

"Is your father involved in this?" asked David. "You don't really have to answer, you know."

Ibrahim shook his head. "No, he is not. My father has been an invalid since he stepped on a mine several years ago. He is a kind man, a gentle man, and he didn't approve of what Alysha and I were doing, but he always let us make our own decisions. Alysha was closer to him than I was."

As usual, Mihali went to the heart of the matter. "We better decide what we are going to do."

David turned to the young Arab. "Would you mind waiting in the next room?" Ibrahim moved to get up, but then sat down again. "Aren't you afraid that I might run away?"

"No," said David with as much gentleness as he could muster. "You love your sister too much to leave without knowing what will happen to her remains."

Ibrahim nodded and left the room.

David poured coffee for Venchiarutti and himself. Mihali, of course, would consider it blasphemous to drink anything but the Greek thick syrupy coffee to which he was accustomed.

"Okay," David started. "First item on the agenda is, what do we do with Ibrahim?"

"I for one would opt for giving him a good kick in the behind and sending him back to where he came from," said Mihali. "We could turn him over to the authorities, but Mother Veronica would have to sign whatever charges will be filed, and I am not at all sure that she would want to do that. Besides, I don't know what we would gain by having him arrested."

"I agree with Mihali," intoned Venchiarutti. "Except for the kick in the behind. I believe that the horrible death of his sister has shaken him enough. How about you, David?"

"That is fine with me. He represents no danger to us, and I have no problem with letting him go. Now, the second item on our agenda is how to dispose of the documents. My instructions were somewhat loose, and it was left to my discretion. I can leave them with the CIA station chief in Athens, who will forward them in a diplomatic pouch, or I can hand carry them to Washington. On one hand, I would prefer to get rid of them as soon as possible. On the other hand, we all agree that there has been a leak somewhere, either within the CIA or at State. What we don't know is the nature, extent, and identity of the leak. Therefore, we don't know if it is really safe to send them home by diplomatic pouch. What I would like to do is get in touch with my CIA contact in Washington, discuss the matter with him, and see what he says. It is now ten in the morning, and I would like to wait until at least three this afternoon before calling him. That will be seven a.m. in D.C., and I know that he will be up and around. This will give us enough time to catch the five-thirty flight this evening to Athens. What do you think?"

Mihali and Venchiarutti looked at each other and smiled. "David," said the old Italian aristocrat, "we appreciate your asking our advice, but this is your show. I came to help you find the papers, and Mihali came because he is a crazy Greek. Now, you make the decisions."

"Okay," David answered, and he called Ibrahim from the adjoining room. "Ibrahim, we understand that you did what you thought was your duty, and we will not hold this against you. You are free to go, and if you will give us an address, Mr. Diamantopoulos here will see to it that your sister's body be sent there, unless you prefer that it be cremated. I will provide the funds necessary."

"No," interrupted Venchiarutti. "The funds that are available to you belong to the U.S. government, and God only knows what questions you may have to answer. Mihali and I will take care of these expenses. I have not consulted with Mihali, but I am sure that he will agree."

Mihali simply nodded, and before David could acknowledge the offer, Ibrahim said, "You are all very generous, and I am so sorry that we are enemies. Yes, I would like my sister's body to be sent back to Beirut, but I am not ready to go back yet, and you are right, of course, I have no money to pay for that." He turned to David. "Mr...."

"Please call me David," interrupted the American.

"David," continued Ibrahim, "you saved my life, you avenged my sister, you spared me the possibility of spending a long time in jail. You offered to pay for the return home of my dead sister's body. And you are a Jew. When I remember what I thought and said about Jews, I want to cut my tongue off and throw it to the dogs." Ibrahim went quiet, looking down at his hands for a long time before continuing. "How can I ever find the words to thank you?"

David suppressed a smile at the young Arab's flowery language, but he sensed his sincerity, and it touched him.

"Someday, Ibrahim, our two people will no longer fight each other, and then, maybe even before then, you may encounter a Jew in need, and you will help him. Your people are generous too. But you said something about wanting to wait before returning to Beirut. May I ask why?"

There was fire in the young Arab's eyes. "I want to go to America first. I want to see this man, this Von Eckardt or Richter, who betrays his friends and sentenced my sister to death. I want to see him face to face, to look into his eyes. Can you help me?"

"Ibrahim, this is a crazy idea," said Venchiarutti. "It will only make you feel worse. What can you do? And besides, these documents are all we need to put him away for a long, long time. In fact, forever."

Ibrahim did not answer but kept staring at David. Of course, it was a crazy idea, but damn if he couldn't understand the young Arab. He would feel the same way. In fact, wasn't his duel with the big German the previous day, in some way, what Ibrahim wanted? David had hurt people in his brief career with the CIA and in his work as a private investigator, but he never relished it, and whenever possible, he avoided it. There was in him the gift or curse of empathy, and he could feel and understand the feelings of other people, their rage as well as their sadness or sorrows. When he had fought Streicher, he had done what Ibrahim wanted to do. He had encountered the enemy face to face, he had looked in the eyes of not only Streicher and Richter but also into the eyes of all those who used their strength to inflict pain and despair on those who did not believe in fighting, to destroy the lives of those who wanted to build, to create, to love and live in peace. He was almost ashamed, almost--but not quite--of having enjoyed inflicting pain upon the German giant. He was almost sorry that their fight had not lasted longer than it did. Oh, yes, he could understand Ibrahim. But to understand how he felt was not enough. To allow an Arab, especially an admitted P.L.O. agent, into the United States was not the easiest thing in the world. However, maybe Bill... Well, he had to call him anyway.

"Ibrahim, what you are asking is not easy," he said suddenly. "However, I have to call a friend in Washington who wields some power. I'll ask him. That's all I can promise, okay?"

Ibrahim nodded.

"Very well," added David. "Let us all meet here at four o'clock sharp. It's a twenty minute drive to the airport. This will give us plenty of time."

℘

David had two more things to do before calling his friend in Washington. From a telephone directory, he got the address of the Jewish community center. It was some distance away, but he decided to walk. He could recognize nothing, no familiar landmarks, no buildings or stores he had ever seen before. It was a totally strange city, but still, it was the city where he was born, where he had spent the early and happiest years of his life. It was the same air that Liza and his parents had breathed before they were gone forever. He would probably never return to Salonica again, and somehow he wanted to experience it as much as possible, even though it seemed so alien to him.

Eventually, he reached the Jewish community center, a small, modern looking house on a quiet street. There were flowers all around it, and two large trees flanked it on either side. He was quite surprised to feel his heart beating somewhat faster. There was a mezuzah on the door. He rang the doorbell and entered without waiting for an answer. It was a large, cool, clean room with many pictures and posters on the walls. Against the wall was a large desk, and behind the desk sat a pretty young woman in her late twenties or early thirties with long dark hair and somewhat gray eyes. A beautiful combination, he thought.

Her smile was pleasant and welcoming. "May I help you?"

"Yes, I would like to see the president of the Jewish community. I don't even know his name. And I apologize for barging in unannounced, but I have a plane for Athens later this afternoon, and I have a communication of the utmost importance for him. Do you think he can see me?"

Her laughter was clear as crystal, and he immediately liked her. Somehow, there was something vaguely familiar about her, and he couldn't figure out what it was. Probably her tone of voice and her mannerisms were reminiscent of Liza's or Mother's.

"You are talking about Mr. Calderon, and of course, he will be happy to see you. We don't have many visitors these days, and he will be delighted to talk with someone from America. I can tell you are an American from your accent when you speak Greek. Aren't you?"

He smiled. "You are perceptive. Yes, I am from the United States. By the way, does Mr. Calderon speak English?"

"Yes, indeed! And quite well, I might say. After the war, he spent a few years in England before returning to Salonica. I'll tell him that you are here, but may I ask your name?"

David handed her one of his business cards. The card simply said David Castro, Ph.D., Private Investigator, and listed his Washington, D.C., address and telephone number. The young woman looked at it, seemed startled, looked at it again, then looked at him. Without any further words, she disappeared behind a door and returned a couple of minutes later.

171

"Please come in. Mr. Calderon is expecting you."

David entered a large, airy office with two wide open windows designed to let in air and sunshine. The office was Spartan; two chairs, presumably for visitors, sat opposite a desk, two chairs sat against the wall, and on the opposite wall stood a very large bookcase overflowing with books, the titles of which David was too far away to distinguish.

A man was sitting behind the desk and stood up as David entered. He walked up to him with an extended hand, saying, "Please come in, come in, Mr. Castro."

The man was not at all what David expected, but then, he really did not know what he expected. Calderon was tall, not as tall as David, but a good-sized man. He stood straight in spite of his age, which David estimated at 74 or 75. His build and short-cropped snowy white hair made David think of a retired marine sergeant, an impression belied by a very gentle face and slightly watery blue eyes with a hint of mischievous humor at the corners. In fact, he reminded David of Francesco Venchiarutti.

"Thank you, sir, and thank you for receiving me without a prior appointment."

"Nonsense," replied Mr. Calderon. "My days are not very busy, you know, and it is good to see someone from the outside." His English was flawless, with a slight but pleasant British accent.

"Please sit down and tell me what I can do for you, but before we get down to serious things..." He opened the door to the reception room and said "May, would you please call the coffee house and have them send up two coffees. How do you take yours, Mr. Castro?"

"Medium heavy," replied David.

Calderon returned to his desk. "Now to business. Is there some way in which I can be of help to you, Mr. Castro?"

"Mr. Calderon, does the name Johann Richter, SS Colonel Johann Richter, mean anything to you?"

"Richter, Johann Richter. Of course, that goes way back. Johann Richter, an SS colonel. I don't know whether he belonged to the Gestapo or the Rosenberg Commandos. Anyway, as far as I can remember, his job was to dispose of the properties which Greek Jews left behind. He was known as 'the vulture.' Like a vulture, he appeared on the scene as soon as apartments and houses were vacated. But why do you ask me this? Richter was killed shortly after the war, and as far as I know, nobody shed any tears."

"Mr. Calderon, Richter did not die. In fact, he is very much alive."

"What, what are you saying?" There was a light tap at the door, and May, the secretary, entered with a silver tray on which were two minuscule cups of coffee. The two men helped themselves to the coffee and remained silent for a few minutes after the young woman left the room.

David commenced. "What I will tell you is an unbelievable but true story known only to very few people."

"Before you continue," interrupted Calderon, "I must tell you that if my conscience or my honor require that I share with others what you will tell me, I will do so. I do not consider myself bound by confidentiality."

"That is how I would want it," replied David. "In fact, you will have to share with others what I will tell you. The only thing which I will ask you to leave out and keep confidential is the source of your information: that is, my name."

"Very well," nodded Calderon. "Your name will remain confidential."

"As you mentioned earlier, it was Richter's job to dispose of Jewish properties. What was not generally known is that Richter kept for himself a large part of what he was supposed to transfer to his superiors. Much of the dead Jews' liquid assets, including gold, diamonds, and other jewelry, found their way into Richter's pockets. He thus amassed an incredible fortune. At that time, there was a person in Salonica named Athanassopoulos. I believe, although I am not sure, that his first name was Dimetrios, Dimetrios Athanassopoulos."

"Of course," interrupted Calderon. "I remember the name. He was a collaborator and was executed by the partisans shortly after the liberation. What does he have to do with Richter?"

"Dimetrios Athanassopoulos was Richter's silent partner. He had warehoused Richter's loot, and when Richter left Salonica--I was told that the German army left Salonica quickly and with very little warning. When Richter left Salonica, Athanassopoulos moved the merchandise to a different location. What Athanassopoulos did not count on was that he would be arrested and sentenced to death. Apparently, a day or two before his death, Athanassopoulos had a change of heart and did not wish to carry to his grave the secret of this wealth. He asked to talk to a respected historian, Professor Assael."

"Yes," said Calderon as if following his own thoughts. "I knew of him. He survived the occupation by hiding in the Italian consulate. As you said, he was a highly respected and admired man. But as I recollect, he died in an unfortunate accident while visiting Israel, which, at that time, was still a British mandate."

"Yes," said David. "And that goes to the core of what I want to tell you. Athanassopoulos told Professor Assael the hiding place of the stolen treasure. Dr. Assael planned to give those instructions to duly constituted authorities in the Jewish community. At that time, I was told, chaos reigned."

Calderon nodded in assent.

"Unfortunately," continued David, "Dr. Assael died before being able to convey the information to the appropriate authorities, and the secret which he shared only with Athanassopoulos, who was already dead, the secret then died with him. It died, that is, until today. Mr. Calderon, I have here with me, in his own writing, Professor Assael's directions to the treasure and a description of the circumstances under which he acquired the information. This document gives the Jewish community of Salonica a legal as well as moral right over this property. I will give it to you under three conditions."

David stopped talking. The old man was no longer listening to him. He was leaning back in his chair, and his eyes were closed. David respected his silence and saw two small tears appearing at the corners of the closed eyes. Eventually, his eyes opened. Mr. Calderon shook his head as if annoyed by the two indiscreet tears. His voice was soft, almost a whisper.

"Mr. Castro, money, gold, jewels, remnants of our past. All this gold, all the diamonds in the whole universe cannot even begin to pay for the tears and blood that were shed. If it were up to me, I would tell you to leave the treasure where it is and forget about it. But the decision is not mine to make. You spoke of three conditions. What are they?"

"The first, as already agreed, is that my name will be kept out of this completely. The second is that there will be some public recognition for the late Professor Assael."

"And the third?"

"I realize that you cannot decide by yourself what to do with all this wealth. I imagine that this will be decided by a board of trustees or whatever in charge of the community's interests. What I will ask you is that you use your influence to see that some of the money goes to the IDF, the Defense Forces of Israel. You see, Mr. Calderon, I always believed, perhaps naively, that if we had actively fought the Germans, perhaps some of us would have survived. The IDF did just that."

Calderon stood up, walked around the room, stayed by the window for a long, long moment, then sat behind the desk again.

"Of course, I accept your conditions. But please, tell me, how did you come into possession of these documents?"

"This I cannot tell you. But I can tell you that it came into my hands in an honorable manner. I will also require a receipt for the document."

"Of course, Mr. Castro. You said earlier 'If we had fought, some of us would have survived.' Were you in Salonica during these days?"

"Yes, I was. My sister and my parents were killed, but I survived."

"Castro, Castro," mused Calderon. "There were many Castro's, but the one who comes to my mind is Isaac Castro, who, among other things, was also a distinguished newspaperman. Are you related to him?"

"He was my father," said David simply.

"I knew your father well, David--may I call you David? He was a bit younger than I. Still, I respected and admired him. Yes, he would have a son like you. He was a most unusual man."

"Thank you, sir."

Mr. Calderon, in bold handwriting, wrote a simple receipt, signed it, and gave it to David.

"Is this sufficient, or would you wish to have it signed by the members of the board?"

"No, Mr. Calderon, that is perfectly sufficient. And now, it is time for me to go." As he was about to leave the office, Calderon called after him.

"David, David. I am glad you survived, I am so glad." There was so much truth in that simple statement that David felt moved.

"Mr. Castro." He was about to close the door behind him and step into the sunny street when the young secretary's words stopped him.

"I'm sorry," David said. "I was still so absorbed by my conversation with Mr. Calderon that I forgot to say goodbye. Will you forgive me?"

The young woman paid no attention to his apology. "Mr. Castro, your first name is David. I know it from your card. I want you to tell me, did you have a younger sister named Liza?"

"Yes I did, but Liza is dead. But how do you know?"

"David, don't you remember me? Of course not. I was such a little girl. I am May, Jacques Cazes' sister."

His knees suddenly felt weak and wobbly. He held himself to the wall, then sat down. He was suddenly transported into the past in a much sharper and acute way than by his visit to the old house. But this time, together with the pain, there was an inexpressible, violent torrent of joy such as he did not remember ever having felt before. It was as if Liza had suddenly come back from the grave. Of course, that is why there was something so familiar about her. How couldn't he have recognized her? As the wave of weakness passed, he was flooded with memories.

Jacques Cazes was one of his two best friends. They had known each other since first grade, played together, fought together, grown together. The first day of their acquaintance had been memorable indeed. They were in first grade and played soldiers during recess. David was the general, and on the way home from school, like every self-respecting general, he had ordered Jacques to carry his lunch box. Jacques had chosen the biggest mud hole (it was raining on that day) and dropped David's lunch box in it, whereupon David had jumped on him, and when it was all over, they were covered with mud from head to toe. The fight had cemented their friendship. He remembered them as ten-year-olds playing chess on a small balcony overlooking the sea in Jacques' home. Jacques' father, a rotund, amiable gentleman, was a physician much respected in the community and a good friend of David's father. Both David and Jacques had sisters of the same age, and each was secretly in love with the other's sister, although they proclaimed to the world that they "hated girls." Jacques, his sister, and his parents had gone the way of David's mother's furniture and suddenly disappeared one day. David had, of course, assumed, that they had been killed.

He looked at May. She was standing, looking at him, tears silently streaming down her cheeks. He felt as if his heart would burst with happiness. He reached for May and hugged her, hugged her tight for a long time. He was just letting go of her when Mr. Calderon came from his office into the waiting room. He saw May's face streaked with tears, David's radiant smile, sensed that something unusual was going on, and looked at them questioningly.

"Mr. Calderon... Mr. Calderon, can you believe it? David and I grew up together. He was my brother's best friend. Can you believe it?"

"Oh, my God. Oh, my God!" said the older gentleman. "It's like a miracle. Look, it's almost noon, why don't you two find a place to have lunch together? You must have so much to talk about. I'll close the place up, and I'll be back by five p.m. May, take the rest of the day off."

Hand in hand, they walked through the sunny streets and sat at an outdoor café. They both were going through an unbelievable experience. It was all the ghosts of the past coming back to life, but this time it was real. Life was born again. Memories came flowing back and forth. *Do you remember this, David? Do you remember that, May?*

May's story was very simple. A gentile patient of Dr. Cazes had taken her in and hidden her from the Germans. Dr. Cazes, although living in Salonica, was a French citizen, and at the end of the war, May had gone to Paris and stayed with an aunt who had also managed to survive the Holocaust. While in Paris, May attended the Sorbonne and graduated with a degree in economics. Two years earlier, she had returned to Salonica to claim some property which belonged to her parents. The property had been taken over by a Greek family, and the legal wrangle took much longer than expected. To support herself, May had taken the job of Calderon's administrative assistant.

"So, Jacques and your father and mother were never heard from?"

"No, David, they probably died with Liza and your parents.   It would be so nice to think that they are all together."

David told her about himself, about his years in Athens, his army experience, his friendship with Bill, but he made no mention of Master

Kwang and his stint with the CIA. He briefly explained, with very few details, his reason for being in Salonica after all these years.

"And what are you going to do now, David?" asked May. "Go back to America?"

"Yes, I must, and as soon as I put some of my affairs in order, I will come back for you."

The words came out without thinking. He didn't regret having said them but he felt terribly anxious about having said them, and felt instantaneous relief when he saw the smile on her face.

"I'll wait for you. I'll be here or in Paris, and before you go, I'll give you both my addresses."

They exchanged addresses and telephone numbers and he walked her back to the Jewish community center building. As he hugged her goodbye, he was reluctant to let go of her; she symbolized so much for him, and he was afraid that he would lose it all for a second time.

It was a little after 1:30, and he had one more thing to do before returning to the hotel and calling his friend in Washington. This time, he hailed a cab and gave the driver the address of the convent. He knocked at the large wooden door, and the same pleasant sister opened it. She recognized him immediately, and instead of asking him to wait, she proceeded to take him to Mother Veronica's office. Mother Veronica was sitting behind her desk.

She must be a very wise woman, thought David. *She does not ask me what she can do for me. I wouldn't know what to answer.*

Instead, Mother Veronica simply smiled and said, "You are here, so the papers are safe. I really would like to know what happened."

David told her everything that had happened--the trap laid for the Palestinians, the fight with Streicher, the death of Alysha, and their decision not to turn Ibrahim over to the Greek police. Mother Veronica listened attentively, without interrupting, then said the very words which David expected to hear.

"That poor, poor child. You did well to help her brother. Yes, you did well."

"Mother Veronica," said David, "you said once, a hundred years ago, it seems, that you entered religious life so that you would not turn into a murderess. When I killed the German last night, I felt no regrets, no remorse. In fact, I wished that I could have killed him twice over. Yet, I am not a bad person, and I do not think of myself as a murderer. Please, talk to me some more."

Mother Veronica stared at him for a long, long moment, and David saw tears in her eyes. "You are a better person than I, David. You have killed in self-defense. You did not start the fight with the intent to kill. Perhaps you

177

have killed before, I do not know, but I am sure that you never intended to kill. Even when you want to kill, you cannot. You feel too much the suffering of others, and you are able to control yourself. I am different. My rage, my need for revenge were such that I knew I could not control them. I had a need, a deep-seated, uncontrollable need to destroy. I knew that I would have succumbed to it, that I wouldn't even have tried to fight it. The thought of killing the Nazi who had murdered my father, any Nazi for that matter, just the mere thought of it would give me the same excitement as an addict at the thought of getting his fix. And believe me, I have worked with addicts, and I know what I am talking about. But then I would have become a killer like them, and that was a thought worse than death. I had to look for controls outside of myself. I found them in my religious vows."

She is right, thought David. *If Streicher had not impaled himself on the knife, I would not have killed the bastard even though I might have wanted to, even though I felt nothing, except perhaps some satisfaction at seeing him dead.*

"So, my friend David, go in peace, and give my love and blessings to your two friends."

David took her hand and kissed it gently. "Thank you, Mother Veronica." He left with a lighter heart.

Chapter 19

Return to Athens

It was close to three o'clock when, back at the hotel, David made his phone call to Washington, and this time, he was put through to Bill fairly quickly; his friend was at his desk.

"David, are you all right? It has been a while, and since we heard nothing from you, I was beginning to worry."

"Hi, Bill! Everything is okay, and we are all fine."

"We?"

"Yes, Venchiarutti and a Greek friend of his. I'll explain when I see you, but in the meantime, I have a couple of small problems that need ironing out."

"Shoot."

"First of all, we have the merchandise. Everything was there as we expected. The problem is that we encountered opposition. Nothing that we couldn't handle, but the opposition was a step ahead of us at every turn. Therefore, there has been a leak: CIA, FBI, or more probably at the State level. I know for a fact that it was our German friend in Detroit who organized the opposition. Find the leak, Bill, and plug it as soon as possible. My second problem is related to the first one. What do I do with the merchandise? Is it safe to consign it at the embassy, or should I hand carry it?"

"Take it to the embassy and hand-deliver it only to the naval attaché commander, Joseph Clark. Joe is the station chief and an old friend of mine. He will see to it that whatever you give him reaches me personally. What is next?"

"I want your friend Joe to have ready an entry visa to the United States, valid for 10 days, for a P.L.O. agent named Ibrahim Khalid."

"A *what*?"

"You heard me, old friend. Another one of the things that I'll explain face to face. Just trust me."

"Okay, if you say so. When shall I see you?"

"In a couple of days. And how are Delores and my godson? Your parents and my friend Annie?"

"They are all fine. Annie is still pining after you, although you may now have a rival in the person of a young man with bell bottom jeans, sandals, and long hair who drives my father crazy."

"Okay," David chuckled. "See you all soon."

"It'll be good to see you again, Dave. Take care of yourself."

ℴ⇛

The phone call completed, David decided to wait for a while before rejoining this friends. He called room service for a beer and something to eat. His mind lingered on his conversation with Mother Veronica, and he remembered one of his sessions with Dr. Rosen.

"Once you told me that you are a Jew, Dr. Rosen, didn't you?"

"Yes, David."

"We are a great race, Dr. Rosen. No other race in history has contributed so much to humankind. Even Jesus was a Jew. Even after the Holocaust, when there are so few of us left, we still get disproportionate numbers of Nobel prizes in the sciences and in medicine."

"David, what are you trying to say? It's not like you to make such generalizations."

"You are right. What am I trying to say? I don't really know. All I know is that, at times, I feel so angry that we didn't fight back. Fifty thousand starved Jews in Warsaw kept the German army at bay for thirty days. They did a hell of a lot better job than the entire Polish army. Just imagine what six million of us could have done. Instead, we allowed ourselves to be massacred. Why, Goddamn it, why?"

"I don't know."

"Then what the hell *do* you know, Doctor?"

"I am wise enough to listen and learn. I was never in the camps, David, but you were. What did you learn? Tell me, and I shall listen."

"I learned that I must fight to remain alive. I learned that my life is as precious as anybody else's. I learned to protect myself. I believe in what Israel is doing. I believe that they will never again let the children of Israel die."

"Tell me, did everyone learn the same thing?" Dr. Rosen asked.

"No, there were those who learned nothing. They still did not believe in fighting back. They repulsed me with their prayers and their rocking and their prayer shawls. Like lambs offering their throats to the knife. They learned nothing."

"Would you have them stop praying, and would you want them to change their beliefs?"

"No, I guess not. Of course not. They were, they are of my people."

"And if today, you saw a hoodlum harassing a Hassidic Jew who refused to defend himself, what would you do?"

"Why, I'd flatten him."

"You see, my friend, the Nazis and those like them use their strength to impose their will on others, to stop them from praying when they want to pray and believe in what they wish to believe, while you, the Israeli soldiers and people like you, use your strength so that those who wish to pray and not fight can do so in honor and without fear, and in the case of us Jews, so that we can die in dignity and among our loved ones."

✑

Mother Veronica, thought David, *in your infinite wisdom, you knew that even though I had killed and would probably kill again, I had not become like them. I am glad our paths crossed.*

The telephone rang. "Four o'clock, Mr. Castro. There is a cab waiting." He took his carry-all and went down to the lobby. Ibrahim, Mihali, and Venchiarutti were waiting for him. Three stocky, well-built men were with them.

"David, Francesco and Ibrahim will fly with you to Athens," started Mihali. "I must stay a little longer to complete all necessary arrangements regarding Alysha and will rejoin you tomorrow or later today. These three gentlemen are friends of mine. They will follow you in another car and see you safely to the airport. *Sto kalo.*"

David nodded to the three policemen, went into the hotel safe, took out the new briefcase, and carefully checked its contents. Nothing was missing. They shook hands with Mihali, paid their bills, and got into the cab. Their ride to the airport and the flight to Athens were uneventful, and in less than an hour they had landed at Hassani Airport. They retrieved their baggage, and on their way to ground transportation, Venchiarutti suggested they drop him at the Grande Bretagne Hotel so that he could take a nap while David and Ibrahim went directly to the American embassy. David agreed wholeheartedly. Indeed, he was anxious to get Dr. Assael's memoirs off his hands as soon as possible. They dropped the Italian lawyer off and, at the same time, left their baggage in the lobby.

The American embassy was an imposing white structure, and at the gate was an even more imposing marine in dress uniform.

"David Castro for Commander Clark. I believe that he is expecting me."

"Please wait," said the marine, who returned a few minutes later and said, "Sir, would you please follow me?"

They walked through some interminable marble tiled hallways with pictures on the walls. Occasionally, what appeared to be aides or secretaries would scurry through, and eventually they reached a beautifully sculpted wooden door. The marine knocked at the door, let them in, and closed the door behind them. The office was a typical stateside CEO's office with its luxurious leather chairs and immense desk, a credenza loaded with what appeared to be coffee paraphernalia, and pictures of the president and the Secretary of the Navy on the walls.

"You might think it beats the deck of a destroyer, but after six months or so, it gets to you, and you'd give anything to be at sea again." Commander Clark came from behind the desk and shook hands with David and Ibrahim.

The latter was speechless and more than a little dazed. No wonder, thought David. After all the terrible things that had happened to him, to see himself, a P.L.O. operative, shaking the hand of a U.S. naval officer within the confines of the U.S. embassy was the stuff of dreams, or perhaps nightmares.

Commander Clark was a handsome, average-built man in his late forties. He was balding a little but otherwise showed no signs of aging.

The Navy believes in keeping its officers trim, thought David.

"How long have you known Bill Sanders?" asked the commander.

"We go back many years," answered David. "We were in the service together, then with the company. He is a good friend."

"He must be. From hearing him talk about you, one would think that you are someone very special."

"Aw, don't believe everything Bill tells you. He does tend to exaggerate, you know."

"No, he doesn't," said Commander Clark seriously. "You see, I have also known him for many years. That is why I consider it a privilege to be of assistance to you."

"Thank you," said David.

"This is a receipt for your briefcase. Since I do not know what should be in it, I'll take your word for that. If you give me Mr. Khalid's passport, I will affix the necessary visas. I think that will take care of everything. Oh, yes. Bill wanted me to let you know that your briefcase will be under the constant guard of my marines. Is there anything else that I can do for you?"

"That's all, Commander, and I thank you from the bottom of my heart."

Commander Clark's handshake was strong and friendly. "Good bye, Mr. Castro, good luck and have a safe trip back home."

When they were out of the building, Ibrahim let go a big sigh of relief. "Until the very end, I wasn't sure that they wouldn't arrest me. You must be a very important person."

"No," David said, smiling, "I am not important at all, but I have friends who are."

It was almost seven in the evening when they arrived at the Grande Bretagne and found out that Venchiarutti had booked an additional room for Ibrahim. As usual, David marveled at the old Italian aristocrat's sensitivity and open-handedness. There was also a message from Venchiarutti informing them that Mihali would arrive at nine and they would meet for dinner at the hotel's restaurant at nine thirty.

Ibrahim wanted to sleep. Since the death of his sister less than forty-eight hours earlier, he had not been quite able to assimilate what was happening to him. It was as if he was walking through a mist and not knowing exactly where he was going. And in that mist, there were two guiding beacons of light. One was his awe of David and his two friends. They were like giants, and how could he have thought of harming them? They had treated him like a younger brother, and that had sustained him through these dark hours. The other was his hatred for Richter. Whoever he was, he would be made to pay.

David, as was his custom, used an empty conference room in the hotel to go through his karate ritual. He felt light of heart, lighter than he had felt in a long time, and as usual, this affected his physical state. His moves were dazzling, powerful, and fast, his kicks were high and elegant. He was not practicing a series of prescribed moves; he was dancing. He was one with the world and with his heart. When he finished, bathed in sweat, he meditated for awhile.

Like wisps of smoke, images and memories came and faded. There was one, however, that kept intruding. It would come, fade away, then come back and come back again. He did not, of course, try to push it away, curious to know what would happen. The image stayed, crystallized--the picture of May. She was a beautiful woman. Her gray eyes contrasted oddly with her jet black hair. She also had a magnificent figure, and the figure and face would, occasionally, shimmer and be replaced by that little girl with the same gray eyes, a skinny little girl with a black pony tail; then she would become a woman again. When she vanished, David stood up.

It was a little after nine. He rushed through his shower, put on a pair of khaki slacks and a short-sleeved white shirt, and hoped that he would not be sent back to his room for more formal attire. He ran into Venchiarutti and Mihali as they entered the restaurant. They were seated without incident, although the head waiter arched his brow at the sight of David.

"They know that you are an American and that Americans have rather peculiar habits," whispered Mihali. "If you were a Greek, you wouldn't have gotten away with it."

Ibrahim joined them five minutes later, and indeed, he wore a light jacket and a tie which fit him rather well and rendered him quite handsome. The three older men smiled their approval. The presence of Ibrahim put a damper on what could have been a joyous celebration. Their mission had been accomplished at no damage to any of them. Alysha's death, however, hovered like a dark shadow over the reunion, and the grief of the young man was evident in the tears that every so often formed in his eyes and which he held back through sheer willpower.

"Ibrahim, your sister's body is in the best funeral home in Salonica," said Mihali. "Here are the address and telephone number. They will keep it until they get word from you and will ship it to Beirut at whichever address you give them. I know that your dead must be buried within 24 hours, but that was the best I could do. I am truly sorry and you might want to contact them right away. By the way, everything has been paid for."

The young Arab, too choked with emotion to speak, put his hand on Mihali's hand and nodded.

"And now," said Mihali, who never lost sight of serious things, "let us order."

They passed on their customary *ouzo* and instead ordered a bottle of *retsina*, a chilled white wine with a peculiar taste of resin, with heaping plates of *mezedes*, Greek appetizers, after which Ibrahim stood up suddenly.

"I am sorry, my friends, but I can't eat. Please forgive me. I must return to my room."

"Of course." David nodded, then he added, "There is a direct TWA flight tomorrow around noon. If we decide to take it, will you be ready?"

"I will, the sooner the better. Goodnight, my friends."

After Ibrahim left, the three friends remained silent for awhile, unable to shake the pall of sadness which Ibrahim's presence had cast upon them.

"The poor kid, the poor little kid," said Venchiarutti finally. "What a horrible thing to go through. Why must there be so much suffering, so much pain in this world?"

"What I like about you, Francesco," said Mihali, "what I like about you is that you don't just lament the ills of the world. You do something about it, sometimes at the risk of your life. As for Ibrahim, I feel sad for him also. But he knew, both he and his sister knew, what they were getting into. This is a deadly game, and when you lose, you pay with your life."

He is right, thought David, *and if I had had to do it to protect Dr. Assael's documents, I would have killed Ibrahim and his sister without hesitation.* Those are the rules of the game. But in their case, the rules were not followed. They were betrayed by their own people. Not only could he understand Ibrahim's rage and grief, but because of Liza, his own sister, he felt a real bond with the young Arab.

They ordered roast lamb for Mihali and David, layered eggplant for the Italian diplomat, and a large country salad for all three of them. The waiter also brought two bottles of red wine.

This will be a memorable night, thought David.

And indeed it was. They talked until long past midnight, the old Italian lawyer and the Greek mountaineer outdoing each other with their war stories, their memories of Mavropotamos, the small village in the mountains where their lives had intersected and which had brought them so close to each other.

"I remember that evening in the *cafeneion*, in the village square, when you showed us the picture of your wife and son. I thought to myself then, 'He is a good man. Even an enemy can be a good man.' Then, when we saw all the evacuation and execution orders, I was enraged and felt betrayed. You see, Mihali is never wrong. I was right all along. You are a good man, Francesco, a good man and a good friend."

Mihali told them about his years in the army, the years of happiness with his wife, his sorrow at having lost her, and how close he had come to taking his own life.

"I stayed alive for my daughter. She needed me, and I am glad today to be alive. She is everything a father could wish. I told you that she is in Philadelphia studying medicine. She wants to become a pediatrician. She loves children. She has a boyfriend, another medical student, and they are talking about getting married. I met the boy last fall. I like him. He is a good boy, and he is Jewish. Well, maybe I can convert him, and if I can't convert him, maybe I can teach him to drink *ouzo* instead of those abominable drinks that you drink in America. Here, David." He scribbled a few words on a piece of paper. "Here, her name is Despina, Despina Diamantopoulos, and these are her address and phone numbers. Call her when you go back to America, and be prepared for a high phone bill. She will want to ask you a million questions. Also, if you ever go to Philadelphia, I want you to check this young man out. I wouldn't want him to marry Despina and then have to break his bones for not being a good husband to my little girl."

David could not suppress a smile. "You bet I will, Mihali. In fact, I promise that I will make a special trip to Philadelphia and check out your future son-in-law."

It was then Francesco Venchiarutti's turn. The after-war years had been kinder to him than to most people. Because of his known anti-fascist leanings, his father had quickly risen to a position of prominence in local, then national politics. He had died in his sleep in the late fifties, shortly followed by his wife. Francesco was never attracted by politics and went back to practicing law. Since he was independently wealthy, he could be choosy and do only what he liked to do. As it turned out, he gravitated toward corporate law, consulting, and mediation. Because of his impeccable integrity, he became widely known and respected, a familiar figure at international negotiations involving the Italian government.

"I was lucky and spared unhappiness. My wife, Stella, is still the most beautiful woman in the world, and our son, Bruno, is a physicist, and he does and teaches research in Rome. We have two grandchildren, Laura and Claudio, and guess what, Mihali? I still flash their picture around." Francesco Venchiarutti was not bragging. The photograph showed a stunningly beautiful woman in her late fifties or early sixties with a patrician head and a slim body and on each side of her a young couple and two young children. The young man showed a remarkable resemblance to the old Venchiarutti, while the two children favored their mother.

"How about you, David? Tell us about you."

"There isn't much to tell, my friends. You already know about my experiences in the camp and the death of my parents, and you know, I no longer feel the urge to talk about those days. It's strange. I went through stages. For a long time, I couldn't talk to anyone about those days, although they haunted me day and night. Then, I felt a need to share these memories with people I liked and who liked me. And now, for quite some time, I no longer wish to discuss those days. I can if I have to, but somehow I have made my peace with these memories, and I no longer wish to touch them."

Instead, he told them about his friendship with Bill and some of his CIA experiences which were not classified and which he felt free to share. He also told them of his relationship with Master Kwang and the role of karate in what he called "his recovery."

The latter intensely interested the former Greek colonel. The duel between David and Streicher had fascinated him. A fighter himself, he could appreciate fighting men and David's strength. His ability as well as his agility had left an indelible impression on him.

"Your teacher, Master Kwang, must have been a remarkable person. How old was he?"

"I never knew his exact age. You are right, he was a remarkable person. At the same time, a very tough and very gentle man. In some ways, you remind me of him, Mihali. You are both capable of ruthlessness and great tenderness. He spoke very little..."

"In that respect," interrupted the Greek, "he was not like me at all."

"No, I guess not," said David, smiling. "But he had a way of expressing his feeling without words as eloquent as yours with words. When he and I parted, he was around seventy-five or seventy-six years old. As I said, I never knew his age for certain. In our sparring session, he could toy with me like a cat with a mouse. He must be in his mid-eighties now, and I am sure that he still can."

"I would have loved to meet him," Mihali said.

"And I am sure that he would have liked you very much. He could read people at first glance."

"My friends," interrupted Venchiarutti, "I am not as young as you are, and I need my sleep. David, if you wish, I could get you two first class seats on that TWA flight. The plane is half-empty, I was told, or you can stick around for another day or two. What do you prefer?"

"I know it's a little abrupt," answered David, "but I think that we shall leave tomorrow. I wish to go home, and I want to put Ibrahim safely back in a plane for Beirut. His visa allows him only seven days in the States."

"All right, then, we'll meet in the lobby tomorrow morning at eleven a.m. The plane, I believe, leaves at one p.m. Good night, then, my friends."

The old gentleman stood up and left, followed closely by David and Mihali.

Chapter 20

The Way Home

It was nine-thirty a.m. on the next day when David spotted Ibrahim in the lobby. Venchiarutti and Mihali would probably sleep late.

"Come on, Ibrahim, let us have breakfast."

They sat at a small table, a little out of the way, and David realized that he and the young Arab were alone for the first time.

"Why have you helped me and done so much for me?" asked the young Arab. "Alysha and I would have killed you if necessary to get the papers."

"I know, and you also know that I would have killed you both to protect the papers."

"Then why?"

"I don't know. Perhaps because you no longer represented a danger to us. Perhaps because my own sister was killed. Perhaps because I don't like a big man to abuse others. Who knows?"

"Still," insisted Ibrahim, "this does not explain why you were so good to me after you saved my life. You know, we were told so many bad things about the Jews. I guess my father was right. You are just people like us, perhaps a little better. I don't know. What I know for sure is that I'll never hate Jews again. Still, I will continue to fight for my people. You understand."

"Of course, I understand," replied David. "Someday we may still find each other at the opposite ends of a gun, but I hope that such a day will never come. In the meantime, we can be friends. But tell me," he added, changing the topic, "Why is it so important for you to see Von Eckardt?"

"I want to see his face. I want to see the look in his eyes when I call him a murderer and a traitor. I want to put my hands around his throat and strangle him. I want to see him dead and know that it is I who killed him. I want to see him dead and spit on his body."

David nodded, "I understand, and often I have felt that way. You know, I don't speak Hebrew, but I was told about a Hebrew word: *Rachamim*. I don't know its precise meaning, but I believe it means something like mercy, compassion and forgiveness, all put together. I always thought that it was a beautiful word but alien to me. At the same time, it is something that I would want to understand, and if someday I can achieve it, I'll feel that I will have become a better person. Hey, look who is there. Mihali and Mr. Venchiarutti are finally awake."

ço

It was time to part. The plane was beginning to board. Ibrahim stood a little aside and watched them curiously. The three men seemed to have a hard time letting go of each other. They had known each other for only a few days. They had known each other all their lives, for all three were men of strength and understanding, of courage and integrity, of violence and compassion. They were human beings in the full sense of the word, and they had encountered the reality of each other. Each had seen part of himself in the other two, and they had become brothers.

"Last boarding call..." said the loudspeaker.

"Good bye, Mihali. Good bye, Mr. Venchiarutti. Thank you."

David hugged the two men and felt tears forming in the side of his eyes, and the eyes of his friends seemed misty also, or was it the effect of the sun of Athens?

"Let's go, Ibrahim."

The young Palestinian ceremoniously shook the hands of the two men. "Thank you, thank you very much," he said and followed David onto the plane.

The first class seats were wide and comfortable, and the plane was half empty. Ibrahim soon fell asleep, and after awhile, David asked the stewardess for a tablet and wrote these words:

> *Dr. Rosen,*
> *It has been a long time, and this is my first letter ever to you. I know that in spite of time and distance you still remember me--maybe not as clearly as I remember you, but then, I did not affect your life as you affected mine. And even as I write, I wonder. Am I really writing because I want you to know what I am doing, or am I writing because I want to clarify*

189

my thoughts and feelings and writing is the next best thing to talking with you? I suspect that it is mostly the latter with a little bit of the former. Well, does it really matter?

Right now, I am on a plane from Athens going to Washington. I just completed a mission in Salonica. Yes, Salonica, you read it right. As missions go, this one was fairly simple and straightforward. In terms of the emotional upheaval which it generated, that is another story, and that is what I wish to talk to you about.

I visited my home, the one I told you about so many times. It is old now, old and decrepit, and it will be demolished soon, and you know what? I really don't care. In a way, it's very symbolic (although I can hear your voice saying "David, stop intellectualizing."), but it is true. It is symbolic of a past which is gone, will never come back, and must give way to the future. And yet, how can one forget the past?

Well, something extraordinary happened. I don't remember ever telling you about my friend Jacques Cazes. Jacques and I went to school together since first grade. He had a sister about Liza's age, a skinny little girl with pigtails named May. I was secretly in love with May, while naturally, Jacques was secretly in love with Liza. I was certain that they had been killed, and all these years, I seldom thought of them. Well, Dr. Rosen, May survived, and I ran into her. How would make an interesting story, but it would be irrelevant and too long to write about. Suffice it to say that I met her again, and my heart almost burst with joy. It was as if Mom and Liza had suddenly come back to life. It was the most extraordinary feeling that one can imagine. Ever since, I haven't stopped thinking about her. All these days, she has been consistently in my heart and in my thoughts.

"All these days," what am I talking about? It has only been two days. I am in love with her--not I think I am in love with her--I know that I am in love with her. Yet, I am bothered. Am I in love with the person she really is? Am I in love with a dear past which she

*resuscitates? Am I in love with the beautiful woman
that she is? Am I in love with the skinny little girl that
she was? Or perhaps I am in love with her because
she is at the same time the past, the present, and the
future? The skinny little girl and the beautiful woman?
Or does it matter??*

*All I know is that since I met her there is a feeling
of happiness in me such as I did not know could exist.
I trust that you are well, Dr. Rosen, and that many
other Davids have followed me in your office and have
left as I did, not healed but healing, not happy but
hopeful. So many times I keep rehearsing our meetings
in my head, partly because it helps, partly because I
have no one. Maybe someday, in the very near future,
I will have someone to talk with when I am troubled
and sad, late in the evenings or in the middle of the
night. Then, I shall relegate our sessions with my other
memories, to be kept preciously, but revisited rarely.*

*Affectionately,
David Castro*

He did not reread what he had written. The words had flowed, and
he knew that he had written exactly what he felt. It was only business and
professional correspondence and articles that needed rereading and rewriting.
He looked at Ibrahim asleep by his side, and his eyes closed also. It was one in
the afternoon when the plane landed in Washington, D.C.

ભ

It was a beautiful day in Washington, warm but not too humid. He had
slept on the plane and felt refreshed and rested. Orange juice, good American
coffee, and two croissants before deplaning had done the trick. It felt good to
be home again and to see Bill's face smiling but looking a little anxious. Bill's
presence, in some miraculous way, facilitated all customs and immigration
formalities.

The two men embraced, and David's first words were, "The
documents?"

"Safely tucked away," replied Bill, and David heaved a long sigh of
relief.

This was it then. Mission accomplished. Now he could look after his own interests. He introduced Bill and Ibrahim to each other and his friend knew better than to ask questions. All in due time. Bill had made reservations for Ibrahim at the Mayflower.

"I can pay," said Ibrahim. "I have money left."

David had planned to shoulder all of Ibrahim's expenses, but he sensed the young man's pride.

"Okay, but if you need extra money, let me know, and when you go home, you can send me the money back by wire transfer."

Interesting, thought David, *he did not seem to mind the money spent on him by Mihali and Francesco Venchiarutti. Perhaps because I am American and a Jew, twice the enemy. Or perhaps simply because they are so much older than he is.*

It really did not matter; he just wanted to protect the young Arab's sensitivity yet make sure that he would not lack in anything. They drove him to the Mayflower and helped him register.

"Ibrahim," said David, "you have a day and a half to yourself. Rest, visit Washington, and if you need to get in touch with me, here are two telephone numbers at which you can contact me. The day after tomorrow, early in the morning, we'll fly to Detroit. Afterwards, you can either go back to Beirut right away or you can stay for a few more days in Washington."

"I want to get back to Beirut as soon as possible, because of Alysha, you understand. Perhaps there is a plane day after tomorrow in the evening?"

"I understand." David nodded. "Of course, I'll do my best, and I'll pick you up here at seven-thirty a.m. day after tomorrow. Goodbye, Ibrahim."

"Goodbye, David."

Back in the cab, the two friends looked at each other with evident happiness. It had been only a few days since David had left Washington, but so many things had happened that those few days seemed to David like an eternity. As for Bill, he had been truly concerned about his friend's safety. The mission seemed easy, but Bill was quite aware of all the possible unpleasant ramifications whenever former Nazis were involved.

"You are in luck, David," he said with his usual friendly smile. "Mom, Dad, and Annie are visiting us from Pittsburgh, so you will get to see all of them together."

"Will you have room? Perhaps I should reserve a room at the Hilton."

"Yes, perhaps you could, but who is going to face the wrath of Annie and your godson, not to mention Delores and my parents? No, I think that for your own safety and mine you better come to the house."

David smiled. "Okay, whatever you say! I would not want to be responsible for all this mayhem. But before we go home, you and I better go somewhere quiet and have a heart-to-heart talk. This way, we won't have to talk shop when the family is there."

"You got it." Bill turned the car around onto a side street and eventually stopped at Angelo's, a small, nondescript Italian restaurant ensconced between two large buildings. "I know the owners," said Bill. "They are nice folks, and we can just have a glass of wine, then go home for dinner."

The dining room was minuscule but empty; it was still too early for the dinner crowd. The tables with the usual red and white checkered tablecloths gave it a warm and friendly flavor. Angelo himself came to greet them and gave Bill a bear hug.

"Angelo, we are here for just a glass of wine, and I want you to meet David, the best friend I ever had."

"Any friend of William is a friend of mine. Sit down, sit down, I'll bring you a Chianti that you will write home about." The Chianti was indeed superb, reasonably dry, cool without being cold. After Angelo ceremoniously opened the bottle and went through the tasting ritual, he filled the glasses and left the two friends to their own devices.

"Okay, David, take it from the top."

David spoke for a long time. He related the events of the past few days without omitting any detail, even when he deemed these details unimportant. He told Bill about his initial meeting with Francesco Venchiarutti, his encounter with the two Greeks in his hotel room, their kidnapping at the hands of the villagers of Mavropotamos, the "trial" of Venchiarutti, and the ensuing friendship that developed primarily between Mihali and the Italian lawyer and secondarily with himself. He told him about their trip to Salonica, their visit to the convent, and how they had been set on by the two P.L.O. agents.

"I knew that something was amiss as soon as we got off the train in Salonica. You know what I mean, the feeling that you are being shadowed, that you are being watched. Yet, I could see nobody. Either these guys were pretty good, or I was imagining things. The attempt at the convent pretty much convinced me that there was a leak somewhere, and I let you know as fast as I could."

"I know," interrupted Bill. "And you'll be glad to know that the leak has been plugged."

"What?" exclaimed David. "How is it possible?"

"Well, as you know, we are super-people. All kidding aside, the FBI had suspected for a long time that classified information regarding former Nazis was reaching the Nazis in some unknown way. Interpol and German police and intelligence sources had reached the same conclusions. Eventually, suspicions centered upon Steve Harper, the guy you met at the Shoreham with Tom Scorcese. The fact that he was assigned to the Von Eckardt case is another classic example of government snafu, the right hand not knowing what the left was doing.

"Anyway, Harper came to see me on the same day you called to let me know that you had the documents. In fact, I talked to him shortly after I hung up. He said that he wanted to talk to me off the record about an important matter and wanted my word that our conversation would remain confidential. I refused, and he finally relented, and we went out to lunch. I felt sorry for the guy. Apparently, he was heavily in debt and needed money to pay for his daughter's medical school tuition. As we had gathered, Richter was paying him for information that might have helped former Nazis escape arrest and deportation. His life has been a living hell since his pact with Von Eckardt, and he has been wracked with guilt at the possibility that you might have been killed in Richter's attempt at stealing the documents. After my talk with him, I called the embassy, and my friend Joe Clark told me that you had left and the documents were safely in his possession. I felt greatly relieved, since Richter was after the documents and not after you. Anyway, that is the story."

"What happened to Harper?" inquired David.

"Not much. We did not have enough evidence to indict, let alone convict him. He was very careful not to leave a paper trail of any kind. He will resign his position at State and live with his conscience for the rest of his life. I don't envy him."

"Okay, enough of Harper and let me get back to my story." David then told him about the trap they had laid for the Palestinians, his fight with Streicher, and the manner in which the man had died. He told him about the rape and murder of Alysha, their joint decision not to turn the young Arab over to the Greek police, and Ibrahim's insistence at coming to the States and confronting Richter. Finally, he described his visit to the embassy and the turnover of the papers to the naval attaché.

Bill listened in rapture. He poured some more wine. "That is some story. I only wish I had been there with you. But what was your reasoning in bringing this P.L.O. guy back with you? You know that I wouldn't have done that for anyone but you. What will he gain by confronting Richter? What if he kills him? Then we'll really be in the soup."

"You are absolutely right, Bill, and it was an impulsive gesture on my part and one hard to explain. You know how many times I had fantasies of grabbing by the throat those who killed my parents and sister, of looking them in the eye and asking, 'Why?' Ibrahim was betrayed, his sister was raped and killed by the same people. True, the perpetrator died in front of him, but he seems to believe--and I agree with him--that the real murderer is Richter, and he wants to look at him. Besides, I'll be with him at all times. I don't believe you have to worry about him."

"Okay, let's go home." Bill picked up the check and started to get up.

David stopped him. "Not quite yet, my friend. There are two more things that won't go into my official report that you must know."

Bill shot him a quizzical look. "My God, David, you look serious. Okay, let us have one more glass. What is it?"

"One thing that neither the Mossad nor you or I were aware of was that Richter had not been a model of Teutonic integrity. As you know, his duties were to dispose of all goods and properties which the Jews left behind when they were taken away. Richter, or SS Colonel Richter as he was then known, diverted to his own use a large part of the loot. He had a Greek associate who warehoused the stolen properties. When the Germans had to flee Salonica, the Greek transferred everything to a different location and never shared the whereabouts of the new location with Richter. Bill, I found the instructions to the new location as I was transferring the documents from the old briefcase to the new one. I believe that the rightful owners of all this money are the few Jewish survivors still in Salonica. They lost not only all their dear ones but also everything they owned. I took it upon myself to take the document and hand-deliver it to the president of whatever is left of the Jewish community in Salonica. If I hadn't, it's certain that they would still get it in several years, and by then, they would all be dead of old age. Anyway, that is how I handled it, and if you wish me to, I'll include this in my official report."

Bill continued to sip his Chianti in silence for several seconds, then said, "My old friend, we'll share the risk and the satisfaction of knowing that it was in our hands, especially yours, to do some good, and we did it, and screw the system. As far as I know, this conversation never happened. I am sure that the rest of the documents are sufficient to extradite, indict, and convict Von Eckardt ten times over. Now, what is the second item?"

"Bill, do you remember my mentioning a childhood friend, Jacques, with whom I played chess at the age of nine?"

"Yes, of course. I also remember my telling you that you were crazy playing chess instead of baseball. But what about him?"

"Jacques had a little sister, a skinny little girl with pigtails with whom I was, of course, desperately in love. Bill, I found her."

"You what? Are you saying that your friend survived?"

"No, they were all killed. May alone survived, having been hidden by a Greek gentile woman. When I visited the Jewish community in Salonica to share my information about the treasure, she was there. She was the assistant to Mr. Calderon, the Jewish community's president. She is no longer a skinny little girl with pigtails but a very beautiful woman. I have only known her for three days, but cliché as it may sound, I feel as if I have known her all my life. In fact, I *have* known her all my life, with a long interruption. Bill, as soon as I take care of a few things here, I am going back for her. Maybe as soon as next week."

"David, do you think your feelings toward her have something to do with Liza?"

"I have given it a lot of thought, and frankly, I don't know. Then, I thought to myself, 'Does it matter?' I don't even know if I am in love with her. I don't even know what that means. All I know is that when I am with her, I feel whole. Do you remember once, a long time ago, you got angry with me when I said that even though I feel deeply the love that you and your family have for me, I would always feel on the fringes, that there would always be something missing? Well, when I am with May, there is nothing missing. She is the last piece of the puzzle." David was surprised to see a brimming of tears in his friend's eyes.

"David, I am dying to meet her so that she also can become part of us. Let's go home."

As always, David was moved to tears by the reception which awaited him. Mrs. Sanders' hug and kiss were as affectionate as those she reserved for her son. Mr. Sanders shook his hand, and Delores, Bill's wife, opened the door with a glass of *ouzo* in her hand before David even had time to sit.

"David, mi hermano!" she exclaimed. "I am so happy to see you."

What then sounded like a cavalry regiment made all heads turn. It was Annie, bounding down the stairs like a wild, healthy animal. Annie was no longer a nine-year-old but an attractive teenager with the obligatory braces. David felt a little embarrassed when, oblivious to all decorum, she jumped on David's lap as if she were still the child of old. Bill caught David's momentary awkwardness and chuckled but said nothing. It was at that very moment that the doorbell rang. In a flash, Annie was off David's lap and at the door.

"Uncle Dave, I want you to meet my boyfriend, Ted. Ted, this is my Uncle David. He is the greatest karate champion in the whole world."

David repressed a smile and looked Ted over critically. Ted, all of sixteen, was a tall, lithe youth with fashionable long hair and neatly and cleanly dressed. He had an open face and a friendly smile but wore sandals and bell-bottom jeans. That was what bent Annie's father out of shape. Well, we can't all be perfect, can we?

He extended his hand to the young man. "I am very pleased to meet you."

The boy shook David's hand vigorously, with an obvious sigh of relief, and said, "Thank you, sir." Before David could formulate an adequate sentence, Ted and Annie had vanished.

Well, thought David philosophically, *that is what I get for becoming a decrepit old man. But there is always Frank.* "Where is my godson?" he exclaimed.

"Karate class," answered Delores. "And it is all your fault. Bill just went to get him."

It wasn't long before the doorbell rang again and Frank ran in, resplendent in his ghi with a green belt, which his father had asked him not to take off so that David could see it. He was a tough-looking five-year-old with short-cropped blond hair and the dark eyes of his mother. His shoulders were square, he stood straight, and when he saw David, he ran to him with squeals of delight.

"Uncle Dave, Uncle Dave!"

It was one of the finest evenings in David's life. He was wanted, loved, and it would have been perfect had he had May by his side. But this would come before long. In the meantime, he abandoned himself to complete and utter relaxation and well-being. It was late when he said his goodbyes before retiring and promising to return very soon. Bill accompanied him to his room and took out of his pocket a .38 snub-nosed revolver.

"I know that you dislike firearms, but with people like Richter, you never know. Better be prepared. Here is also a permit to carry. This will get you through the airport."

જ

The next day dragged on interminably. David had given himself a full day to write his report, to recuperate and take care of matters that might have arisen since his absence. He kept a minuscule office in Washington without the luxury of a secretary. Nothing, however, awaited him except a few bills, which he paid. He had left the Sanders' early in the morning while they were all asleep, wanting to avoid prolonged goodbyes and having to explain why he wasn't staying with them.

It was early afternoon when he dialed the number of Despina Diamandopoulos, Mihali's daughter in Philadelphia. Mihali, of course, was right. Despina kept him on the telephone for over forty-five minutes, thirsty for every detail he could remember regarding Mihali. The young woman's deep love for her father was so evident that it warmed David's heart and made him feel that he would be blessed, indeed, if a child of his would someday love him the way Despina loved Mihali or--and the thought suddenly came to him--the way he loved his father.

He had to promise Despina that he would come to visit her in Philadelphia and "check her boyfriend out."

She laughed and said, "I can hear the words of my father."

He then locked his small office, checked himself into a small hotel in Bethesda, spent two hours practicing karate, showered, and rang room service for a steak, fries, and two beers. He called Bill to let him know where he was and fell asleep, dead to the world.

Chapter 21

Tomorrow

He arrived early at the Mayflower and was surprised to see Ibrahim already waiting for him at the hotel restaurant. The boy looked more rested but nervous.

"I went to bed very early, I was so tired. So I woke up early and came down for coffee."

David was at a loss for words. He truly liked the young Arab. There was something honest, dignified, and proud about him, and David was sad at the knowledge that sooner or later Ibrahim would die, perhaps not in the brutal way in which his sister had died, but he would die anyway. David was uncomfortable and terribly conflicted at the thought that Ibrahim looked up to him and felt in his debt.

As if he had read his thoughts, Ibrahim said, "It is so hard for me to think of you as the enemy, David. You are so strong and so gentle, and sometimes I feel like a younger brother to you. You have saved my life, avenged my sister, and, with your two friends, helped me through these horrible hours. I cannot hate you, ever. But you are a Jew. Your people took our homes, and someday, I may have to kill you or at least try. I'd rather kill myself first."

"Ibrahim, I am not your enemy, nor are my people. Yet, I understand why you believe that. Perhaps, in your place, I would feel the same way. Still, there is something that I must try to explain. You just lost a sister. Imagine if, at the same time, you had lost your father and mother, your grandparents, your cousins, all your school friends--all at the same time--and you were put in a camp. Not a refugee camp, mind you, but a death camp, which you could leave only as smoke through a crematorium, a camp where a crust of bread was an inestimable treasure, where guards could and would shoot you for target practice. Imagine, then, being the only member of your family to survive, you and a few more like you. First, you don't want to live. You feel guilty for being alive. You want to die also. Then, you get angry, and you swear that what happened to you will never happen to your children and your children's children. That is what happened to me. That is what happened to my people. Some of us, like me, chose to come to America, but most of us who survived went to Israel. They believe that the land still belonged to them after being dispossessed for two thousand years. They were willing to share the land, but their neighbors were not, and when Israel was declared a nation, it was invaded by Arab armies. The Jews fought and, in the process, occupied what they had initially been willing to share. And who can blame them?"

Ibrahim listened patiently and intently, then replied, "My father said that, at the beginning, we wanted to take what belonged to the Jews, and in so doing, we lost what was ours. That may be so, but we still want what is ours back, and we shall fight for it."

"And maybe you will get back what is yours. But does it have to be at the point of a gun?"

Ibrahim chuckled. "My father also told me once that we could achieve our goals if we go back to Israel with a branch of an olive tree. The two of you would make a fine pair, and we would spend the rest of our lives arguing."

"Well, Ibrahim, maybe age has made us wiser, and someday I would truly enjoy meeting your father. But on another topic, my friend, this evening, or tomorrow at the latest, we shall pay a call to Mr. Von Eckardt, that is, Colonel Richter. What do you think will happen?"

"I don't know. I truly don't know. When I think of Alysha lying half-naked in a pool of blood, I feel myself going mad. I want to kill him. As I told you before, I want to see him dead at my feet, know that I killed him, and spit in his face. That is how I feel, but I know that in your country that is impossible. Maybe I just want to see him, just see how a monster like him looks."

"I understand, Ibrahim, because this is how I feel and have felt for a long time. Most of the time, I can control my anger, but sometimes I can't. You know, I don't speak Hebrew, but once, a long time ago, I ran into a Jewish army chaplain, and we spent an evening together. There was a Hebrew word which he told to me and which I mentioned to you two days ago. I couldn't figure out its exact translation. The word is *Rachamim*, and as I told you, I believe that it means forgiveness, compassion, and mercy all rolled into one. I always thought that to show *Rachamim* was to reach the highest level of humanness and decency. I don't think that I am capable of it... Well, we better get moving if we want to catch that plane."

As the two men stood up, a bellboy approached them.

"Are you Mr. Ibrahim Khalid?"

Ibrahim, surprised, nodded.

"There is a call for you, sir. The desk manager knew that you had checked out but had seen you coming out of the restaurant. He thought that the call might be important."

Ibrahim thanked him, followed him into the lobby, and returned a minute later.

"The call is for you, David. I believe it is your friend Bill."

"David," said the voice at the other end of the line, "your friends in Athens work really fast. They got the information not long ago from Interpol and the German Geheime Staatdienst. The man you killed in Athens is a former Gestapo thug and executioner named, as you know, Otto Streicher. He was presumed dead, killed by Yugoslav partisans in '43 or '44. We'll never know how he survived, but fingerprints don't lie. Take care of yourself, and call me as soon as you can."

"You look preoccupied. Bad news?" asked Ibrahim upon David's return.

"No, not really. Rather good news. I just found out that the man who killed your sister deserved to die many times over."

⚬⚬⚬

The plane ride to Detroit was short and uneventful. The two men spoke very little, each absorbed in his thoughts. David was thinking of May. In his thoughts, she was always a woman, and the little girl in pigtails was becoming dimmer and dimmer in the recesses of his memory. Truly, it was the woman he was in love with. Perhaps--not perhaps but surely--what she symbolized, the fact that she was a bridge to his past, was part of the love that he felt. Perhaps it even made that love stronger. He smiled, thinking that while his sessions with Dr. Rosen had no doubt saved his life and preserved his sanity, they had a minor drawback. He had learned to analyze things too much. He must relearn, he thought, to accept his feelings as they were, such as his love for May, and enjoy them without trying to dissect them. In his heart, he knew that he could do it.

He missed his friends, Francesco and Mihali. For obvious reasons, he had not become as close to them as they had become to each other, but he liked them, respected them, and above all, he trusted them. He remembered with amusement one of his favorite novels when he was a child, *The Three Musketeers*. Huge, outgoing, friendly Mihali could be Porthos. The aristocratic Italian lawyer was a perfect match for Athos, and he could be a passable D'Artagnan. If it weren't for the fact that his ideals were taking him in a different direction, Ibrahim could make a reasonable imitation of Aramis. He felt sorry for the

201

young Arab. He wondered if he had been right in acceding to his request that he accompany David to America. But then, if he were Ibrahim, that is exactly what he would have wanted. Not facing Richter would have haunted him to the end of his days.

Ibrahim's thoughts mirrored David's. It was, indeed, important for Ibrahim to confront Richter, not for himself, as David believed, but for his father.

Ibrahim was afraid. He had never been more frightened in his life. He would rather die than see the look on his father's face when he would hear that Alysha had been killed. But he could not die, and he could not avoid facing his father. He, and only he, had to tell him that his beloved daughter was dead. He had thoughts of running, but he knew that his father's sorrow would always pursue him, and his voice would always ask, "What have you done with your sister?" At least, he wanted to be able to say, "I saw the assassin, and he will be punished."

They rented a car, and with the aid of a map, it did not take them long to find Richter's residence. It was truly a mansion, all in white bricks, a large front lawn surrounded by a wrought-iron fence, a huge sculpted wooden front door.

No wonder he was so eager to lay his hands on Assael's papers, thought David. *The bastard has done quite well, and it won't be easy to give all this up.*

David rang the bell, and the door was opened by a young maid in a black uniform and a white apron.

"Mr. Von Eckardt, please."

"Is he expecting you?"

"No, he is not."

"May I ask who is calling?"

"No, you may not."

He gently pushed the young maid aside and ignored her protestations. The foyer was large and pretentious, but David paid no attention to it. There was a leather padded door to their left, and they entered without knocking.

A man was sitting behind a very large desk, and he stood up when the door opened. He was a fairly tall man, somewhat thick around the waist, with gray, thinning hair. He was wearing an expensive red satin gentleman's smoking jacket, and he must have been quite handsome at one time. His face was triangular, his traits regular, but his eyes were disconcerting. David could not tell whether they were gray or blue; they were opaque and certainly not "the window to the soul."

So, thought David, *that is what the vulture looks like, and he probably has no soul.*

"Who are you and what do you want? Tell me quickly before I call the police."

"Ibrahim, are you a good shot?" asked David.

"Excellent, but why do you ask?" Ibrahim replied.

David handed him the revolver which Bill had given him. "If you so much as hear a siren or see a police car, shoot this scum between the eyes. And lock the door."

"Mr. Von Eckardt--or if you prefer, Colonel Richter--my name is David Castro, and as you know, I occasionally do odd jobs for the CIA. My, you look surprised. After all, why wouldn't you? But you see, there are a few things that you don't know, and it is my pleasure to enlighten you. In the first place, our common friend Otto Streicher is dead. I killed him with my own two hands. Actually, he impaled himself upon a knife which I had taken away from him. Why, you look positively incredulous. He died hard, Colonel Richter. It was even harder when I told him that I was a Jew. Oh, yes, I see, you didn't know that. Not only am I a Jew, but I am from Salonica."

Richter had become deathly white. "What is this nonsense?" he asked and tried to push past David. The slap on the German's face resounded like a pistol shot. It was only an open-handed slap but applied with such force that Richter fell on the floor. David was on him like a tiger; David lifted him by the lapels of his satin coat and pushed him onto his leather chair.

"Sit down, you bastard! Shut up and listen. Professor Assael's documents existed. I saw them, and there is enough in them to convict you ten times over as a criminal of war."

"Oh, my God!" moaned Ricther. "My home, my family, my... my business."

"All lost, my friend, all lost," David added cheerfully. "But I have a young friend here who wishes to ask you something and satisfy his curiosity. Go ahead, Ibrahim, old friend, talk to the nice man, but first give me my gun back. After all, we are all human."

Ibrahim swallowed and came close to the German; his voice was choked with anger and barely audible. His English was passable and conveyed his thoughts quite accurately.

"You asked us to get these documents for you. My sister and I risked our lives to get them for you. Instead, you sent a murderer to take them from us. You told him that you did not care what happened to the P.L.O. agents. He told us that before he died. This man raped and killed my sister. You murdered my sister, and you betrayed us, and you have no right to live."

"Richter," interrupted David, "I think that I'll give my revolver to my young friend here."

"No, please no," moaned the German.

"Well, well, Vulture, how does it feel to be facing death? All right, Ibrahim, let's go. They'll come to arrest him soon."

The two men turned around and started walking toward the door.

"Hold it!" Richter was half-bent over his desk. From a deathly white, his face had turned beet red, his eyes rolled crazily in their sockets, and he held a heavy Luger in his hand. He was screaming, and his high-pitched voice made him sound like an hysterical old woman. "She was raped, was she? She was killed, was she? I am sorry he didn't kill you as well. You are nothing, nothing, Arabs and Jews! In the gas chambers, out the crematoria. You killed Streicher! Too late, too late! Did you have a sister, a mother, in the gas chambers, out the crematoria? We killed them, we killed them."

It was then that David jumped. His move was so fast and so unexpected that it took the German by surprise. A flying side-kick hit him in the chest, and the Luger fired at the ceiling, then dropped to the floor. David caught the German by the throat, bent him over the desk, and raised his fist. Later, he remembered that his mind was clear as a bell, empty of all thoughts but one: *This man must die.* He was not angry; he was in another world where nothing mattered except *this man must die.*

He raised his fist... and something tugged at his other sleeve. He whirled, like a cobra ready to strike, but was able to hold his blow. Ibrahim was standing beside him, and for a split second, he reminded David of Francesco Venchiarutti when confronted by his Greek judges. His face was gentle and peaceful and caring.

He looked at David and haltingly said, "*Rachamim.*"

It was only then that David realized how tense he was. He slowly lowered his fist and it took a while to let his muscles gradually relax. He looked around, almost in a daze. He felt as if he were coming back from a trip and became increasingly aware of his surroundings.

The German was not dead. David no longer wanted to kill him. *Rachamim.* He had become a better man with the help of the Palestinian. He tousled the young man's hair.

"Thanks."

The two men left without a backward glance at the unconscious German.

cs

The plane for Paris was ready to depart, and Ibrahim was among the last passengers to board. He and David looked at each other, and David drew him gently against him and hugged him.

"Go in peace, my little brother. Someday, your father and I will have a drink of Arak together. Go with God."

He stayed in the lounge until the plane disappeared over the horizon. He got out of the terminal and into the sunshine, walking toward his car. He felt free, and he felt happy. Tomorrow he would fly to Salonica for May. He started skipping and dancing on the sidewalk. People smiled and stared, but he did not care. Tomorrow, tomorrow. His life would begin tomorrow.

<end>